WARS OF CONTRITION

CAROLE YORK

Copyright 2016 Carole York

All rights reserved

DEDICATION

This book is dedicated to my dear friend Toni Ellis. I will never forget you, Toni.

10 November 1945 - 27 November 2016

PART ONE - ZULULAND

MARCH 1878

CHAPTER ONE

My mother sat at the end of the *stoep* in Oupa's rocking chair, clutching the tiny baby to her breast. Its crumpled face was yellow and its mouth opened in a little gasp every now and again. She raised a hand to push a strand of hair away from her eyes. Then she picked up a damp cloth and began to wipe the baby's chest. Nothing stirred in the soft, greasy heat except a small, fat gecko which wriggled across the *stoep* and disappeared into the wall of the house.

I wondered if the baby would die tonight or in the morning. The last one had died just before dawn but this one looked as if it wouldn't last till sunset.

Below the *stoep*, amongst the verbena, mignonettes and stocks, grew a small frangipani tree. Some of the flowers were already going brown at the edges and I picked one and rubbed the creamy petals between my fingers, releasing their perfume into the thick, heavy air. Frangipanis were the smell of death.

I hitched my dress above my knees, let it fall between my legs and settled down to watch an antlion digging a pit below the steps. When the funnel was ready it would bury itself at the bottom so that only its head and open jaws could be seen and there it would wait until a careless fire ant appeared and tumbled over the edge. Escape was impossible but I always hoped that someday an ant would manage to get out. They never did. With every frantic movement they just slipped deeper and deeper until they disappeared into the hungry mouth of the antlion. I felt a kinship with that ant.

I could hear the rhythmic sound of steel chopping through flesh coming from the shed beside the hide store, where my father and grandfather were butchering the carcass of an eland. I loved eland. We smoked the haunch and made *dytong* and ate it sliced thinly, like paper, on bread and butter. But eland was a mixed blessing because its fat was prized for the making of soap and there was no job that I hated more.

I would be fourteen years old the following day, but there would be no celebration and I cast a resentful glance at my mother for, once again, turning my birthday into a period of mourning.

As the sun was dropping behind the hills, the baby uttered an almost inaudible squeak, like a mouse caught in a trap, and died.

"Jacoba. Go and call your father," my mother said. Her voice was cracked and dry, drained of all emotion, as lifeless as the baby lying in her arms.

I dawdled across the hundred yards which separated the house and the butchering shed, scuffing up the sand with my bare toes. I was in no hurry to be the bearer of bad news.

Strips of meat dripped from iron hooks set into the roof of the outhouse and the smell of fresh blood hung in the air. My father and grandfather stood on opposite sides of the scarred bench, not looking at each other, not talking, not doing anything except chopping and cutting and sawing, and throwing slabs of meat from one end of the bench to the other.

I stood in the doorway until my father looked up and saw me and put down his knife. A pool of congealing blood lay at his feet.

"The baby is dead, Pa."

I saw the little muscles in his jaw twitch as he wiped his hand over his forehead, smearing the dead eland's blood across the bridge of his nose. My grandfather had also put down his knife and turned his back to me to wipe his bloody arms with an old pillowcase. A yellow flower embroidered in the corner quickly turned bright red. Until quite recently that pillowcase had lain under my head at night and I wondered why my mother had given it to my grandfather for rags. I waited for my father to reply but he said nothing and after a little while I turned and walked back to the house.

The women working in the pumpkin field had ceased their customary chatter, and stopped to lean on their hoes, lifting their skirts to wipe their sweating faces and I could feel their eyes following me. In the distance, just visible in the fading light, a small herd of horses made its way down from the ridge of hills, and I paused to watch them. The herd boys were already putting the sheep in the kraal for the night, counting them as they skidded through the entrance and I walked over to take the tally. Dead baby or not, farm work never stopped. Our house was built against the slope of a hill, from where rolling pasture lands, crisscrossed with streams and pocked with aardvark holes stretched away towards the Batshe Valley, home of Sihayo, chief of the district, who had given the farm to my grandfather many years before I was born. Thorn trees covered the sides of the hills and valleys and here and there a huge granite outcrop thrust itself out of the ground at the top of a hill. My grandfather had already shown me the piece of land where he would build a house for Jaap and me as soon as we became engaged. I wrote down the sheep count on a piece of slate and went back to the house.

The baby lay on a blue blanket on the table in the front room. It was very small, hardly bigger than the farm cats which lived amongst the zebra skins in the hide store. It had no hair, and pale blue veins covered its scalp like a spider's web. Its head looked too big for its body. The light from the candle cast flickering shadows against the walls as I watched my mother wash each tiny limb in turn, all its fingers and toes, its eyelids and lips and nose. Through the open window I could see my grandfather holding aloft a paraffin lamp while my father drove his pick into the ground.

After a while the digging stopped and my father came in carrying a wooden box. His hair and beard were full of earth, his knuckles bloodied and bruised. He sat down in his chair and watched my mother wrap the baby in the blanket and put it in the box. No one spoke to me and they did not appear to notice when I backed out of the door and went in search of my grandfather. I did not want to see my father nailing the lid on the coffin.

My grandfather was sitting on a bench under the fig tree outside his house, smoking his pipe, wearing his funeral clothes, ostrich skin waistcoat and short black jacket over a white linen shirt, and I could see that he had combed his hair and beard. He patted the bench and I sat down next to him and rested my head against his shoulder. His beard smelled of liquorice and aniseed and tobacco.

"Why do the babies always die, Oupa?"

"It is God's will. We cannot question the ways of the Lord."

And that was the end of it. I knew that once the Lord entered a conversation, there was no more room for talk. I snuggled against him, feeling the rise and fall of his chest, until he tapped out his pipe against the sole of his shoe.

"*Klim af, nou.* It is time."

My father led us through the peach orchard, up to the cemetery, holding the coffin in his arms. Behind him walked my mother, staring straight ahead, her eyes fixed on some invisible point beyond his right shoulder. Once the baby was in the ground and the grave filled in, Oupa began to pray. I stared at the little mound of rocks, wanting it to be over, there was a litter of black and white kittens in the wagon house, almost ready to leave their mother and I wanted to take one and tame it before it became wild.

We trooped back to the house, Oupa took the Statenbijbel down from its stand and put it on the table where the baby had lain only an hour before, snapped open the metal clasps and turned back the black leather cover. All the names of the family were written in the front of that Bible, right back to the day in April 1652 when the first Swanepoel had stepped into a boat and been rowed ashore at the Cape of Good Hope.

He took a little bottle of ink and a dip pen out of his pocket.

"What name did you give the baby, Jan?"

"Tertius."

A wooden calendar hung on the wall behind my head, next to a framed portrait of Queen Victoria. It was my job to move the peg to the next hole every morning but I had forgotten to do it and I wondered if my grandfather would notice. Of course he did.

"Best you get up and move that peg, Jacoba, or your brother will have died before he was born."

He waited, pen poised above the page, until the date was corrected. He wrote:

Tertius Swanepoel

Geboren 3 Maart 1878. Oorleden 3 Maart 1878.

The bible lay open, alone on the table while the ink dried and Oupa poured two tots of peach brandy into wooden cups. My mother took up one of my father's shirts and began to sew. I sat on a folding stool against the wall, drumming my feet on the floor, waiting for a chance to escape.

"Stop that, Jacoba," said my mother, without looking up from her sewing. It was the first time she had spoken to me since the baby died.

A spider had woven a web directly above the open dresser, where my mother's tea service was displayed. I watched it twirling slowly round and round as it descended, hovering a few moments, while it made up its mind, before dropping onto the top of the dresser. It was a very small spider. Nimblefooted it scurried into one of the Delft teacups and did not emerge again.

Nobody stopped me when I got up and went outside. The crickets were starting to chirrup in the grass and a swathe of stars swirled across the sky above me. Years before, when I was very young, my grandfather had told me each star was a dead person's soul and as I looked up I wondered which one was my little brother. I sat on the steps for a while, fighting back the urge to cry, hoping my grandfather would come out but he didn't. Eventually I got up and went down to the wagon house but I couldn't find the black and white kittens.Later, I lay on my bed, listening to my mother's sobs and tried to imagine a different life in which all the babies lived and my mother laughed all the time.

The death of a baby was always followed by soapmaking, a laborious, dirty job which left little time for idle chatter. For the making of candles the fat had to be clean and hard but for soap any kind of fat was used, and it was mostly rotten and stinking before we even began. Boiling and stirring and hacking off layers of bones and skin. It took eight days, from start to finish, to make soap, and another eight before the smell of it left my clothes.

Once the soap was packed away my mother devoted herself to her kitchen garden, harvesting rocket and endive, weeding between the white and red cabbages, cutting tarragon and marjoram to hang from the rafters in the cook house. Somewhere between the starting of the soap and the finishing of the garden, she stopped mourning her dead baby and began to pack Oupa's oxwagon for our journey into town for *Nagmaal*.

I was planning to sell my four year old stallion. He was a stocky animal, fifteen hands high, almost pure white with a grey mane and tail and black hooves and he could triple all day without raising a sweat. His mouth was so soft I could ride him with only one finger on the reins, but as beautiful as he was, Oupa said there was no point in breeding horses if we weren't going to make some money out of it. I thought I might get thirty pounds for him, which was the most money I had ever seen.

CHAPTER TWO

We arrived in town, loaded up with enough food to last us for a month, *mieliemeel*, coffee, sugar, smoked eland haunch and boiled sausages, four chickens swinging from the bedplank in a wooden cage, and every cookpot and kettle we owned. Wagons were rolling into town from all directions, flocks of sheep and herds of cattle churning up the dust, clogging my eyes and nose. The noise was deafening. The dam on the hill had been opened and the townspeople were raising the little gates to draw in the water from the channel which ran on either side of the street, waving to us as we rumbled past. Rows of white tents filled the Church Square, the smell of wood smoke rose from the cooking fires, and the whole place stank of smoke and sweat and manure. We made the weeklong journey only one or twice a year and I was wriggling with excitement by the time we parked next to the van Tonder wagon.

Tannie van Tonder came out of her tent followed by the three younger children.

"Fanie has a new baby!" they announced." His name is Karel!"

The baby was only two weeks old and the pulse on the crown of his head beat in time with his breathing. He lay in a little fur basket, like a kitten. My mother put out a hand to stroke his cheek and I saw the ache in her eyes.

"I was so sorry to hear about your baby, Elizabeth," said the *tannie*

My mother shrugged and sighed.

"I am grown used to it by now, Marijke."

Tannie van Tonder turned to me and smiled.

"There is a surprise for you behind the wagon. Go and see."

Jaap stood beside a blackened tin coffee pot hanging on a hook over the fire. His curly black hair was long, his skin darkly tanned and he looked much bigger than when I had last seen him.

My marriage to Jaap was assumed more than arranged. The van Tonders were our closest neighbours, although not close enough to make regular visiting possible. Sometime around my seventh birthday, when Jaap was nine, his mother lent him to us for a year. She had five other sons and perhaps she felt sorry for my mother when it became apparent that she was unlikely to produce any more viable children. Oupa had just given me my own horses and Jaap helped me to put my brand on them. He was gentle and kind and good with the horses, and by the end of the year we knew we were going to marry each other one day.

I walked over and tapped him on the shoulder. and he turned and smiled at me.

"Jaap," I said. " I didn't expect you see you. I thought you were only coming back from the school at the end of the year."

"My father needed help on the farm."

I thought it was an odd thing to say. Jaap had two older brothers, Fanie and Tielman, big, beefy boys with simple faces and broad smiles, and I found it hard to believe that they could not manage without Jaap.

I watched him as he measured out a cupful of coffee beans and threw them into a grinder mounted on a table. He turned the handle and the grains rattled into the small tin cup below. As he went to empty the cup into the hissing pot he knocked it against the edge of the table and some of its contents spilled onto the ground. He glanced at his father before rubbing the grains into the dust with his foot and then his father slapped him across the back of the head.

"Careless bastard," he said and Jaap's face turned a deep red.

I turned and walked away, embarrassed. No boy would want the girl he was going to marry see him get a *warmklap* from his father.

Boys had been calling on me while Jaap was away, arriving dressed up in their best clothes, with bottles of schnapps for my father and slabs of butter for my mother, and I went through the motions of sitting on the *stoep,* talking to them until the candle my father had lit burned down and they went home. It was called the *opsitting*, it was the custom and we all had to do it. I had no intention of marrying any of them but I had every intention of flirting while I still could.

I put on my best dress and the new pair of buckskin *spogskoene* my grandfather had made for me, and while the other girls cast hateful looks my way, I paraded around the square, basking in the boys' admiration until my father came and marched me back to our wagon where I got a long lecture from my mother.

Jaap ignored me for the next two days but I thought nothing of it. Boys who, only twelve months ago, had challenged me to shooting competitions and pony races now flocked around me like sheep around a salt pan and I was in no hurry to give up my sudden popularity.

Everything changed on Sunday. The church was the biggest building in town, bigger even than the magistrate's offices, built of stone with a wooden gallery upstairs and an organ at the front. The men sat on pews along the inside walls and the women and children on chairs in front of the pulpit. I hated church. The *dominee's* sermon soon put me to sleep and when I woke up my *oupa* was staring at me with a look that told me I would be spending the afternoon learning Bible verses.

Jaap was waiting for me when I came out and as we walked back to our wagons he took me by the wrist.

"I have heard that Hendrik van Rensburg wants to marry you," he said. Hendrik had been particularly persistent in his pursuit of me and I could tell by Jaap's tone of voice that he was angry but I thought nothing of it. Even as a child he had been prone to the occasional temper tantrum but I had always managed to tease him out of it. This time it didn't work.

"Oh yes. And Piet Greyling and Anton Louw and Dirk Meyer. But I am not going to marry any of them."

"And who are you going to marry?"

"I don't know. I haven't made up my mind yet."

I had a pet baboon that I had reared from a baby and we were halfway across the square when I saw him running towards me, skipping through the crowd, between people's legs. He danced about in front of me, chattering and barking and pulling at my dress and everybody started laughing. I wanted to kill him. I probably would have, had I known then all the trouble he was eventually going to cause me. I grabbed his hand and dragged him back to our tent, where I had a temper tantrum of my own, tearing off my church dress and shoes and putting on my trousers and shirt . My mother found me crying.

"I am finished! No more boys will call on me now. Nobody will want to marry me."

"Don't worry," my mother said, stroking my hair, "they will have forgotten about it by tomorrow. And besides that, what does it matter? Everybody knows you are going to marry Jaap."

But they didn't forget about it and the next day, as I was walking down to the stock pens with Jaap, Hendrik van Rensburg appeared in front of me, capering around on all fours, scratching under his arms, making barking noises and pulling faces. Jaap stormed over and punched him in the stomach. Hendrik was younger than Jaap and small for his age and as he doubled over, clutching his arms around him, Jaap snapped his knee up into his face and he fell to the ground, blood pouring from his nose. Then Jaap began to kick him.

"Jaap! Stop!" I shouted. " He was only making a joke!"

I rushed forward and jumped onto his back, but he shook me off and I fell backwards into the dust. It took three grown men to subdue him.

"Are you quite mad?" *Oom* van Tonder roared, as he marched him away.

I sat in the dust, watching them go, hardly able to believe what I had just seen. This was not the same quiet boy who used to follow me around into all kinds of mischief and swim with me in the hippo hole, and admire my riding and shooting skills.

People stood around Hendrik, murmuring amongst themselves as my mother lifted me to my feet.

"What is wrong with him, Ma? To beat Hendrik like that? Hendrik is my friend He said he wanted to marry me."

"Well, now, you have answered your own question. I warned you about flirting with the boys. Now see the trouble you have caused."

But there was worse trouble coming, which could not be blamed on me. Two weeks later we heard that the British High Commissioner had ordered a Boundary Commission to settle the ongoing dispute between the Zulus and the Transvaal Boers over the land immediately north of Rorke's Drift, where our farm was located. Lord Chelmsford had arrived at the Cape to take command of all the British forces in South Africa and the Royal Navy was patrolling off the coast of Natal, which could only mean that the rumours we had been hearing for years were about to come true. The British were going to invade Zululand.

Oupa was furious.

"Three times the *verdomde* British have hunted me off my land! First in the Cape, then in Natal and now they want to chase me out of Zululand? No. Sihayo himself gave me this land and I will not be turned off it."

He stormed up and down the *stoep*, waving his arms around and shouting and his face became so red, that I thought he would have a heart attack at any moment.

In May, Jaap came to ask my father's permission to marry me, and my father and Oupa started building a house for us. All that remained was to give our consent letters to the *dominee* and then we could be married. But the incident at Nagmaal had unsettled me and I was no longer sure I wanted to marry him.

SEPTEMBER 1878

CHAPTER THREE

The pedlar's covered wagon was pulled by two elderly black mules called Barnabas and Mathilda. Mathilda was a bad tempered animal who could strike out in any direction and kick you with any one of his four feet. I never did find out why the pedlar called him by a girl's name. He once told me that the mules knew every farm in Zululand and he had only to show them where he was going on a map and they would find their own way. I was never quite sure whether to believe him or not. He unhitched the mules and set them loose and they brayed their way to the river, kicking their heels and shaking their long black ears. Asjas hopped down from his hammock and began to walk after them.

"Don't!" I warned him.

For a moment the baboon looked as if he would try me and then changed his mind and went back to the fig tree, showing me the two little bald bumps on his backside as he walked past.

The pedlar was a small, round man, with a full beard and long, dark ringlets hanging over his ears. He always wore a suit and hat and when he took off his jacket his arms were the colour of a snake's belly. His name was Yitzak Isaacson but everyone called him the English Jew. A little monkey called Japan, clung to his right shoulder. Asjas hated that monkey. There would be war before the day was done.

"Where have you been? We expected you a month ago," my mother asked.

"I have been to England, *mevrouw*, to look for a wife!"

"And did you find one?"

"I did. We are to be married next year in London."

I knew where England was, I had seen it on the globe that my mother kept on a small table in a corner of the sitting room. The globe was one of the things my grandfather and my mother disagreed about. Oupa was a Dopper and as far as he was concerned the world was flat and the sun revolved around it. No one had ever managed to persuade him to a different point of view.

I couldn't imagine why the pedlar would go so far for a wife. We did not often speak about England in our house and when we did it always set my father and grandfather to cursing. My grandfather blamed the English for his brother's death. He blamed them for his parents' death. In fact, Oupa blamed the English for almost everything. I sometimes wondered what he said when my father came back from Grahamstown with two French Merino rams and an English wife.

Everyone looked forward to the pedlar's visits, for he brought news and gossip and messages from the neighbours, some of whom lived hundreds of miles away. But none looked forward more than my mother, who was not of the same Dutch stock as my father, and brought with her the more sophisticated cooking of the Cape when she married him. Only the pedlar could supply what she needed to make the delicately flavoured stews and spiced casseroles which she set before us every evening

I climbed over the tailgate, breathing in the bitter aroma of coffee beans and the smoky, sweet odour of tobacco. Strapped to the sides of the wagon were wooden boxes containing spices, muslin bags of lemon leaves, strands of delicate saffron and bottles of rosewater. Crates of apples and dried figs, imported from Mauritius, jostled each other in the middle of the bedplank, under piles of brightly coloured blankets and rolls of copper wire. The pedlar brought out a folding table and Japan jumped in and out of the wagon, bringing him tins of snuff and tobacco, and packets of buttons and needles and thread, which he set out in neat little rows for my mother's inspection.

Finally he lifted up the lid of the wagon seat and pulled out a glass jar.

"Hold out your hand, meisiekind," he said.

With a tiny shovel he scooped out a handful of striped sweets and poured them into my outstretched palm. I closed my eyes and breathed in the smell of aniseed and liquorice before putting one of the striped balls onto my tongue. I would try to make it last for at least half an hour.

It was almost dark by the time my father and Oupa returned, carrying the roughly butchered carcass of a *bontebok* between them. My father jumped off his horse and patted the dust off his thighs as he landed. I watched him run up the stirrups and loosen the girth and take off the saddle and saddle cloth. The steam rose from the horse's back and he shook himself from poll to croup and I rested my head against his neck and inhaled the smell of his sweat, keeping an eye on both ends of him. I wanted more than anything to ride that horse and my father had told me that if I could get on him I could ride him. But I never could. I couldn't even manage to catch him. Now he flattened his ears and swung his head around to bite me, but I was ready for him and dodged out of his way.

"So, *Jood*, what have you brought for us today?" my father said

The pedlar reached behind the wagon seat and drew out an oilskin wrapped package, which he opened with a flourish and laid carefully on his folding table.

"A Sharp's Carbine.It can stop a rhinocerus in its tracks at one thousand yards."

I leaned forward between the pedlar and my father. I had never seen a gun like it before and I was desperate for my father to buy it. He hefted it in his hands, measuring its weight, and looked along the top of the barrel before slipping a cartridge into the breech and handing the rifle to me.

"Try it. I think this will suit you very well," he said.

I flipped up the ladder sight and fired at a *dikkop* about five hundred yards away and the bird disappeared in a puff of black and white feathers.

"Do you like it?"

"Yes, Pa, I like it very much."

"Very well, it is yours."

"Really, Pa? Mine?"

"I said I would buy you a rifle when you turned fourteen. That birthday is long past and I do not break my promises. I'm sure you will find it easier than your *oupa's sanna*."

I grimaced as I remembered the first time I had taken my oupa's gun without permission. I was ten years old and it was sheep shearing time. Everyone was busy and I had taken the rifle from his tent and gone to sit on our veranda until Lukas came looking for me, holding a dead puffadder by the tail. We skinned it together and when we had finished I told him my *oupa* had said I could go shooting in the veld, which was a lie, because I knew my father would beat me if I attempted it. Lukas was an *inboekseling*. His skin was the colour of milky coffee and his eyes were blue and Oupa had got him cheap because he wasn't a full-blooded Zulu. He had arrived a week after I was born and his job was to look after me until I was old enough to look after myself. It was a job he would be doing until the day he died.

"I don't know. The *oubaas* going to kill us if he catches us."

"I just told you, Lukas, my *oupa* gave me permission."

He shook his head.

"I don't believe you.

"If you don't come with me I will tell my father about the time you stole the chicken."

"I didn't steal it! You gave it to me," he protested.

"My father will believe me if I tell him you stole it, and then he will beat you."

That, too, was a lie. We did not beat our *plaasvolk*. But it was enough to convince Lukas and we ran off and jumped on our ponies. Lukas's foster mother shouted at us but we kept going until we couldn't hear her any more.

"We'll get a hiding," Lukas said, when we stopped to rest. "My mother will thrash me and she will tell your father and he will thrash you."

But I didn't care. I was puffed up with the excitement of having my grandfather's rifle slung over my shoulder and the prospect of killing something with it. We had not gone far before we heard baboons barking in the hills.

"Let's shoot him," I said

"Shoot who?"

"The *bobbejaan*, stupid. The one that is killing the sheep."

Lukas looked at the gun and then at me.

"You are a girl, you won't be able to fire that, it's too heavy. You won't even be able to lift it."

He was right but I had a plan. I always had a plan.

"I will if you help me. Look, there he is, the bastard."

Bastard was a new word I had recently learned, an English word. I liked the sound of it but I was careful not to say it in front of my father.

The baboons were sitting amongst the rocks and we rode up a small hill and dismounted. I rested the gun on a large boulder and told Lukas to lean against my back and brace his legs.

Oupa's *sanna* was a Sterloop, made in Birmingham. At that time I didn't know where Birmingham was, only that the best guns came from there. It was five feet six inches long, the barrel alone measured four feet, and my grandfather could drop an eland at three hundred yards. It weighed fifteen pounds. You couldn't really miss with a Sterloop unless you were very stupid. I gently squeezed the trigger, just like Oupa had taught me, but I had never fired it with a bullet down the barrel. It went off with a deafening roar, the barrel flew upwards and the recoil knocked me off my feet. Lukas was no use at all. He fell on his face and I landed flat on my back on top of him, and by the time I got up and smacked him across the head the baboons were half a mile away chattering and shouting in the *krans*. All except one which lay on the ground under a thorn tree. The shot had taken away half its head, but stuck to its stomach was a tiny hairless baby and it was screaming its little bald head off. It was a horrible sound. I sat down and started to cry. Then Lukas tapped me on the shoulder and when I looked up and saw his eyes rolling back in his head, I thought the baboon leader had come back, seeking revenge, but it was worse than that. It was my father.

"If you were a boy, Jacoba, I would take the *sjambok* to you,"

He leaned down and pulled the terrified baby from its mother's body.

"You have shot away its ear,"

He handed it to me and it bit me. I dropped it and it lay in the dust, clutching its head with its paws. I was horrified as it tried to scramble away on three legs, whimpering all the time, holding one tiny paw to its bleeding ear. My father remained silent, watching me watch the baboon.

"So what is it to be, Jacoba? Will you rear it or shall I break its neck now? It is your decision."

It was the first time in my life anyone had asked me to decide anything .

"I am waiting," my father said. I had never seen him looking so angry. Lukas stood behind me *tjanking* and I wished he would shut up. I studied my father's face to see whether there was a right or a wrong answer and if so, which was which, but he gave me no hint. I got angry then.

"I will keep it, Pa,"

I picked it up and it screamed and bit me again, but this time I did not let it fall.

"Best you get on your ponies and get home before the baboon father comes back to claim his baby," my father said, his eyebrows pulled together over the top of his nose.

He rode away, taking the rifle with him and I put the baboon inside my shirt. It gripped my stomach and its ear would not stop bleeding and by the time we got home its head was stuck to my shirt.

"I told you, " Lukas moaned."We're going to get battered now."

"Don't be such a baby, "I snapped, but later that evening I heard him howling in concert with the rhythmic slapping of his foster mother's hand and I thought he had got off lightly. My father took his belt to me and my arse was red for two days.

The carbine was a trim, dainty thing, weighing just six pounds, less than half the weight of Oupa's *sanna* and with a considerably shorter barrel. It had a steel barrel band around its pewter tipped forearm, and a delicate filigree pattern covered the breechblock, lever and trigger guard. It was the most beautiful thing I had ever seen.

That night, Oupa roasted slabs of eland over the fire and after we finished eating the pedlar brought out a bottle of Hennessy brandy and my father jerked his head at me.

"Go inside and see how your mother is."

My mother was pregnant again and her pregnancy was not going well. Lately her ankles had swelled up alarmingly and she spent a lot of time lying down. When I peeped in the door of her room she was fast asleep so I went out of my bedroom window, crept through the shadows and crawled under Oupa's wagon. My father sat on the ground leaning against the tree, his long legs straight in front of him and I could see Asjas's tail hanging from a branch above his head.

"Did you hear anything about the Boundary commission?" my father asked, his face changing expression in the firelight every time the breeze shifted direction.

"Not a thing. They were not there when I passed through Rorke's Drift. Reverend Witt says they finished up in July. But what I did hear is that Sihayo's sons crossed the river into Natal and clubbed to death two of their father's wives for adultery. Bartle Frere and Chelmsford are spreading rumours of a Zulu invasion of Natal and the settlers are barricading their towns. Pietermaritzburg is crawling with soldiers."

"Then they are stupid. The Zulus have no interest in Natal," Oupa said.

"True. But the British seem to have a great interest in Zululand."

"I do not understand. The British have been friends of the Zulus for years. More than once they have chased the *burghers* back into the Transvaal themselves."

The pedlar shrugged his shoulders and refilled everyone's cups.

"Why? Why are they doing this? For over twenty years we have lived in peace with the Zulus. The British have the Cape, they have the Transvaal. What more do they want?" Oupa shouted.

The pedlar paused and stared into the fire before he replied.

"They want it all, *mijnheer*, the Transvaal, the Orange Free State, Natal, Zululand. Even Matabeleleland. The British want all of Africa."

As the pedlar finished speaking Asjas leapt from the tree and snatched a piece of eland off the fire. Oupa whipped around and reached for his rifle.

"I'm going to shoot that *bliksemse bobbejaan*!" he shouted and I took advantage of the commotion to creep out from under the wagon and return to my room. At the time I did not fully understand what they were talking about. My small world was circumscribed by the boundaries of our farm and I had never left it except to go into town for *Nagmaal*. The Transvaal and the Cape might as well have been on another continent and I had never even heard of Matabeleland.

CHAPTER FOUR

Our farm lay on the road between the port of Durban and the diamond fields in the Northern Cape and once every two months, a coach pulled by ten horses drove past. It was driven by Hannes Vosloo.

Hannes was almost seven feet tall with a long black beard and a gold ear ring in his right ear and his hands were as big as soup plates. He wore canvas trousers, a long moleskin coat and a red and green kerchief around his neck. Hannes could consume, in one sitting, a whole fried pickled tongue rolled in breadcrumbs, and a bowlful of chard, boiled with salt and butter. Everyone liked Hannes Vosloo. He was the gentlest man I have ever known.

There was little room for luggage in Hannes's wagon and the passengers sat with their cases cutting into their knees, while loose canvas bags containing food swung from the roof and every jolt of the wagon put them in peril of being knocked senseless by boiled hams or tins of potted meat and sardines. By the time they reached our farm they were glad of an opportunity to stretch their legs, tumbling out of the wagon, their limbs stiff and swollen. On this occasion they had no choice, as one of the wheels had lost two spokes coming over the pass at Laing's Nek. I watched from the *stoep* as a woman stepped out of the vehicle, announcing, in language that threatened to strip the paint off the wagon wheels, that she would never ride with Hannes again. Behind her toppled out a black and white piglet, pursued by a short, fat man in a shiny, black suit.

"God strike me dead if I ever again get on that bone shaking contraption you call a coach! Bloody disgrace is what it is!" the woman shouted. "Travelling with a pig inside. Never heard the like of it! You can sling yer ruddy 'ook, Hannes Vosloo, yer brass polishing sodger!"

I was enchanted. Nobody I knew spoke like that and I looked forward to an entertaining afternoon.

She marched up to the house, Hannes running behind her like a puppy dog.

"Please, Mrs Yudelman, calm down," he pleaded.

"Calm down? Calm down? You get rid of the bloody porker before I set foot on that coach again!" the woman snapped. Hannes gave up and stalked over to the smithy, muttering obscenities under his breath, while the woman mounted the three steps up to the *stoep* and subsided into Oupa's rocking chair.

"Fanny Yudelman, pleased to make your acquaintance," she said, holding out a gloved hand. "Speak English, ducks?"

"Oh yes."

"Well, ain't that a mercy. Make a cup of tea?"

I nodded and ran to the cookhouse to call my mother.

"Ma, there's an Englishwoman sitting on our *stoep*. She says she wants a cup of tea. And she curses worse than Oupa."

"Indeed," my mother replied, putting down her rolling pin and adjusting her bonnet.

Fanny Yudelman was not a small woman and her wide brimmed black straw hat, embellished with lace, netting, red feathers, roses and beads made her look even bigger. By now she was heartily regretting the petticoat, camisole and underskirt she had put on that morning. The whalebone reinforced corset which simultaneously constricted her waist and pushed her bosom upwards and outwards, was severely restricting her breathing. As she rearranged her skirts, I caught a glimpse of low heeled laced black boots and black striped scarlet petticoat. By comparison, my mother, in her plain chintz dress and leather shoes, seemed so slight and colourless. Fanny removed her gloves to reveal soft, delicate hands, quite at odds with her bulk. I looked at my own work- roughened hands and dirty fingernails and shoved them into my pockets.

Fanny was on her way from Kimberley to London. On business, she said. I had never heard of a woman who had business, Boer girls spent their childhood reading the bible and learning how to cook and clean and sew and then they got married and took care of their husbands and children. They didn't have business.

"What is Kimberley like, Mrs Yudelman? Can you pick up diamonds in the streets like Hannes says?" I enquired.

Fanny burst out laughing.

"Not bloody likely. If you could I'd be long gone back to the East End."

She produced a tiny glass bottle, opened the silver lid and pressed it to her wrists, and I closed my eyes as the rich, earthy fragrance swirled around me. My grandfather said only the godless wore perfume. A godless Englishwoman with business. I hung on every word she said.

Fanny said she had gone to the diamond fields when she was fifteen, shortly after a Griekwa shepherd boy had found a diamond weighing 83 carats on the banks of the Orange River and sold it to a farmer for five hundred sheep, ten oxen and a horse.

"Then that rake, Fleetwood Rawstorne, came up from Colesberg, with his friends. Called themselves the Red Cap Company. July of '71 it was. Found a handful of diamonds on a little hill and before you could say Jack Robinson they had the place pegged out in all directions. Course the news spread like a bushfire and in a week there was tents grown up like mushrooms in the middle of the *veld* and before you knew it that hill had become a great big hole in the ground. It's a stinking place, the miners camp, reckon there's twenty thousand of 'em living there, people and dogs and horses shitting all over the place. No lavatories, you see. Lavatories is the mark of civilization, ducks. No civilization where there's no lavatories."

I thought of the pit in the outhouse behind the shearing shed and wondered if Fanny would think us uncivilized, too, if she saw it.

"And you? Did you also dig for diamonds, tannie?"

Fanny let out another great roar of laughter.

"Dig? Not me, ducks. There's easier ways to make money out of diamonds than digging for them yourself, if you know what I mean. Course I'm well past that kind of carry on. Got a gentleman's club now. Nice little earner it is, too."

I didn't know what she meant but it seemed my mother did.

"I think you have asked Mrs Yudelman enough questions, Jacoba," she said. "I'm sure she would like to rest before she continues her journey."

But there was no stopping Fanny. She fixed her attention on me and I listened, spellbound, as the words gushed out of her mouth. For the first time in my life I realised that there was a world beyond the confines of my strict, Calvinist upbringing, a world where women ran eating houses and saloons and wore perfume. I tried to imagine what it must be like to live in such a frightening, exciting place. I didn't want her to stop, but the other passengers were already clambering back into the wagon, the man in the shiny black suit now sitting at the back with the guard, clutching his piglet to his chest. Fanny heaved herself to her feet and picked up her parasol. She produced a small tortoiseshell box, took out an embossed card and handed it to me.

"You're as smart as a whip, you are. You ever come to Kimberley you make sure and call on me," she said.

My mother stood next to me as I watched her sway back to the coach.

"I hope she comes again. I liked her," I said.

That night we ate dassie in ginger and cinnamon flavoured gravy made from the pot scrapings of the rock-rabbit and thickened with milk and breadcrumbs. After we had eaten and the dishes were washed and dried and put away I sat outside, holding Asjas on my lap, and wondered whether Hannes and Fanny and the black and white piglet had reached Pietermaritzburg yet.

CHAPTER FIVE

The next day we saw a column of soldiers marching towards the house.

"What do you think they want? They are a long way from home," my father said.

"I have no idea, but no doubt we shall find out soon enough," my *oupa* replied

At the head of the column rode an officer wearing a white helmet and a scarlet patrol jacket and as he drew closer I made out a double row of gold braid around his cuffs and a gold embroidered crown each side of his collar opening. The sunlight glinted off the long sword which hung by two slings from his waist.

"He is very beautiful," Oupa said." He will make a fine target for the Zulus once they learn how to shoot the guns that damned John Dunn has been selling them."

The officer dismounted and handed the reins of his horse to one of his men. Off his horse he was a small man and when he removed his helmet his red hair flowed down into a luxurious growth of whiskers. His name, we shortly discovered, was Evelyn Wood.

"So, colonel, where are you going? We are not accustomed to seeing British soldiers so far from Natal," my father said.

"To Utrecht. I hope you will have no objection to our making camp here for the night?"

"Certainly," Oupa replied. He might despise the English but he would never deny them his hospitality.

Suddenly my mother stepped forward and extended her hand.

"Colonel Wood. My father was a great admirer of yours. He served with you in India during the mutiny and before that in the Crimea with the Lancers. I used to play with your sister Kittie at the lovely house at Rivershall Place."

Wood looked at her closely and then, as he recognized her, his eyes lit up.

"Good Lord, yes, you are Elizabeth Rawlings are you not? Captain Rawlings's daughter. You were only a scrap of a girl then, and I a mere stripling in the Navy. Did you know Kittie married Captain O'Shea and has three children now?"

"No, I did not, but I am delighted to hear it."

My father and grandfather stared at her, a look of astonishment on their faces but my mother ignored them.

"But I am forgetting my manners, Colonel Wood. You must be tired after your march. Perhaps after you have rested you will join us for dinner this evening? And bring your officers with you?"

I could see by the look on my grandfather's face that this was too much hospitality but he said nothing.

"It will be my pleasure, my dear," the colonel replied, bending his head to kiss her hand.

"Come, Jacoba," my mother said, ignoring the stunned look on my father's face, "we have work to do."

The cookhouse was a little way from the house, in case it caught fire and took the house with it, a rondawel, filled with three legged cauldrons and copper pots and ladles. It was a place I usually tried to avoid.

A row of dogs and cats sat hopefully outside the door watching our every move and in the middle of them sat Asjas, a cat held firmly in one hand, while the other picked fleas off its back.

"I did not know you lived in England, Ma," I said.

She smiled at me.

"That was a long time ago. Before my father brought us to Grahamstown. Now go and kill a chicken and make sure you pluck it properly. I don't want to see a single feather."

There was a lightness about her which I did not often see.

While the chicken bubbled over the fire, with milk and finely crushed almonds, I dipped fresh eland steaks in melted butter, rolled them in parsley, thyme and chopped lemon peel, and handed them to my mother to wrap in buttered paper. I picked fresh rocket leaves, wild chicory and borage flowers and my mother uncorked the best olive oil and wine vinegar and mixed it into the salad. Every so often she held out a ladle of this or that for me to taste. All afternoon, we stood side by side, chopping and grating and frying. I didn't want the day to end.

Asjas had thrown aside his cat and gone to investigate the soldiers' camp and I was eager to investigate myself. These were the first British soldiers I had ever seen.

"Asjas has gone down to the camp. I am going to fetch him."

"Do," my mother replied. She was humming a tune to herself and I could see her thoughts were elsewhere.

The soldiers stared at me as I walked towards them. I was surprised at how small and young they were, not one of them was as tall as me.I remember thinking they must feed them very poorly in England.

"Your baboon, miss?" said one, a little taller than the rest, who was busy shoeing a horse.

"Yes."

"He's a cracker."

"I hope he is not making a nuisance of himself."

"Not at all. He's been holding the horses for me."

His eyes were a deep blue, beneath a shock of black hair. He straightened up and offered me his hand.

"Shoeing smith Conor O'Reilly, at your service, ma'am."

One of the soldiers whistled.

"Want to be watching him, miss, he's a right charmer with the ladies."

"Don't heed him," Conor replied, grinning at me.

"That is a nice horse," I said.

"He is. Name's War Game, belongs to the colonel. Loves him like his own child, so he does."

I had never seen such a big horse before. None of our own horses were more than fifteen hands and this one was a good six inches taller. Asjas was pinching his lip and he did not seem to mind but I knew what came next so I grabbed his hand and pulled him away.

"Leave him off, miss, he's not causing any trouble," Conor said.

"Not yet, but he will. I will take him away."

I walked back to the house and when I stepped up onto the stoep and turned around the soldier was standing as I had left him, the farrier's hammer in his hand. He lifted his cap and saluted me and I waved back at him. I wish I had known then what kind of trouble he was going to cause me.

Colonel Wood brought two officers with him for dinner and a bottle of whisky for my grandfather. My mother looked very tired and I told her to sit down and I would serve them but of course she wouldn't listen to me. My mother never listened to anyone, a character trait I inherited from her.

"Eat," Oupa said, when he had finished thanking God for every meal we had ever eaten. "My daughter in law is a famous cook. She will entertain your bland English stomachs."

The table fairly groaned under the weight of the food. Eland steaks, potatoes roasted in pork fat, sweet potatoes baked in the ashes of the fire and served with apricot gravy and sugar and cinnamon. More potatoes boiled in their skins and served with mint, sultanas, vinegar and pepper. Chicken casserole and salad. A steamed pudding made from flour and kidney fat, mixed with currants and raisins, and served with brandy sauce. I remember it well because it was the last meal my mother ever cooked for us.

"So what ,precisely, is your business in Utrecht, colonel?" my oupa asked.

"The Zulus are getting restless over the land dispute. We are afraid they may attempt to invade the Transvaal and do harm to the

German missionaries at Luneberg. We are hoping to enlist the help of a burgher commando to keep them in line."

"Hah! Well you may forget that. There is not a Transvaal Boer who will lift a finger to help you if you start trouble with the Zulus. We may be living in Zululand but we are still Transvaal burghers. You stole our land from us and we will not help you until you give it back. We will pour sheep dip in our eyes before we help you."

Colonel Wood's face threatened to match the colour of his hair and I let out a snort of laughter and received, in return, a warning look from my father.

"If you do that again, you will leave the room," he said. My mother jogged my elbow and handed me a plate of *koeksisters* to put on the table and Colonel Wood decided to take a different tack.

"We saw a large number of horses on the hillside, might you be interested in selling them?"

"They are not for sale," Oupa replied.

It was exactly what I expected him to say. Our family had bred horses for over two hundred years, ever since Jan van Riebeeck, the first Governor of the Cape, gave the first Swanepoel six horses as a gift in 1653, and Oupa was very proud of his bloodlines. Knowing how much he despised the English, I thought it was highly unlikely he would sell them a three legged goat, let alone a horse. I settled back to see what would happen next but the ferocity of my grandfather's outburst had stopped all conversation in its tracks and the colonel and his officers scraped back their chairs and rose to leave.

"My dear, thankyou for the delightful meal, it was wonderful to see you again. I will pass on your regards to my sister when I next see her."

As he took her hands in his, I thought I saw tears in my mother's eyes.

After they had left, my father turned to my oupa.

"One way or another there will be a collision between the Zulus and the English, Pa"

"Well, if there is, that is not our business."

"How can it not be our business when the land they fight over is ours? We ought not to be so hasty to annoy them, we may have need of them soon. You should have sold them the horses."

There might have been an argument then, had not my mother suddenly gone very pale and collapsed to the floor. As my father pushed me aside and scooped her into his arms, the joy I had felt earlier slipped away into the night.

The next day four Zulu regiments arrived, heading in the opposite direction.

My father ordered me into the house and waited with oupa on the stoep as the *impi* approached. The regiment was young, their hair long, stiffened with clay and cut into shapes to which a pad of otter skin stuffed with a variety of crane, finch and ostrich feathers was attached. Two square pieces of green-monkey skin dropped from under the pad, covering their ears, and cowtails hung from their forearms and lower legs.

Their captain stepped forward and I saw it was Dabulamanzi, the

King's half brother. He had often stopped by to drink coffee with my oupa, and occasionally we had come across him when we were out hunting. I liked Dabulamanzi, he was always laughing. Today he was not laughing.

Oupa put down his gun and the two exchanged the traditional handshake..

"Well, Dabulamanzi, my old friend," Oupa said, "what brings you here today?"

"I am sorry to tell you that there is going to be war with the English and my brother Cetshwayo has ordered all the Boers to leave their farms, " Dabulamanzi replied.

"And if we do not?"

Dabulamanzi shrugged.

"It is up to you, I am only delivering the King's message. But it will be dangerous to stay. The English are very bad people. They want to send our men to work on the diamond mines and and take all our cattle for themselves. They are demanding that the King give up Sihayo and his sons.

"And will he?"

"If he does the English will only demand more to be surrendered. War is inevitable and it is better to fight at once."

"In thirty years I have never had trouble with your people. Sihayo himself gave me this land to farm. Are you telling me he will now send his warriors to eat me up?"

"I cannot say. But we are going to wash our spears in white men's blood and perhaps some of our young men may not know the difference between a Boer and an Englishman."

There was silence between them then, before Dabulamanzi marched back to his warriors.

Dabulamanzi and his men were only the first. There were sixteen military kraals in Zululand and soon we saw thousands of men, in full battle dress, all heading towards Ulundi.

"We should go into *laager*," my father said.

"What? And leave the kaffirs and the English to strip the place bare? No. I will not do it!" Oupa replied.

DECEMBER 1878

CHAPTER SIX

My mother did not go with us to *Nagmaal* in December. By then she was spending most of the day in bed, trying to save the baby she was carrying. At the time, I did not think anything of it, I had seen three pregnancies by then and they always went the same way, and besides that, I had other things on my mind. Jaap and I were going to give our consent letters to the *dominee* and set a date for our marriage but I had not forgotten the fight with Hendrik and I was wondering whether I was doing the right thing.

Asjas spent the entire journey jumping from sheep to sheep, scratching in their wool and twisting their ears when he thought no one was looking. The sheep ran around all over the place and the herdboys threatened to beat him. Everybody was thoroughly *gatvol* by the time we reached town.

"I should have turned that stupid *bobbejaan's* neck around when I had the chance. He will never get any sense," my father muttered.

Jaap was all smiles from the moment I arrived, helping me down from the wagon, taking our oxen onto the veld, offering to help us pitch our tent, herding our sheep into the stock pens, until oupa got sick of him and told him our marriage was already agreed and he could stop trying to make a good impression now and concentrate on how he was going to keep me under control once we were man and wife. I watched him for any signs of the behaviour he had shown the last time but he kept that part of himself carefully hidden. We handed in our consent letters to the *dominee*, accepted everyone's congratulations and talked about the horses I would breed and how many children we would have, all boys, of course.

But, I could not ignore the atmosphere in town, we were all waiting to see whether the British would go to war with the Zulus, and there was the issue of the Boundary Commission, we had still not heard whether they were going to take away our farms.

On our last night in town a portion of the square was cleared and the sides of an oxwagon were taken down. The band sat on top wearing their church suits, their hair and beards washed and combed, hatless foreheads white above their eyes, tuning their guitars and concertinas, while the old *tantes* sat around the square like crows, in their black dresses with their arms folded across their bosoms, their hair wound in stiff plaits around their heads, watching their daughters and granddaughters. Couples sneaked off behind the parked wagons, returning minutes later flushed and excited, the girls straightening their dresses, the boys wearing triumphant smiles, and if they were gone too long a *tante* got up from her high back chair and marched over to call them back.

The band struck up a *vastrap* and the boys rushed en masse to the opposite side of the square and made stiff little bows in front of the girls.I felt so grown up, standing between Jaap and my father.

They were only halfway through the first dance when a rider

galloped onto the square.

"That's Redelinghuys. What's he in such a hurry about?" my father said.

Marthinus Redelinghuys looked as if he had been riding hard for some days. His hat was caked in dust and his horse was blowing hard through bright red nostrils, its neck lathered in sweaty foam. In a minute everybody had gathered around him. Marthinus was only a couple of years older than me, a boy who rarely had anything to say for himself, and he was clearly delighted to be, for once, the focus of everyone's attention.

"The British have delivered an ultimatum to Cetshwayo. They are ordering him to disband his army and abandon the military kraals within thirty days," he shouted.

"What? They are asking Cetshwayo to give them his country. They must be quite mad if they think he will agree to it!" my father replied.

"They are demanding that the sons of Sihayo be sent for trial in Natal for the murder of their father's wives and he is to hand over Mbilini for cattle raiding. He is also fined one hundred cattle for molesting the English land surveyors."

Everybody started talking at once. Dominee Terblanche was waving his arms in the air, trying to make himself heard above the din but nobody was taking any notice of him and eventually I heard my father's voice. My father was an important man in the district and everyone listened when he spoke.

"Zulu business is Zulu business. Sihayo's wives were adulterers.

The sons had hardly to go two miles into Natal before they caught them and brought them back ,the British are making a fuss over notjing. Mbilini stole cattle from the Transvaal Boers, let them deal with it. As for the Land Surveyors, I heard they strayed across the Tugela onto the Zulu side and were only frightened a little by Sihayo's men and cried like little girls before being set free. The Zulus only took their handkerchiefs and pipes to tease them. One hundred cattle? Cetshwayo won't give them."

"Well, if he doesn't there will be war," Redelinghuys said.

"And what about the Boundary Commission? What did you hear about that?"

Redelinghuys paused, and I could tell by the way he drew himself up that he was about to deliver his most important news. Suddenly it was so quiet I could hear the sheep snoring in the stock pens on the other side of the square. Everyone was looking at Redelinghuys.

"They read it out after the ultimatum. They have found in favour of the Zulus," he said, as solemnly as if he were delivering a sermon at a funeral, which, in a sense, he was. Suddenly, I was afraid and I clutched Jaap's hand tighter.

The words dropped heavily onto the ground and Oupa threw down his pipe.

"What? What did you say? We must give our farms back to the Zulus? I won't do it," he shouted.

For a moment I thought he was going to smack Redelinghuys.

"They say we will be compensated."

"Compensated? How will we be compensated? How will they

compensate me for thirty years of work? Where will we go? Who will look after my kaffirs when they have nowhere to live?"

My father picked up the pipe but the bowl was cracked in two and it was useless and I felt sad because I knew how much my grandfather loved that pipe. He said it was given to him by Andries Pretorius at Blood River.

"There will be war now, between the British and the Zulus, and we will be caught in the middle of it. We should get up a commando," said my father.

"You are saying we should support them? Against the wishes of the Transvaal and Free State burghers?"

"Yes, it is the only way."

Oupa was glaring at my father.

"Going to be trouble now," I murmured to Jaap.

"Shhh." he replied.

"What do you mean shhhh?"

"Go back to the wagons. This is man's work."

He let go of my hand and I was about to argue with him but then I heard my Oupa.

"I say we should stay out of it and let the British fight their own war. Cetshwayo will remember his friends when it is over."

"Pa! I have already said it! The Zulus cannot win this war! When it is over Cetshwayo's opinion will count for nothing! And neither will yours!"

And then, right in front of me, Oupa punched my father in the face. He was a big man, well over six feet tall, and my father staggered backwards, holding his hand to his nose, blood pouring from between his fingers. If my father hit my oupa I didn't know what I would do. But he didn't. Instead he turned and stormed back to our wagon. It was the first and last time I saw my grandfather hit my father and I think he regretted for the rest of his life.

The dance was abandoned and everybody hurried back to their wagons but Jaap held me back.

"It's time you started learning to do as I say," he said, and my temper flared.

"I've never done as you say, Jaap van Tonder, and I'm not going to start now, " I retorted.

My father and oupa were already hard at work, striking the tent by the time I got back to the wagon.

"Where have you been, Jacoba? Go and help Lukas with the oxen. We have no time to waste if we are to leave by midnight," my father snapped.

The blood was still dripping from his nose and his eyes were beginning to close and Oupa told him to sit down, gripped the bridge of his nose and twisted it. I heard a crack as it popped back into place. It remains the most horrible sound I have ever heard.

"It occurs to me," said my father, on the long drive home," that if the British are going to war with the Zulus, we need have no fear about the Boundary Commission. They will have more important things on their minds."

"Precisely," Oupa replied.

I had more important things on my mind, too. Jaap had informed me that he intended to move to Pietermaritzburg and take up articles with a lawyer as soon as we were married.

JANUARY 1879

CHAPTER SEVEN

Three weeks passed before I plucked up the courage to speak to my grandfather.

"What would Oupa say if I said I did not want to marry Jaap any more?"

"I would say that Jaap comes from a good family and if you didn't want to marry him you should have said so before the consent letters were given to the *dominee*. it is too late to change your mind now. You would only bring disgrace on the whole family and certainly no other boy will want to marry you after that."

"But he wants to take me to Natal. He says he is going to become a lawyer."

"Oh? I did not know that. But it doesn't matter. A married woman must obey her husband in all things. It says so in the Bible."

There was nothing more to say. I could not argue against the Bible. I saddled my pony and told my father I was going to check the jackal traps.

It was a hot summer's day , the rains were late, and the sun beat out of a cloudless, pale blue sky. Flat plains stretched out all around me, a sea of wavy grass so high I could barely see over the top of it. In the distance a river broke into a series of cascades, the spray painting a rainbow against the morning sun, eleven separate falls, in the shape of a horse-shoe, divided by pillars of basalt, tipped with bushes, from whose branches hung the nests of hundreds of weaverbirds. As I drew closer the roar of the falls grew louder, jets of water tumbled into a boiling pool beyond which was a thicket of rank grass growing between fallen boulders, wet with spray, and overgrown with clematis. Grasshoppers hopped amongst the feathery grass, and on the summit of a basalt column, mid-stream, a pair of Cape crows perched on their nest, croaking loudly. I paused to watch two tiny klipspringers leap up into the air and bound up the crags, their dappled grey and brown coats merging so perfectly with the veld that when they stood still, I could not see them at all. This was my favourite place to be when I was sad and I had been spending so much time there since we got back from Nagmaal that my mother was complaining to my father that I was not doing my work around the house. I had prayed to God to deliver me from Jaap but so far he had ignored me. Now I knew there was no way to to avoid marrying Jaap and the life I had imagined for myself was in ruins. I turned my pony around and I was almost home when I saw thousands of Zulus trotting past, the plumes on their headdresses waving in the air. They were less than two miles away and they must have seen me on top of the *koppie* but they paid me no attention. Half an hour passed before they were out of sight.

   My father had also seen them and by the time I skidded to a halt outside the house he was already sitting on his horse, two bandoliers of ammunition slung around his shoulders, his rifle in its holster, waiting for my oupa to saddle up.

"Pa! The Zulus are marching towards Natal!" I shouted.

"I know. I have seen them. I am going to Rorke's Drift to warn the British. You will stay here with Lukas and look after your mother. We will be back tomorrow."

I think he expected an argument from me but I was badly shaken and very afraid. I watched them ride away, their bedding rolls strapped behind their saddles, my grandfather wearing his ostrich skin waistcoat, my father a white shirt and yellow nankeen jacket. Perhaps I already knew it would be the last time I would see him, because I remained staring across the veld long after they were out of sight.

When I went into the house my mother was leaning against the table, her face contorted with pain..

"I think this baby is coming, Jacoba. Help me back to the bed."

"It can't be. It is too soon!"

"Trust me, Jacoba, I have had enough babies to know when the time has come. Now stop gawking and help me back to bed."

"I will send Lukas for Tannie van Tonder."

"I don't think this baby is going to wait for Tannie van Tonder. Go and boil water and fetch the rags I keep in the *wakis*."

"You can't have the baby now, Ma, I don't know what to do. You must wait for Tannie van Tonder!"

Even as the words came out of my mouth I knew how stupid they sounded. I had seen enough foals born to know that once the time came there was no waiting to be had.

CHAPTER EIGHT

A long line of artillery horses stood in the early morning sun, tethered to a picket line stretched between two wagons, a pile of feed boxes beside them. Two of the horses stood with their hind legs drawn under their bellies and their forefeet advanced, in an attempt to relieve their painful feet of as much weight as possible. Occasionally they swayed backward, raising their toes and throwing the weight, for a moment, upon the heels of their front feet. A grey horse lay on his side, groaning, his legs stretched out, his body slick with sweat.

"Shit!" said Conor.

Founder in the field was his worst nightmare. He could remove the shoes and pare the soles and apply hot linseed poultices to the feet of the two still standing, but there was no hope for the grey.

Conor knelt down beside him.

"I think you'll have to go, Oscar," he said, stroking the horse's face. He stood up and went to fetch the farrier's axe from the wagon.

In the four months since he had marched to Utrecht with Evelyn Wood, Conor hadn't been able to get the young farm girl out of his mind and had been hoping they would march back the same way so that he could get another look at her. Instead he had landed up at this godforsaken little hamlet on top of a hill, while horses fell sick all around him. He didn't think he'd spent more than half an hour in good humour since leaving Pietermaritzburg.

Situated on top of a plateau in the Biggarsberg mountains, only twelve miles by road from Rorke's Drift, Helpmekaar could hardly be called a village but its natural prominence made it ideal as a heliograph station and starting point for the invasion of Zululand. The mountain top was a series of gently rolling swells, which followed one another like waves, the hollows gradually deepening, becoming valleys, then ravines with scarped sides, many miles in length, until they ended in the central valley of the Buffalo River. Nestling among the fallen boulders at the foot of these crags were the beehive shaped kraals of Zulu villages and beyond the deep valley, plains ran up into hill ranges surmounted by flat topped mountains. The mountain was alive with life. Snakes and grey lizards rustling towards their holes, larks and other small birds springing around, graceful cranes and secretary birds searching for frogs, and snakes.

But its peacefulness was soon shattered.

A steady convoy of supply wagons made its way from the wharves at Durban to Rorke's Drift, passing through Helpmekaar on its way, and as the weeks went by and more and more troops marched up the road from Maritzburg, tents began to spill down the hillside. Helpmekaar's two stone houses and small chapel were soon augmented by three corrugated iron sheds, five thatched sheds and a sod fort, to hold reserve stocks of ammunition and food.

West of Helpmakaar, the mountain descended to a vast sandy plain,and across this plain the Drakensberg range raised its crests to some ten thousand feet, beyond which lay the Orange Free State, the last possession left to the Boers in South Africa.It was in this direction that Conor looked when he stood on top of the hill, the night before they marched out. If you crossed the Free State you would end up in Kimberley, where , so he had heard, you could pick diamonds up off the ground, something he was intending to do as soon as the opportunity to desert presented itself.

Done with the horse, he cleaned the axe and walked over to the forge, where a young lad, his skinny white chest bare, was banking the fire.

"That fire still not ready? For the love of God, Ellis, get a move on, or we'll be pulling the guns ourselves."

Ellis scowled.

"I've only got two hands. If you think you can do better, come and do it yourself."

"Ah, that I can, you idle gobshite, but my two hands are better occupied shoeing horses than minding forges," Conor replied, as he opened his tool chest and took out a clinch cutter and shoeing knife. Every single horse, mule and ox was to be fitted with new shoes before they left for Zululand. It was four o'clock by the time they had finished the first sixteen horses and the bugle sounded for evening stables.

A big, burly man, with short curly hair, and whiskers covering his cheeks strode down the line of horses. A yellow chevron on the upper sleeve of his blue patrol jacket, topped by a horse shoe, a field gun and a crown, identified him as a Farrier Sergeant. His name was Robert Whinham, he was thirty one years old and he would not be returning from Zululand. Whinham did not suffer fools gladly and he was wont to nail a man to the forge floor for a few hours for sloppy work. In the absence of permanent forges on campaign he had yet to think up an alternative punishment but Conor was sure it would not be long coming. Nobody wanted to cross Sergeant Whinham.

All went well until he reached the fifth horse in the line, one that Ellis had shod. He picked up a fore leg and scowled.

"What's the most important thing in this Battery, O'Reilly?"

"The horse, Farrier Sergeant."

"And why is he so important O'Reilly?"

"Because he pulls the guns, Farrier Sergeant."

"And how is he going to pull the guns if his bloody feet are sore?" Whinham roared, seizing Conor by the ear and pulling his head level with the horse's hoof. A nail had been driven too high up the wall of the hoof and Conor cast a venomous look at Ellis as he began to pull off the shoe. Later that night he nailed Ellis's boots together.

A week later they crossed the river into Zululand.

Conor rode alongside his travelling forge. Ahead of him were the six guns, each with a caisson carrying two extra ammunition chests, a spare wheel and extra limber pole slung beneath. The sun glinted off the copper sheeting covering the lid of the ammunition chest, making his eyes water. On either side of the guns, festooned with an assortment of pouches, belts, bayonets and knapsacks marched two battalions of infantry, behind him a train of forty five supply wagons stretched back for five miles and lying tantalizingly in the distance, a craggy, sheer faced rock shaped like a sphinx rose straight up out of the ground for four thousand feet. It was called Isandlwana.

It was late in the afternoon by the time they reached the mountain and even later by the time Conor had unhitched the horses, slipped their nosebags over their heads and checked the feet of every horse on the picket line. By nightfall seven hundred and fifty tents were neatly laid out, company by company, street by street, in the looming shadow of the sheer cliffs. Dinner was a vile stew made from an ox which had died in its yoke the previous day, but it was the first cooked meal they had seen in three weeks and the men fell upon it ravenously Dinner over, Conor sat down, took up a harness and began to scrub it with neatsfoot oil and mutton tallow.

He glanced up at the mountain behind him and turned to the man next to him.

"I'd say we've nothing to fear from that direction."

"Aye, but I'm thinking they'll get a good run at us if they come from over there."

In front of them a rock strewn expanse of open ground stretched away towards the base of a large plateau about five miles away, topped by a few scraggly thorn bushes.

Conor bent to his task, carefully cleaning out the eyelets in the leather straps and polishing the brass buckles, checking every stitch and join before laying the tack across the limber pole, ready for the morning, and turning in, but sleep eluded him and after a while he went outside and crept under the forge limber. A little terrier crawled in beside him, wagging her tail.

"Captain Smith's little dog, ain'tcha? Where's your master, then?"

He fed her pieces of biscuit and scratched her ears until she curled up and fell asleep.

Eventually he got up and went to the latrines. Standing in the darkness he looked over towards the hills opposite. The new moon was a mere sliver in the sky and he thought he saw fires twinkling in the hills. Something was there, he felt it and shivered. Passing by the General's tent on his way back, he saw a tall, bearded, man wearing a pale yellow jacket and moleskin trousers standing in the pool of light thrown by a single lamp. Beside him stood an older man, impudently smoking a pipe.

"I tell you, mijnheer, you are looking for trouble. You have no trenches, no broken glass in front of the camp and what use are your wagons parked behind the tents?" said the younger man.

Lord Chelmsford, seated behind his paper littered desk was annoyed at the interruption. Frederic Augustus Thesiger was an arrogant, Eton educated man who had served in Ireland, the Crimea and India. He knew nothing about South Africa.

"My good man," he drawled, "this is only a temporary stop. We shall be gone tomorrow. My scouts report no native activity in the vicinity and I see no reason to waste time on unnecessary fortifications."

"Then your scouts must be blind. We saw the Zulu army heading in this direction earlier today. At least draw up your wagons in a *laager* and put your cannons in between,"the man replied, throwing up his arms in a gesture of frustration.

The General looked up from his despatches and put down his pen. Tall and thin, he wore an officer's dark blue patrol jacket and riding breeches. A breech loading Enfield six chamber, double action revolver lay on the desk next to his left hand, and he began to caress it as he spoke.

"This is the British Army. We are well versed in the handling of natives. Even if there is an attack, I doubt they will stay and fight after the first volley of rifle fire."

With that he turned back to his papers in a curt gesture of dismissal.

"*Kom*, Jan," said the older man," we are wasting our time.Let us sleep here tonight, it is too dangerous to ride home in the dark when Cetshwayo's impis are all around us."

Conor crept back under the forge limber, lit a stub of candle and began to write in his notebook.

The next day broke hot and windless, the sun invisible in the metallic whiteness of the sky and Conor's eyes watered as he rubbed his dirtcaked eyelashes. He swept his eyes over the rock strewn expanse of open ground in front of the camp. The silence of the place unnerved him.Pushing his fears aside he began to walk down the line of picketed horses, lifting each hoof in turn.

"Now you scallywag," he said, as he fastened a muzzle onto a bay horse intent on biting its neighbour, "we'll have none of that carry on."

He was attending to an unruly mule when a sound like distant thunder made him glance up at the sky. Over the edge of the plateau spilled row upon row of black and white cowhide shields, half a mile deep and four miles wide. Caught completely off guard, troops raced hither and thither as the bugle sounded the 'fall in'. Quartermasters swore as ammunition wagons crashed into each other and half struck tents collapsed in the confusion. Yelping dogs added to the racket as the seven pounder guns were galloped up to the line.

Conor dropped his hammer and stood transfixed as the Zulus trotted towards the British lines. Jesus, Mary and Joseph, he began to bless himself, the words of the prayers sticking, fearbound, to the roof of his mouth.

He saw the Farrier Sergeant running towards him.

"Stop your Papist gabbling and get up on that cart, you idle bastard!" he roared, Conor's mouth worked, but no sound came out as the saliva dried on his palate. The Farrier Sergeant seized his collar and shook him like a terrier.

"Do you understand me, smith?"

Conor nodded as the man picked him up and heaved him on top of the ammunition cart, slapping a screwdriver into his hand.

"Now, boy, start opening those boxes and issue that ammunition to anyone as asks you and don't stop till it's finished."

He broke them open as fast as he could but the lids were screwed down and the lengthening queue of men cursed him from all sides for his slowness.

From the top of his cart he watched volley after volley tear into the charging Zulus and soon clouds of heavy black smoke hung over the field, obscuring friend and foe alike, but still they came, wave upon wave of ox hide shields, blinded and half suffocated by the smoke, clambering over the bodies of their fallen comrades until only a hundred yards of open ground stood between them and the line of waiting soldiers. Then, suddenly, they faltered and a cheer went up from the British lines. The troops stopped firing and began to laugh and joke amongst themselves as the warriors milled around uncertainly. They were still laughing as a gigantic induna ran down from the overlooking cliffs, rallied his men, and led them in the final charge. They were completely overrun and Conor, realising his hopeless position, looked around for some means of escape.

Through the pall of smoke, one of the two guns appeared, its riderless horses galloping frenziedly towards the road to Rorke's Drift, pursued by a crowd of screaming warriors and he made a desperate leap onto the back of the lead horse, urging the panic stricken animal onto the road, just in time to collide with the advancing right horn of the Zulu army. It was all he could do to cling to the horse as the carriage careered down the road, before plunging down the ravine and capsizing on the banks of the river.

CHAPTER NINE

I slumped against the wall, staring at the face of my dead mother. She had begged me to save the baby and I had failed and it lay in the slowly congealing pool of blood between her legs. Asjas sat next to me, holding his white cat in his lap. The smell of blood made me want to retch.

"I am so sorry, Mama," I whispered, half expecting her to answer, but my mother's blue eyes gazed up at the rafters, through half closed eyelids, and I tried to remember what they had done after my grandmother died. I pulled the eyelids down with my fingers and placed a rolled up towel under her chin. I was so tired. A candle flickered on the window sill, while the rain for which we had waited so long, drummed down on the thatched roof.

In the corner of the room, next to the *jonkmanskas*, stood a yellowwood cradle, with hearts carved out on all four sides and I put the dead baby into it, wrapping him up so that only his face was visible.

"You are not even supposed to be here. Why could you not have waited till your proper time?"

The weight of my mother's body made it difficult to pull out the bloodied sheet from underneath her and tears of frustration and anger began to flow down my cheeks.

Hours passed. The candle died. The rain stopped and I went out onto the *stoep* to await the return of my father and grandfather. The women had not gone into the fields and a silence had settled on the farm, even the farm labourers' children were quiet. Hours passed and at midday Lukas appeared with a shovel in his hand and I could see that he already knew. Only a deaf person could have failed to hear my mother's shrieks in the early hours of the morning.

We buried them next to my grandmother and afterwards I walked down the sandy path which wound through the long grass until I reached the hippo pool, stripped off my bloody clothes and leapt off the ledge. The floor of the pool was paved and smooth as polished marble and the river weeds which grew on them were soft, like a rabbit's skin. I let myself sink to the bottom, holding my breath while the water washed me clean. Beneath the ledge was a secret chamber, far beneath the surface, where the hippopotamus had once lived until it ate a child and my grandfather shot it. I dived down and crawled into it and sat there for hours, wondering how I would tell my father that I had let my mother die.

The floor of our house was made of finely powdered anthills mixed with boiled *turksvy* leaves, manure and oxblood, and once a week my mother and I used to carry all the furniture outside, sweep the floor and smear it with a mixture of cattle dung and water. I carried that furniture in and out and got down on my knees and polished that floor every day, for five days, before I heard Lukas shouting.

"They are coming, Miss Jacoba, they are coming!"

Oupa's arms hung by his side as his horse hobbled across the veld, reins flapping loosely against its neck. Behind him walked my father's horse. I felt sick when I saw him. Oupa slid off his horse and grunted as his feet hit the ground, while the horse stood with lowered head, its sides heaving. It had a long gash down its right foreleg. Oupa's face was the colour of sheepswool beneath his beard, and there was a large patch of wet blood on the front of his shirt.

"Oupa? Where is Pa?"

He leaned his head against the saddle and I saw his shoulders starting to shake. The *plaasvolk* in the fields had stopped working and one of the women began to wail, an unearthly sound which bounced off the *koppie* and came to rest on the ground in front of me. I knew then that my father was dead.

"See to the horse," Oupa said, turning his face away from me, and when I examined the horse's leg I knew there was only one way of seeing to him. I fetched my carbine from the house, patted the horse on the neck and shot him between the eyes. He was dead before he hit the ground. He was a good horse, a black Boerperd, but the bone in his leg was cracked from elbow to knee and I knew it was only his big heart that had brought my grandfather home. I stared at him, while my mind emptied itself and numbness spread through my body. My oupa had slumped to the steps of the stoep.

"Call your mother," he said.

"She is dead. The baby came and they both died."

I had never seen my grandfather cry before, and I was angry. There would be no one to comfort me now. Between us, Lukas and I helped him to his house and onto his bed. He had taken a bullet in his neck just under his jaw and I could see where it went in but not where it went out.

"Put your finger in the hole and see if you can find the bullet," Oupa said.

"I can't do it."

"Do it, Jacoba. Unless you want me to die also."

I stuck my finger into the bloody hole and wiggled it around. It felt like meat that had been left too long in the sun and I wanted to be sick.

"I can't feel anything."

"Keep trying," Oupa said, through gritted teeth.

I poked harder and suddenly he screamed and fell back on his blankets, his eyes rolling back in his head and for a moment I thought I had killed him.

"I can't find it, Oupa." I said, but he was unconscious and could not hear me and the flies were beginning to settle on his shirt. I wiped my hands on my trousers but the stickiness remained between my fingers.

Outside, Lukas waited, his eyes welling with tears.

"Cut off the *oubaas's* shirt and burn it," I said, as I walked past him. The women in the fields were still wailing and I thought if another person started crying I would surely hit them. The door to the bedroom stood ajar and I could see my father's spare shirt hanging from a peg on the wall and the wagon chest at the foot of the bed, containing his *kisklere*. I walked past and went to stand at the window where I could see the mound of earth where my mother and the baby lay, next to all the other babies. I thought it was the end but I would soon find out it was only the beginning.

Oupa screamed day and night, from the pain in his arms. He complained of twitching, he said it felt like ants running up and down his arms and he could not move them at all. He said he wanted them chopped off, the pain was so bad. He could not lift his head from the bed unless someone was there to help him and yellow pus began to seep from the hole in his neck, matting his beard and making it stink. I tried to shave him but I was not very good at it and I cut his face so many times that he told me to leave it, he would rather keep the stinking beard than go through any more suffering. Lukas attended to his other needs - there were parts of my grandfather I was not allowed to see, nor did I want to. I spent my nights kneeling on the striped zebra skin carpet next to his *katel* praying for him to get better, and when I was not on my knees I sat in my great grandfather's chair and read to him from the bible. There were times when I wanted to strangle him.

I was almost ready to give up by the time Tannie van Tonder arrived, in a cloud of dust and noise and oxen.

"We heard the news. Dear God, such misfortune," she said, enfolding me in her arms, "Why did you not send for me?"

"I don't know, *tannie,* I did not think," I lied. I could not say that I did not send for her because I knew Jaap would come with her and I did not want to see him.

"Jaap was held up with the sheep dipping. He will be here tomorrow."

At that moment Oupa let out an earsplitting shriek.

"Liewe aarde! What is that?"

"It's Oupa. He is very bad, Auntie, I think he is going to die."

"What? Take me to him immediately!"

She wrinkled her nose as she pushed open the door.

"Dear Lord, the stink, Jacoba, tie back those window shutters and let in some fresh air,"

"He won't allow it, he says it hurts his eyes. He wants to lie in the dark."

"Really? We'll see about that. Now Gerrit, what goes on here? Jacoba says you are dying."

Oupa opened his eyes and I saw a tinge of yellow and my heart sank. Oupa came down with malaria at least once a year. If it came back now it would surely finish the work that the Zulus had started.

"Marijke. What brings you here?" he mumbled.

"What brings me here? What do you think brings me here? Not to see you die, old man. I didn't drive the wagon for four days for that! Now let me see where you are hurt."

"No, don't touch me, don't touch me."

Tannie van Tonder was a big woman, I had seen her throw an ox more than once, my oupa was no problem to her. As she lifted him up and threw him onto his stomach, he cried out and kicked his legs but he was no match for her.

"Be still, Gerrit!"

She pulled down his shirt collar and rolled the fold of wounded skin between fingers and thumb until oupa found enough strength to kick her so hard that she landed on the floor on her backside and for the first time in a fortnight I laughed.

"Stop laughing and bring me your Oupa's *herneutermes*, I am going to stop his nonsense," she said.

Oupa's father had bought that knife from the Moravian missionaries in Genadendal before the Great Trek, it was as sharp as a razor and the only time I had touched it had earned me a hiding.

"Nobody is allowed to touch it except Oupa." I replied.

"Well, it's not going to be much use to him if he's dead, is it?"

She ran her thumb along the blade.

"Go and make it hot in the fire."

At this Oupa started swearing.

"Dear God, Marijke, you are going to kill me!" he shouted

"Well, better that I kill you now than that you lie around dying for months making a nuisance of yourself!"

As I passed the blade back and forth through the flames I wondered what I was going to do when Jaap arrived.

"Sit on his back, child, and you, Lukas, you hold his head and don't let go."

She cut him open where his neck joined his shoulder, and poked about until a bullet popped out and dropped onto the pillow. Oupa roared and passed out. Jaap's mother poured brandy into the hole and, when he woke up, he could move both his arms again. It was a miracle. God had answered my prayers and rewarded me for my kneecaps rubbed raw on Oupa's zebraskin mat. I promised I would never again neglect my *godsdiens*, a promise I would not keep for very long.

Jaap arrived and my grandfather immediately set him to work, checking jackal traps. A few days passed before he raised the subject of our marriage.

Tannie van Tonder was stirring eland fat in a pot over the fire outside the cookhouse and I was tearing up an old sheet into narrow strips for wicks. If we worked quickly we could make a hundred candles in a day. When my mother was alive we would boil *gammabos* berries until they melted and mix the wax ,half and half, with fat and the candles would come out a pretty green colour, but we had no berries that day.

Jaap watched us for a while before he spoke.

"If you are going to stand there and say nothing you can make yourself useful and pour this fat into the molds," his mother said.

"We should make arrangements for our marriage," Jaap replied.

Tannie van Tonder stopped stirring the fat and stared at him.

"Have you taken leave of your senses, Jaap? Jacoba has lost almost her entire family and you want to talk about marriage?"

"All the more reason to get married. Who is going to run the farm now that Oom Jan is dead?"

"Not you, anyway," I blurted out, "Aren't you going off to be a lawyer?"

I think he realised then that I was having second thoughts and perhaps that was why he was in such a rush to marry us before I had time to change my mind completely. His face flushed and I saw him clenching his fists as he tried to control his temper.

"Perhaps we will not go. Now that your parents are dead."

Years later I would wonder whether he ever really wanted to be a lawyer and going to Maritzburg was just a way to get me away from my family and keep me for himself.

Tannie van Tonder put her hand on my shoulder.

"That's enough. There will be no talk of marriage until a suitable period of mourning has passed. Best you leave us alone now, Jaap, and go and look for Oom Gerrit, I am sure he has plenty of work for you to do."

Jaap looked as if he would answer back and I saw his mother raise the ladle she was using to stir the candle wax.

"You are not yet too old to get a hiding, Jaap van Tonder," she said and he turned and walked away, his face still red.

She poured the fat into the candle mold and I carried it outside to set in the shade of the fig tree.

JUNE 1879

CHAPTER TEN

Conor touched the tender spot on his head and winced. Four months previously, he had woken up under the gun carriage on the banks of the Buffalo, his head aching like the devil, to find a black woman bending over him. As she brought an assegai out from the folds of her skirt he closed his eyes and prepared himself to die. A few moments later he felt the blade of the spear scraping across his head and cautiously opened one eye.

When she had finished shaving his hair off she made him put his finger on his skull and he felt a small hole, no bigger than his thumbnail. She washed it out, stuck a reed from the river into it and waited with him until all the blood had poured out, before bandaging him with the shirt off a dead bombardier. He tried to thank her but she put a finger on his lips.

"*Tula*," she whispered, before picking up her spear and walking swiftly away. He crawled up the hill and lay under a wagon at the edge of the battlefield.

Only the buzzing of flies and the moans of the dying disturbed the silence. They had killed everything. Horses, oxen, mules, even the dogs. Sacks of rice and flour, maize meal and sugar lay broken everywhere, amongst cricket bats and pads, hunting guns and artist's materials. He watched as the woman raised her club and brought it down hard on the head of a young warrior who had lost both his legs. It burst like a watermelon and the contents of his skull spattered her dress. The men of the 24th lay in heaps where they had died together and the bodies were already starting to stink. According to Zulu custom a dead enemy had to be disembowelled to release evil spirits and to prevent the swelling up of a corpse and he turned his head away. The victorious warriors plundered the tents and drank the spirits and the *izinyanga* collected body parts from the dead soldiers, pieces of foreheads, rectums and the soft part from the bottom of breast-bones. Towards sunset, drunk and laden with booty, they moved off and Conor crawled out and walked across the bloody grass. The new moon cast no light and he saw dark shapes moving amongst the bodies and heard the crunch of powerful jaws on bones. He made his way to where his tent had been and found the little terrier cowering there.

"Aren't you the lucky one?" he said, wondering how she had avoided a stabbing as he saw the bodies of half a dozen camp dogs littered around her.

He found his notebook next to the smashed tentpole, put the little dog under his arm and began to walk down the road to Rorke's Drift.

He had spent almost four months there before he was issued with a new uniform, a pair of new saddlebags and new tools to replace what he had lost at Isandlwana and two days later he crossed the river into Zululand again. He was now halfway to Ulundi, the Zulu capital.

Most of the men on this second invasion of Zululand were new recruits freshly arrived from England, who talked excitedly about the upcoming battle, and as he listened to them he felt his throat constrict. Their route had taken them past Isandlwana and the sight of the unburied bodies, their skin stretched parchment like over their bones, had unnerved him. Everybody in the camp knew he was the only one there who had survived the battle and he was tired of being asked about it. He could not get the picture of Ellis impaled on a Zulu assegai, screaming for his mother, out of his head. He was considering desertion but he did not think any of the horses would carry him away fast enough. General Wood's horse would do it but he was kept tethered outside his master's tent night and day.

That evening a troop of lancers rode into camp. They were dressed in booted overalls and gold lace, and one of the officers was heard to remark that they looked like a lot of damned tenors in the opera. Conor froze when he saw, amongst them, a blond officer riding a black horse.

"By Jesus," he whispered, ducking quickly behind his wagon, his heart pounding.

"Well, Annie, that's it for us," he said to the little terrier, "got to go now. No choice."

Once he had collected his wits he realised that the solid black horse with a long white stripe extending from its eyes to its nostrils would definitely carry him away with no fear of being caught. He had shod that horse before every point to point it had ever won. That night he walked the horse out of the camp and into a *donga*, and once out of sight he mounted and fled, galloping across the veld, the dead Captain Smith's little terrier running beside him. He knew exactly where he was going, if he could only find his way there.

He had been riding for a week when he saw a spiral of smoke in the distance and pushed the horse into a canter. Five minutes later it stumbled into an antbear hole and went down on its knees, turfing Conor over its head. He got to his feet, cursing, and began to walk.

SEPTEMBER 1879

CHAPTER ELEVEN

I was helping my grandfather and Lukas to brand the new yearlings when I saw Conor walking across the veld towards the farmhouse.

"More visitors," Oupa grunted. "Her Majesty's soldiers don't seem to have much stomach for the Zulus any more. How many do you think, by this stage, Jacoba?"

"I don't know Oupa. Maybe a dozen."

"I hope he has better manners than the last one. Better get your rifle, just in case."

The horse's knees were shredded and bleeding and it could barely put one foot in front of the other and Conor was in no better condition. His uniform was in tatters, his hair hung over his collar and I barely recognised him until he was right in front of me. He raised his hands above his head when he saw the Sharp's pointed at his chest.

"You don't recognise me, miss."

"Oh. The shoeing smith," I replied, lowering the rifle.

"Aye, that's me."

I noticed a large patch of dried blood on the front of his tunic.

"Are you hurt?"

"Not I. I borrowed this jacket off a man who no longer had need of it."

"And the horse?

"He no longer had need of him, either."

"I meant what happened to his legs."

"Oh. He stumbled into a hole."

"Riding hard, were you?"

"You could say that."

I stooped to examine the horse's legs.

"You won't be getting any further on him today."

"I thought I might stand him in the river for a while."

"I wouldn't advise it. The crocodiles are breeding and they will be very cross. Better put him in the kraal and I will poultice him."

Whenever I think of Conor, it is always that day that comes into my mind. Him standing in front of me, the strip of white hair in the centre of his head making him look like a *bontebok*, fielding all my questions in a way that never quite gave me the full answer, but left me believing he had. He was so confident of his ability to wriggle out of every tricky situation.

After I had poulticed the horse, I brought out a plate of cold breast of mutton and spiced carrots, and set it down in front of him but before he could take the first mouthful Jaap appeared from behind the hide shed and I could see straight away there was going to be trouble.

"What is your business?" he asked.

"Just passing through," Conor replied. The broad grin on his face which, I later learned, could disarm almost everyone of even the most hostile intentions did not work on Jaap.

"You cannot stay here," he said.

I stared at him.

"That is not your decision to make, Jaap."

Jaap ignored me and took a step towards Conor. My oupa had never fully recovered from his injuries and was not the man he used to be and Jaap thought he was in charge now. I had all but resigned myself to marrying him now that he had given up his plans to be a lawyer. Oupa was right. A woman needed a husband and I thought that here on the farm I would be able to have the best of both worlds, at least as long as my grandfather was alive.

"You must leave."

Conor stood up and raised his hands.

"Of course. I'll be on my way."

I turned on Jaap.

"You have no right. Look at the state of his horse!"

My grandfather had finished the branding and was walking towards us, wiping his hands on a piece of cloth.

"What's going on, Jacoba?"

Jaap answered him.

"A deserter, *oom*. I am sending him on his way."

Oupa saw the uneaten plate of mutton on the table.

"Without food? Where are your manners?"

"He is a British deserter, *oom*."

"I don't care if he is the devil himself, in this house we do not turn away strangers without food and drink."

Conor was staring at my oupa.

" I know you, sir. I saw you with Lord Chelmsford before the battle at Isandlwana."

I think my heart stopped then, for just a few seconds. Surely he had seen my father, too.

"Did you indeed?" my grandfather replied. "If your Lord Chelmsford had listened to us there would not be nine hundred redcoats now lying in graves on that battlefield. He made a fool of himself."

"He did," Conor agreed.

"Sit and eat. We will talk later."

I glanced at Jaap. It was the same as the day he had beaten up Hendrik, the clenched jaw, the red rash rising above his collar, the fight to control himself. I felt it, more than saw it and it frightened me. Conor tore into his food and I wondered how long it had been since he last ate. Oupa had lit his pipe and poured coffee for himself. And while they sat there my thoughts collided in my head as I waited to see whether I would now discover how my father had died.

"What news do you have of the war?" Oupa said.

"They were on their way to Ulundi when I left, I expect it will be all over soon enough."

"And what will they do then?"

"I don't know, sir, but whatever it is, they be doing it without me."

Oupa stared into the distance.

"You have made a mess of our country and my son is dead because of it."

Conor did not reply and I dared not join in the conversation. To do so would have been an unforgivable breach of manners and earn me a swift rebuke from my Oupa.

"My granddaughter tells me that you are a farrier. I have forty horses in need of shoes. Perhaps you will shoe them for me while you wait for your horse's legs to heal?"

"I can shoe the horses, *oom*," Jaap said.

"Yes, and I can spend the next month picking up cast shoes on the *veld*, what you know about shoeing will fit on the head of a nail. You stick to minding your sheep, you are good at that."

Days stretched into weeks and Conor's horse came sound but he showed no signs of leaving and I made no effort to encourage him to go. We certainly needed the extra pair of hands, the war was over, the British had reversed the decision of the Boundary Commission and we thought our lives were going back to the way they had been. Oupa started to take a renewed interest in the horses and began to talk about getting more sheep. The longer Conor stayed, the darker Jaap became and I knew I was only storing up trouble for myself but Conor was funny and kind and he made me laugh. He made himself useful, and lifted the gloomy atmosphere which had hung over the farm since my mother and father died. I asked him once about Isandlwana and whether he had seen my father die but he refused to talk about it.

Things came to a head when Oupa told him he could stay as long as he liked. Perhaps he saw the growing attraction between us before

I did and when Jaap suddenly announced that he needed to discuss something with his father I thought that he had changed his mind about marrying me and might never come back. I had mixed feelings as I watched him ride away, it was not easy for me to admit that the quiet, considerate Jaap I grew up with had changed into a man of whom I was afraid.

CHAPTER TWELVE

A few miles away, at Isandlwana, a squadron of 17th Lancers, en route to the Transvaal, were camped for the night at the edge of the battlefield. They had taken the opportunity to rebury bodies which had become partially exposed and bury those which still lay in the open. Brevet Major Herbert Webster, annoyed that he had to redo a job which he had already done in March, had just sat down at his field desk to write his report when a soldier appeared at the door of his tent.

"Yes?" he snarled.

"Sir. There is a Boer outside wants to speak to you."

"What about?"

"Won't say, sir. Says he'll only speak to an officer, sir. Says it's important."

Herbert jabbed his pen back in its inkwell.

"Very well. Bring him inside."

Jaap stepped inside the door, looked at Herbert and recognised a kindred spirit. Here, he was sure, was a man who would bear a grudge till his dying day. Earlier that week he had noticed that Conor's black horse bore the letters 17 L burned into its hooves. It was certainly an officer's horse. Perhaps it belonged to the man now glaring at him from behind his desk.

"*Middag, meneer*," he said.

"Speak English, for God's sake, man!"

"My *Engels* is not so good, *meneer*."

"I'll fetch Soames, sir, he speaks their lingo," the trooper said. He returned moments later with a skinny little corporal, who rattled off a string of questions at Jaap.

"He says there is a deserter on a farm nearby, sir."

"Indeed."

"Yes, sir."

"Tell him I haven't time to go on a wild goose chase looking for one deserter," Herbert replied, waving his hand in dismissal and picking up his pen again.

"Says he arrived in July riding a big black horse with a white blaze, sir."

Herbert put the pen down, cursing as ink splattered ink across his report.

"What? Is he quite sure?"

"He is, sir."

Herbert rose from his chair and strapped on his revolver.

"And where exactly is this farm?"

"About twenty miles away, sir. He says he will give us directions. He wants to know if there is a reward, sir."

"There is no reward!" Herbert snapped, "Tell him he is only doing what is expected of every loyal subject of the Crown!"

I spotted the soldiers riding towards the farm and ran the black horse into the shearing shed, slamming the door closed and hooking the chain.

The officer was heavyset and his neatly pressed scarlet tunic and polished boots contrasted sharply with the tattered uniforms of his men. Below his helmet was a white scar, standing out from his sun reddened face and there was cruelty in his washed out blue eyes. I disliked him immediately.

"Good afternoon, madam, we are looking for a deserter," he said.

"There is no deserter here."

"We were given information, madam, that there is a deserter living here."

He heeled his horse a step closer to me and I raised my hand and placed it on the animal's muzzle.

"Step away, please , madam,"

His eyes bored into mine and I felt my palms begin to sweat.

"I have told you. There is no deserter here."

"Then you will not mind if we take a look inside?" he replied, motioning to two troopers, who immediately dismounted and began to walk towards the house.

"I certainly do mind," I replied. It was a reckless thing to say, to antagonise him, but I did not know, then, what the British were capable of, and even if I had, I probably would have acted no differently. My father always said I was *hardegat* from the day I was born and he was right.

"Well, you are hardly in a position to stop us, madam."

He smiled as the troopers mounted the steps, and then the fly screen door swung open.

"Perhaps not, but I am."

Oupa stood in the doorway, his elephant gun pointed straight at the officer's chest. He swayed back and forth, his eyes bloodshot in his jaundiced face but his aim did not waver. The malaria which had struck him down the previous day had taken a firm hold by then.

"You do realise that you are pointing a rifle at an officer of the Queen?" the officer said.

"What I realise is that I am pointing my rifle at a trespasser," Oupa replied, steadying himself against the door jamb, "Even in Africa you must have a warrant from the magistrate to search a private dwelling."

For a moment they stared at each other and then the officer recalled his men. An elephant gun is not something you argue with.

"Very well, sir. We can wait. And I assure you if he is here we shall have him."

They retired and began to pitch their camp next to the road, while I helped my grandfather back inside and onto the bed. I could see the effort had nearly killed him.

I found Conor in the smithy, lacing up his boots.

"I shall have to go, now," he said and I could hear the fear in his voice.

"You cant. You won't get away. They are waiting outside for you."

"I know that man. Your grandfather will not be able to keep him at bay forever. He will wait until he has me and then he will kill me. I think I'll take my chances."

Taking chances was something Conor was very good at, it was a great pity that his chances always had consequences for other people.

"Why does he want to kill you? For deserting?"

He finished tying his laces and stood up.

"No. I'd say I'll only get the cat for that, and a night tied to a wagon wheel. There is another reason why he wants to kill me and I have no time to tell it to you."

He held me then, for the first time, I never forgot that moment, it was when I decided that, no matter what happened, I would not marry Jaap.

"You will come back? When the soldiers have gone? I heard one of them saying they are on their way to the Transvaal. They will surely not return to look for you again."

"I will."

"Promise me."

"I promise," he replied and I believed him.

My grandfather was raving when I got back to the house and I sat, sponging his face with a wet cloth, thinking about what I was going to say to Jaap if he returned.

As Conor walked the horse out of the shed a shadow disengaged itself from the wall of the sheepkraal and Herbert walked towards him, his revolver in his hand.

"You!" he said.

Conor stared down the barrel of the Webley and felt his guts contract.

"Aye, me," he replied.

"Attempted murder, horse theft, desertion. You have made certain of the gallows now."

He stood directly in front of the horse, a smile on his face. Conor remembered that smile so well and it made him shudder.

"Perhaps not," he replied, nudging the horse with his left heel. It rose on its hind legs and struck out with its forelegs, knocking Herbert to the ground and sending the revolver flying into the dipping trough.

"I made a hames of it the last time but I'll do for you now, you bastard," he said.

He drove the horse forward again as Herbert tried to roll out of the way, but the noise had alerted a sentry and the troopers were already pouring out of their tents and he wheeled around and galloped into the darkness.

Herbert picked himself up off the ground, his uniform covered in mud and sheep manure.

"Shall we go after him sir?" enquired one of the troopers.

"Of course, you fool," Herbert screamed, " What are you waiting for?"

Jacoba watched from the window as the troopers galloped in pursuit. The sky was black, clouds obscuring the moon. If Conor made for the hills they would never catch him. It was almost dawn before the troopers returned emptyhanded.

"No sign of him, sir."

"Fire the house."

The man hesitated.

"Are you sure, sir? What about the old man and the girl?"

"What about them?"

"Sir. We can't burn a house with people inside. The men won't do it."

Herbert looked at the faces of the troopers. Most of them were older than him and he could see the thinly veiled disapproval on their faces. He knew they would not do it and he knew he could not make them, and when word got around that he was unable to enforce an order, he would be disgraced and any prospects of promotion would be lost.

"Very well. Burn everything except the house and confiscate the stock." he snarled.

CHAPTER THIRTEEN

All that remained of my grandfather's house was a charred heap of reeds and plaster. He had built that *hartbeeshuisie* when he first came to Zululand, fleeing British rule in Natal, almost twenty five years before I was born

.Made of grass and reeds, thinly plastered with a mixture of cattle dung and antheap, it was supposed to be a temporary dwelling in case he had to flee again but he had never replaced it. Once a year, when my Uncle Andries came down from the Transvaal to graze his cattle, we would whitewash the walls and make repairs to the roof. My grandfather loved that house.

The stink of burned hides under the ruins of the shearing shed was unbearable and made me gag and I turned and walked across the veld to the compound where the *plaasvolk* lived but they had run away, leaving the corpses of headless chickens littered around the burnt circles that were once their huts. One small hen wandered around with her chicks and I scooped them up and brought them back to the house, while the hen ran angrily behind me, pecking at my bare legs. The horses and sheep were gone. All of Oupa's careful breeding had been brought to nothing in the space of a day. By some miracle my oupa's oxwagon was unscathed, although the wagon house lay in pieces on top of it, but the cookhouse had collapsed and as I sifted through the rubble looking for my mother's cooking pots I wondered how I would tell my Oupa that we had lost everything.

He was still out of his mind with the fever and I sat beside him holding his hand, for the comfort it gave me, listening to him rave about people I had never heard of..Two days passed before he came out of his delirium and by then I had questions.

"Oupa. Who is Wynand?"

He sighed.

"Ah. Wynand. Wynand was your father's brother."

I thought he had lost his mind.

"No, Oupa, Pa's brother is Oom Andries. Do you not remember?"

"Wynand was your father's twin. He was not like your father. He was a young buck, always restless, always looking for adventure. He gave me a lot of trouble. The year you were born we had a big fight and Wynand ran away to the diamond fields to seek his fortune. I don't know if he found it for we never saw him again."

And never spoke of him again, either. I wondered what my uncle had done to make his name disappear from my family's conversations.

"Why did you fight, Oupa?"

"It doesn't matter, my child. It was a stupid thing. A small thing but I was stubborn and Wynand was worse. Neither of us would give in. I regret it to this day."

"You could have written him a letter and sent it with Hannes."

"I did. Many times. But he never replied. Perhaps he is dead."

I saw the pain in his old blue eyes and I knew that if I told him what had happened to his horses it would be the end of him.

"I will bring Oupa a cup of coffee," I said.

When I went outside Lukas was standing on the stoep.

"It was Baas Jaap," he said.

"What was Baas Jaap?"

"Baas Jaap told the soldiers about the *rooinek*."

It took me a few moments to fully comprehend what he was saying.

"No," I replied.

"Yes, *missies*, I was looking for stray sheep and I saw him at the place where the *baas* died, talking to that *moerskont* that burned the farm."

"Are you sure?"

I knew Lukas did not like Jaap and I thought perhaps he was making it up. I hoped he was making it up because my brain refused to believe that Jaap would do such a thing, no matter how jealous he was..

Lukas nodded his head.

"And where is he now?"

I saw his eyes shift towards the road.

"There, Miss Jacoba."

As I watched Jaap cantering towards me, I tried to rein in my temper, something I had never been very good at.

"What have you done?" I said, as he stopped in front of me.

"What do you mean? What happened? Who did this? Where are the sheep? And the horses?" he replied, staring at the still smouldering ruins of my grandfather's house.

"I think you know very well what happened," I replied, struggling to contain my fury.

"I don't know what you mean."

"No? Was it not you who sent the soldiers here, Jaap? It was they who burnt the huts and took the stock."

"I know nothing of that!" he protested.

"Don't lie to me, Jaap. I am not a fool."

His face flushed with anger, but this time I was not afraid.

"Don't call me a liar," he replied.

"Why not? That is what you are. Lukas saw you talking to the soldiers."

"You will take the word of a *kaffirboy* over mine? It is Lukas who is lying."

I felt my self control slipping away and I still do not know how I stopped myself from hitting him.

"Oupa got that *kaffirboy* from the magistrate when I was born. He took care of me when I was a child. Yes, I will take his word over yours."

I pointed to my empty land.

"Look, Jaap, look what you have done. They have taken everything."

"It is your own fault, you should never have allowed him to stay. At least now he is caught and will get his punishment."

"No, Jaap, he is not caught. He got away and then they burned the farm. You were jealous of him and now we have lost everything. Go! Get off my farm!"

"What?"

"Get off my farm."

"You can't…. you can't…you can't chase me off this farm, we are going to be married," he shouted.

"No we are not Jaap."

"You have to, you have to marry me."

I saw him bring his weight into the stirrup as he prepared to dismount and I grabbed his horse's bridle.

"Don't get off your horse, Jaap."

"I am going to speak to your grandfather."

"No, you are not."

I saw that look in his eye, the same one I saw at Nagmaal. I thought he was going to hit me and I let go of the horse and walked into the house. I gripped the table, my heart pounding in my ears and then I heard the flyscreen door slam and suddenly he was upon me, tearing at my clothes. I scratched at his eyes and kicked his legs but he was too strong for me. I couldn't get my fist back to punch him but still I thought he would not get the better of me. I did not yet know what he was going to do and then he threw me to the floor and I could not keep him out of me. After a time I stopped struggling and let him do what he wanted. When he got off me he started to cry.

"I am sorry, Jacoba, I am sorry, I am sorry."

He picked up my shirt and tried to put it back on me and that was when I began to lose my reason.

"Get away from me Jaap," I said, picking up my grandfather's hunting knife from the sideboard.

"Please, Jacoba, put down the knife. I am sorry, I am sorry."

"I am telling you, Jaap. Get out before I kill you."

He walked backwards to the door, still crying and then Asjas came running out of nowhere and jumped at him and Jaap kicked him hard, and I heard the bone crack. He ran away across the veld screaming and as I saw Jaap get on his horse and go after him something inside me snapped as neatly as the baboon's broken arm.

I took the Sharp's down from the rack and went, half naked, onto the stoep. Jaap had cut Asjas off by then and the horse was standing up on its hind legs, striking out with its front feet. I knew that trick well, my grandfather had taught it to me and I taught it to Jaap. We used it to kill snakes in the *veld*. I felt something boiling up inside me, burning my throat and nose. He was half a mile away when I shot him.

"What's going on, Jacoba?" Oupa called out

I heard a thump and I knew he had fallen from his bed again but I had no energy to go into him.

"*Niks*, Oupa," I replied, as I sank to the floor.

I lay on the floor of the livingroom for a long time, feeling the coolness of the *misvloer* against my cheek, before I heard the flyscreen door bang open again and in an instant I was on my feet and reaching for my rifle, but it was only Asjas, making the chirruping sound he always made when he had hurt himself.

After I had splinted his arm I went to the cemetery and sat in front of my mother's grave, cradling the baboon in my lap, trying to feel some remorse for what I had done, but I could not. The sun was setting by the time I gave up, and when I got back to the house my grandfather was dead. I stood next to the bed as numbness spread across my chest, clamping down on my lungs so that I could hardly breathe. It was dark by now but the moon was full and as I sat on the stoep, I could see Jaap's horse still standing next to the body of his master. After a while I began to imagine that he was not dead, after all, and was crawling towards me, through the long grass. Asjas started chattering and I shrank against the wall, clutching my rifle but it was Lukas who appeared from the shadows and I was so relieved to see him that I started shouting.

"Where the hell have you been?"

"I went to look for the oxen, *missies*."

"Well, I hope you found them because we will be needing them soon. The *oubaas* is dead," I replied, and saw his eyes fill with tears.

"Stop *tjanking*! Crying is not going to help us," I snapped.

"What we going to do with him, Miss Jacoba?"

"We are going to bury him. What else are we going to do?"

"I mean the other one. Baas Jaap. What we going to do with him?"

I had not given any thought to this and I paused for a moment, before I replied.

"We will put him in first and the *oubaas* on top of him."

When we were done I poured myself a measure of my grandfather's peach brandy. It was the first time I had taken alcohol and the fiery liquid caught in my throat making me cough but I forced it down and then I poured another one. I woke up many hours later with a blinding headache and a plan. Jaap's horse had run home and it would not be long before his brothers came looking for him. We would go to my Uncle Andries in the Transvaal. Nobody would ride so far to look for me there.

Oupa's wagon was a huge machine, twelve feet long and four feet broad, the body low, the hind wheels as large again as the front ones, all put together with wooden pegs so that it could be dismantled to be carried piecemeal up and down the mountain passes and reassembled on the other side. It was covered with a wooden frame and a canvas sail which formed a curtain at each end. Fourteen oxen were needed to pull it, yoked in spans of two.

We packed the wagon, grabbing whatever was to hand. *Oupagrootjie's* stinkwood chair, a folding table and two *riempiestoele* ,my mother's foot stove and my father's kist. Water casks, shovels, a tar bucket, the twisted cookpots and kettles I had managed to retrieve from the remains of the cookhouse. A hundred pound bag of mieliemeel, a fifty pound bag of coffee beans and my grandmother's medicine chest. I put Oupa's *sanna* and the Sharp's and all the ammunition I could find, behind the wagon seat, where I could reach them easily, put my good saddle and bridle in on top of everything and threw Asjas and Conor's little dog up onto the wagon seat.

I was frantic to get away and almost forgot to go down the line of waiting oxen. My oupa had taught me that if you did not remind each ox of his name, he would forget who he was halfway through your journey and refuse to go further. Perhaps it was just a story but we never left home without doing it.

"*Laat waai. Missies, laat waai!*" Lukas shouted as I cracked the whip above my head. The *spoggertjie* on the end of it made a high pitched scream as it flew through the air and the wagon lurched forward as the oxen leaned into their yokes. I did not look back.

CHAPTER FOURTEEN

It was raining and the river was in spate when we got to Laing's Nek and there were over one hundred wagons waiting to cross to the other side. Boers from the Free State and the Transvaal, huddled in their tents while they waited for the water level to drop and the women in their print dresses and embroidered black aprons stared as we drove past. A young girl travelling alone with a baboon and a black man was not a common sight.

Lukas outspanned our animals and turned them loose and I watched them lumber off until they were out of sight, lost amongst the two thousand oxen grazing on the waterlogged veld. It had taken me more than a week to get there and I was close to exhaustion. I ate some *biltong*, crawled into the wagon and fell asleep immediately, with Asjas on one side of me and Conor's little dog on the other, still in the clothes I was wearing when I shot Jaap. I woke up before everyone else and went to wash myself in the river in the early morning darkness, hugging the trunk of a tree wedged between two rocks, letting the freezing water wash over me, while Asjas sat on the riverbank, nursing his arm and crooning softly to himself. As I watched my clothes float away down the river I wondered how long it would take before they passed by our farm and would Conor return and see them washed up on the riverbank and think I had drowned. I didn't want to touch myself there, I was afraid of what I might find. I didn't want to think about what had happened to our farm, what had happened to my parents and my oupa and my life..

And I didn't want to think about what Jaap did to me and what I did to him.

It rained and rained and we were stuck for weeks, watching the river rise higher and higher every day and the higher it went, the lower my spirits sank. The strength I had summoned up when leaving the farm evaporated and left me wondering how I was going to make the one hundred and fifty mile journey to my Uncle Andries's farm in Lydenburg. I was saved by the arrival of two transport riders who had sometimes called to the farm. They had six wagons between them, filled with goods for the Transvaal and they said they would help me over the mountain pass and escort me as far as Dullstroom. They were rough and dangerous looking, these transport riders, wearing ear rings and bright red neckerchiefs, armed to the teeth with rifles and pistols. Surly and uncommunicative, they did not ask me what I was doing, alone, so far from home.

Eating was my biggest problem. I had coffee and sugar and *mieliemeel* but no means of cooking it in the continuous, pouring rain and I wished I had stayed an extra day at the farm and baked bread and *beskuit* before I left. My mother would never have left on such a long journey without adequate provisions. Women came to offer me their help but I turned them politely away, afraid they would ask me about my family and I might let slip something about Jaap. I sat inside my wagon listening to the rain beating down on the canvas, expecting Fanie and Tielman to arrive at any moment. Asjas and the little dog agreed an uneasy truce and sat miserably at opposite ends of the wagon, ignoring each other. Lukas spent his days with the other *voorleiers*, returning only at night to sleep under the wagon on Oupa's *katelbed*. For the first time in my life I had no one to confide in.

I used the time to rearrange the wagon which we had packed in such haste. In the bottom of my father's kist I found a cloth wrapped parcel and when I untied the strings I discovered a photograph of my mother sitting on a chair, my father standing behind her, his hand resting on her shoulder. His face was clean shaven and he looked so young and happy. I stared at the photograph for a very long time, and tried to imagine what he must have felt when he first saw my mother. I knew the story, of course, I had pestered it out of my mother while she was laid up in bed expecting the baby which had killed her. Her father had emigrated from England to the Eastern Cape at the end of a distinguished military career, lured by promises of a farming paradise. He had arrived full of hope but after four years of failed crops he abandoned his small allotment of land and moved into Grahamstown where he became a wealthy merchant. My mother attended Mrs Blackburn's Academy for Ladies, where she learned to play the harp and the piano, to sing in English, Italian and French, and to dance and draw. When she wasn't copying poetry or playing whist she attended concerts and race meetings and took part in amateur theatricals. Courted eagerly by the officers of the local garrison, the most important decision she had to make was which dress to wear to the ball.

Then my father arrived to buy two imported French Merino rams. His rough farmer's ways excited her in a way that the foppish English officers were unable to do and he, in turn, was bowled away by her sophistication. The union had been welcomed by neither side of the family but they had stood their ground and got married anyway. I remembered asking my mother whether she had ever regretted her decision and she had told me no, never, my father was a good man.

Two months passed before the rain stopped and the sun came out and the first thing I did was make a fire, emptying a thimbleful of gunpowder onto a scrap of cloth and hitting it against the wagon wheel with a stone until it flared and set alight the *kapokbossie* I held in my other hand. Soon I had a mass of glowing coals and I set the coffee pot to boil. Everything in the wagon was damp and every scrap of leather was furred and mouldy. The constant downpour had also revealed places of perished canvas, where the water had dripped through, which would have to be repaired before I could go any further. We began to empty the wagon of its contents. Everybody else was doing the same thing and as the sun shone down steam rose from every corner of the camp and my spirits began to lift. By then I had discovered Fanny's card amongst my father's things, how it got there, I will never know, but when one of the transport riders came and told me to be ready to leave by the following evening I thanked him for his trouble and told him I had changed my mind.

We followed the game paths over the *nek*, passing many wagons hopelessly stuck. Some were completely overturned or sunk down to the axles in the mud, people unloading their goods, cursing and shouting. We managed only three miles an hour. I had bought two ponies and a pack mule from one of the Orange Free State Boers and these plodded along behind us, tied to the back of the wagon.

Once over the mountains, the transport riders turned towards Harrismith and we turned west, towards the Northern Cape. I was on my own now with nothing but treeless *veld* and *spitzkoppies* in front of me and my dead family behind me. I opened my hand and studied Fanny's card.

Mrs Frances Yudelman

Clean rooms, fresh linen

All night - £1

No 5 Loch Street, Belgravia, Kimberley.

As soon as we came to the rolling grasslands of the Orange Free State, I shot a *blesbok* and roasted the juicy, dark red meat over the fire with a gravy seasoned with spinach and wild sorrel. I had not tasted fresh meat for over two months and I ate until I was nearly sick, allowing the juices to flow down my chin. I made the rest into *biltong*, hanging it at the back of the wagon where the breeze could blow through it, and threw the entrails on the ground for Asjas and Conor's little terrier to squabble over.

In the following weeks the countryside gradually changed and the ground became hard and sandy, covered with low, woody scrub and dotted with saltpans. Sometimes I left Lukas to lead the oxen while I rode one of the ponies across the veld with Asjas and the dog, I was used to my own company and there was no shortage of game and we ate well off the buck I shot. I was free now, free to do whatever I pleased and I began to imagine what life would be like in Kimberley. I hardly noticed my belly beginning to swell and it was only when I woke up one morning and began to vomit that I realised I was pregnant. I should have expected it but I didn't and the shock threw me into a panic, not least because I thought one of us might die. I did not want to give birth alone with nobody to help me and I bullied the oxen unmercifully, giving them no rest, until Lukas told me to stop before I killed them and we all died in the *veld*.

And then the springbok came.

We were plodding along a dry riverbed in the middle of the morning, when Asjas became very agitated, jumped off the wagon and ran up a tree, baring his teeth and chattering. I followed his gaze and saw a faint haze on the horizon many miles away.

"What is it, Lukas? A dust storm?"

"No, Miss Jacoba, they are *trekbokke* and they are coming very fast."

I knew about *trekbokke*. Sometimes, for no reason at all, springbok gathered in great herds and migrated across the country, destroying everything in their path and they were going to destroy us if we did not get out of their way. I lashed the oxen out of the riverbed towards a nearby *koppie* . Halfway up the hill I got off the wagon and walked the rest of the way to the top with Lukas and then I could see them coming. They would be upon us within the hour. While I outspanned the oxen, Lukas started building a six foot palisade of camelthorn branches. We set fires around the wagon and drove the ponies, the mule and the oxen inside the boma

By now the dust was only a few miles away, and rising higher with every passing minute. It was at least three miles wide and the midpoint of it was headed straight at us and for the first time, I felt afraid and I considered escaping with Asjas and Lukas on the two ponies but I could not chance losing my oxen, without them we would get no further. Soon rock rabbits and jackals, families of meerkats and tiny fieldmice began to race past. Even snakes were out in the open, slithering under the rocks on the hill, I had never seen puff adders move so fast.

The buck were still hidden by an enormous cloud of dust when, at last, I heard a faint drumming and then I saw the first springbok, running faster than galloping horses and I told Lukas to light the fires. The stock milled around inside the boma, the fires were driving them into a panic and Asjas was screaming and chattering like a mountain parrot. Solid groups of buck swept past on both sides of the hill, making for the river and the open country beyond and I clung to the wagon hood as the animals crashed through the fires and were jammed in the wheels. The wagon swayed on its axles and I was sure it would turn over at any minute. Then the thorn barrier broke and the ponies and oxen stampeded and vanished into the dust and Asjas jumped onto the mule's back. They ran down the riverbed, all mingled together, getting under each others' hooves and were soon lost to view. Everything in the wagon was an inch deep in pale yellow dust and Lukas and I got under a blanket to keep from smothering. The noise was overwhelming and I put my hands over my ears to shut it out. Long after sunset, hundreds upon hundreds of exhausted, crippled stragglers staggered past until, just as I thought it would never end, they were gone.

At daybreak, I climbed to the top of the hill. The morning air was so clear and the day so bright but all that remained of what had been trees the day before were stumps. Every *donga* leading into the riverbed, was filled with dead antelope, even tortoises were crushed to a pulp. I found the body of Conor's brave little terrier caught between the spokes of the wagon wheel, her neck broken, and I cried.

There was no sign of a pony, or an ox or a baboon and I slumped down against the wheels of the oxwagon. The vultures were already circling overhead as packs of wild dogs tore at the soft, white bellies of the dead buck.

Lukas stood next to the wagon, shaking his head.

"I will go to look for the oxen, Miss Jacoba," he said.

I fell asleep and woke up in the late afternoon with pains in my stomach, which quickly got worse until I thought I would burst apart. Then I felt wetness between my thighs and when I lifted up my dress there was blood. Hours passed before the baby escaped from my body. She was about twelve inches long, covered in white fat with tiny fingers and fingernails and fine hair growing on her head. She was so small, I did not even know if she counted as a person. I folded her inside a piece of cloth to keep away the flies and after a while, I took the shovel out of the wagon and made a space amongst the dead springbok and buried her and everything that came with her and piled rocks on top of the grave.

It was a full three days before Lukas returned with Asjas, one pony and the mule and by then I was very sick. I sweated all day, I could hear my heart beating in my ears and I vomited all the time. I lay on a blanket under the wagon, sure I was going to die, while Lukas covered my head with wet cloths. All around me lay the stinking, rotting carcases of the dead buck. I was being punished by God for what I had done to Jaap.

When my fever broke I asked Lukas how long I had been like that and he held up ten fingers.

"The oxen?"

"Gone, *missies*."

Our water was almost finished and there was no grazing for the animals, the pony was chewing the bark off the treestumps.

"Come, Lukas," I said, dragging myself to my feet. "We must pack what we can onto the mule and get going or we will die out here."

I had nothing left except a *bobbejaan*, a pony and a loaded pack mule. I did not even have my name for I had decided that from now on I would go by my mother's name of Rawlings, just in case Jaap's brothers came looking for me. I didn't realise it at the time but I gave up my Boer heritage along with my name and it would be many years before I got it back.

PART TWO - KIMBERLEY

APRIL 1880

CHAPTER FIFTEEN

I rode into Kimberley in a daze of pain, my stomach cramping, the sweat pouring down my face, stinging my eyes. Slapped on either side of the road was a great white canvas town, straggling across the veld, amongst the camelthorn trees. Teams of half naked men, scratching through mounds of red earth, stopped to stare at us as we rode past. Soon the town came into view but here was no broad, treelined main street leading up to the church, no fancy houses with Cape Dutch gables, no smiling faces waiting to welcome us, only a dusty, potholed road lined with rows of brick and iron buildings and not a single tree to be seen.

I found Number 5 Loch Street easily enough, it seemed that everyone in Kimberley knew Fanny. Constructed out of orange brick, the house was set well back from the street, sprawled over large grounds on which nothing grew except a large fig tree, whose branches rested on the red and white zinc roof which covered the wraparound verandah. A black man, with a deep scar across the bridge of his nose, opened the door and I showed him Fanny's card.

"The madam is not here, she has gone to Ingrand," he said, shutting the door in my face. I stood for a while staring at the door and for the first time I thought I might give up.

Then Lukas tapped me on the shoulder.

"*Kom,* Miss Jacoba, we must find a place to sleep for the night," he said.

We were halfway down Main Street when I fainted and fell off my pony.

DECEMBER 1880

CHAPTER SIXTEEN

I might have died had it not been for Mary O'Hara, who saw me topple to the ground outside the Grand Hotel and brought me to the hospital, where they told me I had childbed fever and would never have any more children, a diagnosis which would later prove to be wrong and cause me a great deal of trouble.

Mary's husband had fallen down the mine when a large piece of reef collapsed, breaking nearly every bone in his body when he hit the bottom. He had left her with a claim on the outskirts of town and three freckle faced boys called Albert, Michael and Jimmy.

Our tents were pitched on a rise, close to a tree, surrounded by a thorn bush fence, beyond which plains, carpeted in long silvery grass and dotted with thousands of umbrella-shaped thorn trees, stretched away to the horizon. As soon as I was well enough I went to look at the mine. Overshadowed by mountainous dumps of blue earth, it was over three hundred feet deep and the men on the sides looked like a swarm of flies on a gigantic sugarbowl. Looking down into it made me dizzy. The rasp and clatter of shovels, the whine of the windlasses and the roar of buckets tipping their contents at the surface in a cloud of smothering dust was deafening. The natives, almost naked, wearing a greasy, gaudy handkerchief twisted around their heads were easily distinguishable from the white miners in their plain suits of brown corduroy, and broad-brimmed straw hats. As I stood there, a ladder came adrift from the side of the hole and plummeted downwards, taking half a dozen screaming labourers with it. Fanny had not exaggerated about the miners' camp. It was a filthy place, where scavenging dogs roamed amongst the rotting carcases of animals, and flies clustered on the insides of tents, waiting to pounce as soon as a plate of food appeared. I was glad I did not have to live there.

Mary's claim was thirty feet square and sixty feet deep and a knotted rope dangled into it from a post set in the ground near its mouth. At the bottom of this pit Lukas split the soft, greenish rock with a pick axe and shovelled it into a bucket which we hauled up to the surface by means of a rope stretched over a crude windlass.Mary's eldest boy emptied it onto the ground and beat the lumps of earth with a shovel after which I screened it in a round sieve of coarse mesh, to separate the worthless larger stones. After this screening Mary's two younger boys sifted the ground a second time, in a rocking sieve of fine, strong wire, set in an oblong frame, stretched between two upright posts, until all the sand and dust had fallen through the wire mesh, leaving a layer of fine chips and little pebbles of limestone. They brought this to a sorting table where Mary and I scraped it over. The diamonds came in every colour, white, brown, pink, mauve, and green . Sometimes we found deep yellow and pale blue stones, as well as the black diamonds used for setting drill-crowns. I quickly learned how to recognise a good stone, and estimate its value without even putting it on the scales. Asjas also turned out to have a fine eye for the shiny stones. At first he plucked them out and ran off with them but before long I had taught him to put them in a little pile at the end of the table.

"Clever little beggar, ain't he?" Mary remarked.

"Brave,too. He's afraid of nothing," I replied, remembering how he had tried to defend me from Jaap.

Hot winds blew in clouds of red dust mixed with powdered white limestone from the ridge above us, inflaming our eyes, and clogging our noses. Our skin was coated through our clothes and Asjas looked as if he had been sprinkled with flour.

Once a week Mary sent me into town to the diamond dealers. Whether it was my good looks or my bargaining skills I cannot say, but I always obtained a good price. Perhaps my unusual height, I was almost six feet tall by then, also played a part. It is difficult to argue with a woman who looks down on you, something I quickly learned to use to my advantage.

Sunday was the only day we did not work and Mary exchanged her faded print dress and coalscuttle *kappie* for a bustle and bonnet and led her children off to church but I never went with them. I did not think God would be pleased to welcome me into his house after what I had done.

One Sunday in the middle of December she returned from church bursting with news. Five thousand Transvaal Boers had held a meeting, at Paardekraal, hoisted the Vierkleur and declared themselves a republic again. I remembered the time when I was eleven years old and Uncle Andries had arrived from the Transvaal in a towering rage. It was 1877 and Theophilus Shepstone, the native agent in Natal, having tricked the Boers into believing that the Zulus were about to invade, had recently marched into Pretoria with twenty five policemen, run up the Union Jack and declared the country under British rule. The Boers who had who had trekked away from their British rulers in the Cape and settled in the Transvaal some forty years before were an argumentative people and bickered endlessly amongst themselves over the most trivial matters. They weren't really a nation at all, simply a collection of quarrelsome Dutch speaking farmers spread over a vast area, and a few towns occupied by shopkeepers and petty officials, most of whom were foreigners. They refused to pay taxes and they would not obey the law but the annexation had finally united them in a common cause and now they were taking back their country.

The British response was to declare them rebels and over the next two weeks I saw a constant stream of troops passing through Kimberley on their way to put down this rebellion. I wondered whether my uncle and my cousin Etienne had been at Paardekraal.

For the first time I missed the heated arguments which had formed such a huge part of my childhood, whenever my uncle came to Zululand to graze his cattle.

CHAPTER SEVENTEEN

Shortly before midday, at Bronkhorstspruit, twenty miles outside Pretoria, Conor waited in a thicket on top of a ridge . Inside his saddlebags were a gross of sharpened pencils and a ream of paper. Earlier that day he had presented himself in the Boer camp as a war correspondent. At first they had thought him an English spy but he had allayed their suspicions with a masterful lie about his part in the assassination of the Earl of Leitrim and been told to do as he pleased as long as he didn't get in the way of the fighting.

"No fear of that. I had a bellyful of fighting in Zululand. This time I'm going to watch," Conor replied.

The burghers of the Transvaal had no standing army. Their fighters were made up of heavily bearded farmers, dressed in odd coloured, loose fitting corduroy working clothes. Everyone of them was required to provide himself with a rifle, fifty rounds of ammunition, a horse, and eight days rations and report for duty whenever he was called upon. They knew little about military discipline or drills but they lacked nothing in the use of firearms and field-craft. Most of them had learnt to ride before they were six years of age and were crack shots by the age of ten. They could move through the veld as silently as shadows. The British forces, still riding high on the success of the Zulu war, were in for a shock.

Next to Conor, Paul de Beer sat on his horse, smoking his pipe. A stick with a white flag was balanced across the pommel of his saddle and a piece of paper stuck out of his jacket pocket. They had not long to wait before Conor heard the familiar strains of Kiss me Mother, Kiss your Darling, wafting across the veld and began to hum along.

Soon a column of scarlet and blue uniforms appeared, their white helmets bobbing in the sunlight, followed by a long line of wagons. Still haven't learned your lesson, have ye, lads, thought Conor. They'll pick ye off like hens in a coop. The band stopped playing and went for their rifles as soon as they saw the line of waiting Boers on top of the ridge.

"How many do you think?" said Paul.

Conor narrowed his eyes and stood up in his stirrups.

"Over two hundred, I'd say. How many are ye?"

Paul shrugged.

"It is difficult to say. One hundred and fifty, perhaps more."

He set off with his flag of truce and his letter. Conor had written the letter himself, at the request of Commandant Joubert, and he was quite proud of the way he had worded it. The gist of it was Stop where you are or you will be at war. They wouldn't, of course, and he slid off his horse and crouched behind a tree.

De Beer stopped about a hundred yards from the troops and Conor heard him call out in both Dutch and English that if there was anyone who would come out and speak to him they should come now. Waste of time, no point being polite to them bastards, thought Conor.

"Do you think they will shoot him?" said the lad next to him. He was a young boy called Kieser and Conor could feel the nervousness coming off him, as his horse shifted from one foot to another.

"I wouldn't say so, it would look bad for them to shoot an unarmed man," Conor replied, "and they do not consider ye worthy opponents. They do not think ye can fight. But you should get off your horse now, just in case."

De Beer pushed his horse forward another fifty yards and then three officers walked out to meet him. One of them was Herbert Webster and Conor stiffened when he saw him.

Their colonel glanced at the letter, words were exchanged, and then De Beer turned around and began to trot back but Conor, his eyes fixed on Herbert, barely acknowledged him as he rode past. The British had told them to go to hell, they were marching to Pretoria and moments later, the Boers opened fire.

"Kneel down!" Conor shouted to Kieser but the boy was too slow and fell dead, moments later, a bullet between his eyes.

It didn't last long. Within minutes, all the British officers were hit and the soldiers began waving their handkerchiefs and throwing up their hands to surrender. Fifteen minutes was all it took to inflict the first defeat of the war. The Boers lost only Kieser and five wounded and Conor wrote down their names in his notebook. The British had lost thirty men killed and another eighty wounded but he was only interested in one of them. Herbert Webster lay amongst the wounded, blood pouring from a large hole in his thigh. A young black boy, dressed in a drummer's uniform knelt over him, trying to staunch the flow.

"Well, young master, I never thought I'd see you again, this side of hell," Conor said.

He placed his boot on Herbert's thigh and saw him wince.

"I'll have you shot when this is over," Herbert snarled.

"I don't think you'll be having anyone shot anytime soon. You'll be lucky if they don't amputate that leg."

He leaned his weight into his foot and Herbert grunted and bit through his lip.

The black boy tapped his arm.

"What?" said Conor.

"Please, *baas*, can you take me with you?"

"I'll ask the commandant but I don't think so. Who's going to feed you?"

The boy looked as if he were about to burst into tears, Conor made him no more than twelve years old. He brought his full weight into his foot and heard the bone in Herbert's thigh crunch as he screamed and passed out. By now Joubert had given permission for the British to send to Pretoria for ambulances and the men were preparing to move out, leaving twenty soldiers behind to care for their wounded.

"*Kom, rooinek,* we must leave now, before they send more soldiers from Pretoria," shouted De Beer.

Conor was halfway to Heidelberg with the plundered wagons before he remembered Herbert's black boy.

It proved to be not as easy as he had thought to sit and write on paper which insisted on slipping and sliding off his knee, with pencils which kept on breaking and in the end he wrote everything down in his notebook, promising himself that he would write his report once he was in more comfortable surroundings.

It was a very short war and by the end of February, the British garrisons at Marabastad and Rustenburg were under siege, the Boers had been the victors at Schuinshoogte and now they waited at Laing's Nek for General Colley to pass by on his way to Pretoria with reinforcements. Opposite them stood Majuba Hill, its steep sides dotted with rocks and bushes. Below them lay Mount Prospect where Colley was preparing to advance. The Boers' earlier suspicions had subsided, Conor had made friends and so far he had not fired a single shot from the Martini Henry they had pressed upon him. Neither had he submitted any articles to the newspaper. He stared across the plains to the east. It couldn't be more than three days ride to Jacoba's farm.

On the night before the battle, as they sat around their campfire, one of the men turned to Conor.

"Is it true that you fought against the Zulus at Isandlwana, *rooinek*?"

"It is."

"I had an uncle who died there. Perhaps you met him. His name was Johannes Swanepoel."

"I might have seen him and his father talking to Chelmsford the night before."

"He was a good man, and so was my grandfather. The British came to the farm and burned it later. My grandfather died, and my cousin also."

Conor felt his stomach jolt.

"What's that you say? Your cousin died?"

"Yes. When we heard the news my father and I came immediately from the Transvaal. Someone must have buried my grandfather but there was no sign of my cousin. We cannot be sure but we assume she is dead. She was only a girl of fifteen. Tomorrow I will kill twenty British soldiers in their memory."

Conor's heart lurched and he turned away to hide his emotions. Perhaps, if he had not run away, Jacoba might still be alive. He pushed the thought from his mind and turned back to the man.

"What's your name?"

"Etienne. Etienne Swanepoel.

The following morning Conor woke up to discover that the British had scaled Majuba during the night and were standing on top of the hill, waving their fists and rifles and throwing down insults. He joined the ascent and while his companions rushed to the summit, killing a small group of Gordons on the way up, he tucked himself in behind a small knoll from where he could see everything and scribbled furiously in his notebook. He watched as the troops broke and ran wildly to the other side of the hill, where some of them, not seeing the drop, threw themselves over the edge and tumbled to their deaths. Afterwards, where the dead and wounded lay piled up in the shallow basin on top of the hill, Conor stared at the body of General

Colley. A bullet had gone through his helmet above his right eye and come out behind his left ear and three men were arguing over who had shot him.

"Why don't ye toss a coin for it?" said Conor, and then he saw Etienne Swanepoel lying beside him and stopped laughing.

Majuba had knocked the stuffing out of the British and after General Colley's body was handed over for burial General Jorrissen clapped Conor on the shoulder.

"Come with me, *rooinek*, we are going to make peace now and you will interpret for me so that these English ruffians cannot deceive us."

The war was over and the Transvaal was independent once again. The British had not won a single battle but they would never forget Majuba and twenty years later there would be another war which would end very differently.

FEBRUARY 1882

CHAPTER EIGHTEEN

Two years after I arrived in Kimberley, Lukas had dug Mary's claim as deep as he dared without the walls collapsing and killing him and we were finding less and less diamonds. Soon there would be barely enough to support us all and I decided to visit the outlying claims where the poorer diggers worked. I had heard there was a living to be made from buying up the diamonds from these men who could not afford to come into town.

Kopjewalloping was hard work, sometimes we were gone for a fortnight, just me, Asjas and the yellow pony. At night we slept in the open under a camelthorn tree and I gazed up at the stars and wondered what would become of us. Most of the diamonds I bought were of poor quality and I was barely scraping a living. It didn't help that the prices of diamonds were falling and the dealers were becoming more and more reluctant to part with their cash. From time to time I went to Number Five but the black man always gave me the same story. The madam is in England. I don't know when she will come back.

In the middle of the year a storm came and destroyed half of Kimberley. It tore buildings in half and ripped the roofs off offices, sending them flying through the air, flattening tin shacks as they went. We did not escape either. It crashed into our camp, an enormous cloud of sand and grit, whipped up from the dumps, carrying everything before it. My tent was blown away, and its contents scattered everywhere and my yellow pony fled into the veld. My blankets were reduced to a sodden, green, mildewed heap and the box of diamonds I had just spent three weeks collecting was lifted into the air and blown up to the ridge where it broke apart, scattering the diamonds where not even Asjas could find them. Perhaps it was this that finally made me break Mary's only rule.

Lukas shook me out of my sleep.

"*Missies, hier's mense,*" he whispered.

I jumped off my cot and reached for my revolver.

"Who is it? What does he want at this hour of the night?"

"I don't know. I never seen him before."

I knew John Corcoran slightly. He owned a useless claim well out of town and I visited him every two months. He wasn't a bad man, just a foolish one and he rarely had any stones worth buying.

"Oh, it's you!" I said lowering my gun, "What do you want?"

"I've got something for you."

He opened his fist and showed me a very large uncut diamond. I did not need to put it on the scales to see how valuable it was and it was certainly not come by honestly or John Corcoran would not be standing squeezed between my camp bed and my paraffin stove in the middle of the night. He was sweating and his hand kept moving to the handle of a knife in the waistband of his corduroys.

"Put it down there," I said, pointing to my table.

I put the stone on my scales and picked up my magnifying glass.

"Where did you get it John? I don't imagine you found it on that miserable claim of yours."

"Can't say."

"How much do you want for it."

"Two thousand pounds,"

I burst out laughing.

"Two thousand pounds? Are you crazy? I don't have that kind of money."

There was a rattling outside the door and he spun around, looking for another way out.

"What was that?"

"Probably my baboon. Unless you are expecting someone else?"

"How much have you got? I'll take whatever you've got."

Before I could answer him the flap of the tent flew open and a short, ginger haired man burst in, followed by two others. I recognised Baas Fox, the chief diamond detective. Up until now our sole interactions had consisted of a raised hat and a nod whenever we passed each other on the street. I had nothing to fear from the diamond detectives, I still had morals then.

"There you are, you blackguard. I'll have you now," he shouted.

John tried to make a run for it but they brought him down, sending my table and all that was on it into the dust.

"Where's the blazer, John? I know you've got it!"

"I swear I haven't, Baas Fox. God strike me dead if I'm tellin' a lie."

The diamond detective grabbed John by the collar and shook him like a terrier shaking a rat.

"Tell me where it is, John, or by God I'll beat it out of you,"

"I'm telling you I don't have it."

While I tried not to let my eyes stray to my upended table, they pinned back his arms and turned out his pockets and slapped his face but all they found was a half a crown and a half used bag of tobacco. Baas Fox was an annoying man but he was not stupid and in the short time he had been head of the detective department he had caught a number of notorious thieves. His gift was the ability to read faces and now he turned and studied mine.

"I'm sorry to ask you this, but I don't suppose you would have the diamond, Miss Rawlings?"

"Of course not. You know I won't have anything to do with stolen diamonds. Mary would kill me."

He seemed satisfied with my answer.

"Of course, Miss Rawlings. You don't mind if my men take a look around? He may have dropped it."

"Help yourselves," I replied.

They got down on their hands and knees and scratched in the dust for over an hour, their suits were filthy afterwards, but they found nothing.

Mary stepped inside, an overcoat thrown over her nightdress.

"What do you want, Fox? Turning decent people out of their beds in the middle of the night."

"This scoundrel has stolen a diamond and I mean to find it."

"Well, you won't find any stolen diamonds here."

She looked at me and I held up my hands and shrugged.

They left with John in handcuffs, still protesting his innocence.

"You didn't take it did you?" Mary said

"Of course I didn't. I know the rules, Mary."

"Might as well have a cuppa, then. Nearly time to get up."

We sat outside Mary's tent, in the moonlight, drinking tea and complaining about Baas Fox and when I returned to my tent Asjas was sitting in the corner, turning something over and over in his hands. He bared his teeth at me and barked and then he held out his hand and lying in his palm was John Corcoran's diamond. I should have handed it in to Baas Fox immediately but I didn't, I sewed it into the waistband of my trousers.

Six months went by before Fanny's black man walked into our camp. He caused quite a stir as he walked down the road, wearing a grey suit and top hat, beating off stray dogs with an ivory handled cane.

"Mrs Yudelman's boy. What does he want?" said Mary.

I felt a tremor of excitement, I knew very well Fanny had sent him to find me, but to Mary I just shrugged my shoulders.

"Who knows?"

"The madam is back from England. She has sent me to bring you to her house," he said.

Mary turned to me, a question mark on her face.

"You know Mrs Yudelman?"

"Not exactly. I only met her once."

"Fanny Yudelman is a piece of work, Jacoba. Been rumours about her for years. Why do you think she's been in England the past two years. I heard she only just made it onto the boat, and Baas Fox screaming and yelling on the quayside in Durban. Why does she want to see you?"

"She visited our farm once. She gave me her card and told me to call on her. That's why I came here. I had nowhere else to go."

Mary's description of Fanny differed so much from the fantasy I had created in my head that I rejected it immediately. Fanny had not appeared to be in a hurry when she passed by our farm in Hannes Vosloo's coach and in my mind that was proof that she was not running away from anyone.

"You're storing up trouble for yourself if you get yourself involved with her. If she wants to see you it's only because she has a use for you. I was you I'd tell him to sling his hook," Mary said, but I had no intention of doing that. I had almost given up hope that Fanny would ever come back from London and now here she was, looking for me. I didn't care if she was a thief. It could only mean that my fortunes were about to take a turn for the better and I wasted no time washing my face and hands, brushing my hair and following the black man back to her house.

SEPTEMBER 1882

CHAPTER NINETEEN

He led me down a short passage, into a sitting room where Fanny sat in a wingback armchair, in front of the window. A cat with black paws and face, lay on her lap, and as I walked in it opened its mouth and let out a cry which set my teeth on edge.

"The girl, madam."

"Thankyou Johnson, you can bring us some tea."

Fanny's gaze moved from my face to my feet and back to my face.

"You look like you've seen a bit of life since I last saw you, ducks."

She gestured to a chair.

"Sit down."

I was very aware of my dirty clothes as I sat down and as Fanny sat back in her chair and studied me, my confidence began to evaporate. In the camp I was respected as an honest dealer who would pay a fair price, but sitting in this bright, sunny room with its highly polished floor, strewn with sheepskins and bamboo mats, I was just an eighteen year old girl, wearing trousers and a grubby man's shirt. Everything about this house reeked of wealth and something else I would later recognise as corruption.

Johnson reappeared carrying a tray set with a silver teapot and milk jug and two delicate little gold rimmed china teacups, decorated with roses. A bowl of sweets lay on the tray next to the teapot and my mouth started to water as soon as I saw them. It had been a very long time since I had tasted sweets and I couldn't take my eyes off them. Jelly babies and Pontefract cakes nestled amongst Turkish Delight and French nougat. Even the *smous* had never had such an assortment. Fanny pushed the bowl of sweets towards me.

"Try the nougat, ducks, only good thing to come out of France."

France. I wondered whether it was a town or a country. The taste of honey and roasted almonds spread across my tongue as I bit into the soft confectionery. Fanny popped a piece of Turkish Delight into her mouth and licked the sugary coating off her lips, as she poured the tea.

"There's a rumour going around that a very big blazer was stolen from De Beers. Word is John Corcoran slipped it to a young girl when the peelers caught him," she said.

"Really?" I replied, and that's what gave me away. I should have said I'd heard the rumour, all of Kimberley had been talking about it for months, but I was still naive in those days.

"Rhodes is in a right old snit about it. Willing to pay a good few bob to get it back, so I hear."

"I imagine he is."

Fanny smiled at me, over the rim of her teacup.

"Do you have the diamond, ducks?"

Her directness took me by surprise and I felt my heart beat faster, as I forced myself to look her in the eye.

"No I don't."

She put down her teacup and sighed in the same way my mother used to sigh when she found me out in a lie.

"All right, ducks, let's say you do have it. How do you imagine you're going to get rid of it?"

"I'm sorry, I don't have it," I repeated.

"You've got balls, I'll give you that. Rhodes will never stop looking for that diamond, he's got Fox tormented, and when he finds it, which he will, whoever has it is going to wish they'd never been born. Ten years in the Breakwater will see to that."

I knew about the prison at the Cape, where the prisoners spent all their waking hours walking on treadmills. Mary used to threaten her boys with it whenever they misbehaved.

The cat was purring loudly, almost drowning out the ticking of the clock on the mantelpiece. Fanny rang the little bell and Johnson appeared with more tea. When he had gone she rummaged around in her cleavage and produced a blue velvet drawstring bag which she emptied onto the table between us. The diamonds which scattered across the table were much bigger than the ones I was accustomed to seeing on the claims and my surprise must have shown on my face.

"Not used to these are you, ducks? What do you make of them?"

.I picked one of them up and weighed it in my hand.

"I'd really need my scales to be sure, but I'd say this is worth about £300."

She made me value half a dozen assorted stones and I was so proud of my cleverness.

"And this one?"

She pushed a small stone towards me and I saw immediately that she was trying to trick me

"That's a garnet. It's not worth very much."

She scooped up the diamonds, dropped them back inside her dress and giggled then, a small childish sound, and it made me giggle too. I was so happy to have gained her approval.

"Diamond detectives not going to be sticking their fists down a lady's bosom are they?" she said.

There was a knock on the door then, and Johnson came in.

"Mr Cooper is here to see you, Madam."

A look of irritation passed across Fanny's face.

"What does he want?"

"He didn't say, madam."

"Tell him to come back at four."

"He says it's urgent, madam."

Fanny clicked her tongue and heaved herself out of the chair, tipping the cat onto the floor where it wandered around protesting loudly, before settling down on the sheepskin rug and fixing its blue eyes on me. I waited until Fanny had gone before I leaned forward and hissed at it but it was made of sterner stuff than our farm cats and did not move a muscle. As I looked around at the richly patterned carpet and the large framed portrait of Queen Victoria on the wall, flanked by paintings of men on horseback surrounded by brown and white dogs, I wondered whether I had ruined my chances with Fanny by not owning up to the diamond. Here was my chance to escape the squalor of the camp, I could see no other way out, and yet I hesitated.

Fanny returned, humming a tune under her breath and I could see that she was pleased about something.

"*Kopjewalloping* to your liking, is it?" she said, putting another piece of Turkish Delight into her mouth. I wondered if I dared take another piece of nougat.

."I am making a living."

"Not much of one, so I hear."

"It's enough for my needs."

"What do you think of my house?"

"It's a lovely house, Mrs Yudelman."

"What would you think about coming to live in it?"

She took me completely by surprise. I would find out later that hidden under Fanny's jovial exterior was a mind as sharp as my grandfather's *herneutermes*. Mary was right. She had seen something in me which she could use.

"I don't know. I....I will have to think," I replied.

She picked up the little silver bell and shook it again and Johnson appeared immediately. He must have been listening outside the door.

"You may clear, Johnson, Miss Jacoba is leaving now."

"Don't think for too long, ducks, all the balls in the world ain't going to do you any good in prison," she said, as I reached the door.

I took a long time walking back to camp, looking in the shop windows as I went. In the window of a dress shop a headless mannequin balanced on three wooden legs wearing a silk taffeta dress of blue grey and cream with velvet buttons down the front. The high neckline with its pleated stand up collar gave it an almost human air of elegance. I wanted that dress.

When I got back to the camp Mary had struck her tent and all its contents were piled in a heap next to it. Her boys were gathering up the picks and shovels and Lukas was dismantling the rocking sieve. The mule was already hitched to the cart.

"Mary? What's going on?"

"Thrown me off, haven't they?" Mary replied waving a piece of paper at me, " feller that rented me this claim has sold it to De Beers, the bastard! Got to be off here by this evening or the bailiffs will come in and take it all. "

"How can that be? I thought you owned the claim. Wasn't it left you by your husband?"

"Only left me the lease, dearie. Never belonged to me."

All around her, other diggers were striking their tents and packing them onto wagons. Those that had no wagon were tying their things into bundles. I saw a group of men standing on the perimeter, carrying pick handles, holding dogs on leashes.

"No! You can't go and leave me here on my own!"

"No intention of that, lovey, tell your boy to strike your tent and pack your pony. We're off to Jagersfontein, they've just sectioned off claims there. Australians, so I hear."

"But that's a hundred miles away! I can't go there."

"Well, you can't stay here, you're trespassing on De Beers land now. What else are you going to do?"

I hesitated a moment before replying.

"Mrs Yudelman has offered to take me in."

"You'd want to be getting a move on, Mary, before all the claims are gone!" someone shouted.

Mary gripped me by the shoulders.

"Please, Jacoba, you are making a mistake. Come with us. They're picking stones up off the ground at Jagersfontein. You can buy your own claim. Besides, how am I going to get to Jagersfontein without your mule?"

I shook my head. I was done with digging for diamonds and done with riding about the countryside buying up inferior stones and arguing with diamond merchants. Fanny had told me in Zululand that there were easier ways of making money and I wanted that. It would be many years before I found out that easy money had a way of exacting its own price.

There is no way to excuse what I did to Lukas after all his years of faithful service.

"Take the mule, Mary. And the pony and Lukas. I won't be needing them any more."

Mary hugged me and I suppressed a sob. Over her shoulder I could see Lukas's face, his hurt plainly visible.

"You be careful, Jacoba. Mrs Yudelman isn't all she seems to be."

She climbed aboard the cart, and tipped the mule with her whip and he opened his mouth and let out a loud bray as they moved off. It was only then that I realised I had no idea what Fanny wanted of me.

OCTOBER 1885

CHAPTER TWENTY

Fanny was a dazzling creature. Compared to the black dressed *tantes* of my childhood she appeared almost mythical and I was in awe of her her. In the space of two and a half years she transformed me from a rough, Boer farmgirl into a glamorous English woman. I became more English than the English themselves and I could not remember the last time I spoke Dutch.

I spent my days choosing what I was going to wear and my nights in Fanny's saloon, keeping an eye on the customers and playing chemmy. The young men who worked at De Beers flocked around me like silly chickens waiting for morsels of food. I received half a dozen marriage proposals within the space of twelve months and I accepted none of them. Kimberley was thriving, the Kimberley Club, where the rich men went to eat every evening, had more millionaires to the square foot than anywhere else in the world and the richest of them all was Cecil Rhodes. John Corcoran's diamond rested behind the skirting board in my room. Fanny had never asked about it again.

Fanny's saloon was squashed between a Salvation Army hostel and a dressmaker's. It was a wild place full of rough looking men standing on the sawdust covered floor, cheering on girls doing cartwheels and splits on the bar, their petticoats flying over their heads, revealing their frilly pantaloons. The first time Fanny took me there, she had to drag me through to the back or I would have watched them all night, oblivious to the lecherous stares directed my way as soon as I walked in.

But the saloon was only a front for Fanny's real business. Behind it was the Privee, where the wealthy men came to play cards. No sawdust here, a red plush carpet covered most of the floor and heavy red curtains hung from rails at the windows. A rich mahogany billiards table squatted in the middle overhung by two chandeliers, but I never saw anyone playing on it. Most of the time it was laden with trays of smoked salmon and cucumber sandwiches. There were women, too, in spectacular dresses, who lounged around on the comfortable sofas and occasionally accompanied men to the rooms upstairs. I never asked what they did there, I didn't want to know.

The entire town was now supplied with water pumped from the Vaal River and Fanny employed a gardener called Bloody Fool, whose complete ignorance of all things horticultural became immediately apparent the day he started work. Nevertheless, despite his efforts, flowers now bloomed where before there was only sand.

And so it went on, the endless round of balls and race meetings and card playing and all I had to do was write a letter, every three months, to the Atherstone family in London whose son, Freddie had been sent to Africa because of some misbehaviour. Even this was no hardship since Fanny dictated all the letters and all I had to do was write down what she said, sign them and post them. The letters were always the same, a paragraph about the weather, another one about the state of the diamond industry and a glowing report about how well Freddie was doing and what a reformed character he had become since going to work for De Beers, and there was always a postscript, written by Fanny, which invariably made mention of Bloody Fool's flowers.

I enjoyed writing the letters, sometimes adding my own little comments and even though I never met him, and nobody I knew had ever heard of him, I became quite fond of Freddie Atherstone and I was always asking Fanny about him.

"Where is Freddie? Does he never come to Kimberley?"

The answer was always the same.

"He's in Mashonaland, ducks, on business for Mr Rhodes. I expect he'll be back at the end of the month."

Every morning I walked the short distance into the centre of town to the Grand Hotel, where I had lunch on the verandah, watched the passing traffic, and invited whoever I liked to join me. One day I spotted a familar figure amongst the crowd.

"Mary? Is that you?"

Mary O'Hara looked up and her face split into a broad grin.

"Jacoba! By God, don't you look fancy."

"Come up and have lunch with me, Mary. I haven't seen you for so long."

Mary looked down at her faded dress and men's boots.

"Dressed like this? They won't let me in."

"Oh never mind that, they won't dare turn you away if you are with me."

"Have to say I could do with taking the weight off me feet," she said, as she dropped into a white wicker chair.

"You will have tea, first? And then we'll get menus and order. I want to hear all your news."

"Don't bother with the menus, love, I can't read anyway. Just order me whatever you're having for yourself."

I decided on roast beef and Yorkshire pudding and Mary tucked in as if she had never seen food before. I was so pleased to see her.

"I hear you're living quite the life now, Jacoba." she said

There was something in her tone which made me feel slightly ashamed, as if I didn't deserve to have done so much better than her.

"Yes, Fanny has been very good to me."

"People are talking, you know."

"Oh? What do they say?"

"They say Fanny is heading for a fall and she'll take you with her."

"I don't know what you mean."

"Yes you do. Everyone knows the diamond detectives are watching her like a hawk."

"I have nothing to do with that"

Mary looked me in the eye.

"You might think you don't. But Fanny is as cute as a pet fox and you can be sure she has you involved somehow, even if you don't know it. There's some as says you're grown too big for your boots, Jacoba. Swanning around town like you own the place."

I did not know how to answer her and we finished our meal in silence and then Mary wiped her lips with her napkin and got up. She reached over the table and put her hand on my arm.

"I've offended you now, haven't I? But I only wanted to warn you. I'm fond of you, Jacoba, and I don't want you to come to any harm."

"I know, Mary."

As I watched her walk down the street, I felt uneasy but I had ignored Mary's warning once before and no harm had come to me. I saw no reason not to ignore it again.

Late one night, we were sitting in a dark corner of the Privee, with Martin Cooper, while Asjas lay asleep under the table. Laid out in front of us were enough uncut diamonds to buy half the new suburb of Beaconsfield. I never had any direct dealings with the buying and selling of illicit diamonds but I enjoyed picking them up, just to see whether I could still tell a good one from a bad one. And I enjoyed Martin Cooper's company, there was an air of danger about him which excited me, but tonight he wasn't paying me any attention and I became bored.

"I have a headache, Fanny. I think I'll go home," I said.

"Yes, do. And take that bloody monkey with you. Snoring's driving me mad."

As I got up, the door burst open and Baas Fox dashed in, followed by half a dozen diamond detectives. Nobody said a word as he marched triumphantly across the room. They were halfway across when Asjas woke up and started running from one detective to the other, shaking their hands, and while he was at it, Fanny calmly gathered up the table cloth, glasses and all, swept it off the table and

Johnson spread another one. Baas Fox saw it all and he was apoplectic.

"Mrs Yudelman! Mrs Yudelman!" he shouted but Fanny had disappeared through the back door and by the time he pushed the baboon out of the way, and negotiated the obstacle course of chairs and feet which suddenly appeared in his way, she had returned empty handed and I knew that wherever they searched they would find no trace of a diamond. Martin Cooper carried on drinking his scotch and soda winking at me over the rim of his glass.

"Bloody baboon. What's a monkey doing in a gambling saloon anyway?" Baas Fox roared.

"Playing cards, Mr Fox. With all the other monkeys. What else would he be doing?" I replied.

"I should arrest him for disturbing the peace!"

This provoked numerous catcalls from the players, urging him to make good on his threat and right at that moment Asjas held out his two hands and that was the end of it. The saloon exploded with laughter, the tears ran down Fanny's face and she declared herself quite out of breath, which didn't surprise me since I was the one who laced up her corsets every evening and I had lately been forced to place my foot in the small of her back to get the job done.

Baas Fox wagged his finger in Fanny's face

"I know what's going in here, Mrs Yudelman," he said, the ends of his ginger moustache twitching, "and one day I am going to catch the big fish. The big fish, mind you."

"Well, ducks, I hope you have an appetite for it when you do catch it. Would you like a drink? Must be thirsty work catching diamond thieves."

Baas Fox raided the saloon regularly after that and Fanny took me with her to De Beers to complain to Rhodes. It was the first time I had seen him up close and I was surprised by his appearance. He wore a badly fitting old suit, with half the buttons missing and his shoes were dirty. This was the man who was worth more money than I could conceive of?

"Come now, Mrs Yudelman, you can hardly expect me to intervene on your behalf?" he said, smiling behind steepled fingers.

"And why not? I'm running a decent establishment. Your employees have been enjoying my facilities for long enough," Fanny snapped.

"Let us say I prefer not to mix business with pleasure. And by the way, Martin Cooper was arrested this morning on a charge of illicit diamond buying."

Fanny glared at him, but I could see she was shaken.

"And why would that be of interest to me, Cecil?"

Rhodes shrugged.

"I just thought you might like to know."

Fanny stormed into the house, tore off her gloves and flung them at Johnson.

"Bring tea. And go and find Mr Cooper."

"Which shall I do first, madam?"

"Don't be cheeky." Fanny replied.

Johnson returned two hours later with the news that Martin had vanished.

"What do you mean you can't find him?"

"He is not at his rooms, madam, and nobody has seen him since yesterday."

"Of course he's not at his rooms. He's in bloody jail ain't he?"

Johnson shook his head.

"Not there either. The judge gave him bail."

Fanny stormed up and down the parlour, swearing. I had not heard her use such language since the day she had the man with the piglet thrown off Hannes's wagon.

"Just like that godrotting Cooper to get himself arrested and do a runner," she shouted.

"Where do you think he might have gone?"

"Halfway to Cape Town by now, I imagine. With a ticket on the next boat to England if he has any sense. What the hell am I going to do now?"

I, too, wondered what I was going to do. Martin and I had grown very close over the preceding months.

We were still trying to find a replacement for Martin when the railway arrived at the end of November. It had taken them a year to complete the last section of eighty five miles from Orange River Station. Now we would be linked to Port Elizabeth, Cape Town and East London and hopefully the price of everything would go down. The goods shed would be the largest in the whole of the Cape and the engine shed was to house nine locomotives but the station was not yet finished and they had built a temporary platform of railway sleepers in the cricket ground. None of this had discouraged the citizens of Kimberley in the slightest and we were beside ourselves with anticipation. Every shop, office and public building was draped with flags and bunting and Fanny ordered an enormous Union Jack strung between two pillars across the verandah, a job which took an entire day and ended with Johnson and Bloody Fool rolling in the dust, hitting each other. Every time I walked under it I imagined my Oupa turning in his grave.

It was as hot as hell itself when I woke up and I was not overjoyed at the thought of standing out in the sun to watch the train arrive and listen to the hours of speeches which would surely follow, but the excitement of lunching with the Governor soon made me forget my discomfort. Fanny spent half an hour primping in front of the hall mirror before she finally stepped out of the front door and allowed Johnson to help her into the spider. He handed me up beside her and Fanny took my hand and laid it on her knee. The material of her new dress slid under my fingers and I closed my eyes and let my head fall back against the leather headrest. I could already feel the perspiration collecting between my breasts.

The train was two hours late and by the time it chugged up to the platform, and the balding and rotund Sir Hercules Robinson and his wife stepped off the train, to loud cheers from the hundreds of people gathered on the De Beers debris heaps, I had a pounding headache.

"Well, I'll be damned, I never thought he'd have the nerve," Fanny murmured.

"What do you mean?"

"That's Charles Spalding, as big a ruffian as you could hope to meet. Half the town's after him for salting claims. Ran off with a small fortune in '79," Fanny replied.

She pointed to a slim, clean shaven man, dressed in a fashionable suit, standing in the open doorway of the carriage. He looked about him, before stepping onto the platform and turning around to extend his hand to a girl about my age. I should have paid more attention to Charles Spalding, he was about to change my life forever.

Sir Hercules made his speech short but the answering speeches went on an on and it was only after the Mayor had smashed a bottle of champagne on the engine that we were released to follow the Governor's party into the luncheon tent where the ferocious heat almost bounced us backwards. Then some fool ordered the Fire Brigade to hose it down and we were all drenched. They set up tables under umbrellas and Fanny sat down, while Johnson tried to wring out the hem of her dress and I tried, unsuccessfully, to stifle my giggles.

"Oh stop it!" she snapped, popping him on the head with her parasol.

I read the menu. Asparagus, salmon in a creamy sauce, roast beef and Yorkshire pudding, brandy tart and fresh fruit salad. In this heat? I thought. In between courses I saw Fanny scanning the crowd and as we got to the roast beef and Yorkshire pudding she beckoned to

Johnson and he bent down as she whispered something in his ear. Moments later I saw him making his way towards the Public Gardens.

"Where has he gone?" I asked.

"To find Charles."

"What for? You said he was a thief."

Fanny turned to me and arched her eyebrows.

"Exactly. And ain't we short of a thief at the moment? Charles Spalding could be the answer to all our problems."

She was wrong about that. He turned out to be the beginning of all of mine.

When we arrived back at Number Five, Charles and Amelia were sitting on the wicker chairs on the verandah, tall glasses of lemonade in their hands.

"Well, Charles, how nice to see you. Been a while." said Fanny.

"Indeed it has, Fanny. I must thank you for your very kind offer of lodgings."

" I thought you'd be wanting to stay out of the public eye. And I have a business proposition for you."

"How delightful. I look forward to hearing about it."

"Get into the parlour then, you know where it is. No time like the present. Johnson, take Miss Amelia's trunk to the room next to Jacoba's."

They vanished into the house and left Amelia and I there, on the verandah, staring at each other. Petite, with long dark hair scraped back into a bun at the nape of her neck, dressed in a shapeless skirt and a loose fitting blouse, covered by a dusty travel coat, Amelia was hardly the picture of fashion, but she had eyes of such a deep violet they seemed almost black and these were what captivated me. She returned my gaze, a lazy smile spreading across her mouth.

"Have you known Mrs Yudelman long?" she asked.

"Long enough. And you?"

"Papa has known her for ages. They used to do business together."

"Yes. Fanny mentioned it."

"Oh good. Then we shall understand each other," Amelia replied. Her smile dazzled me.

NOVEMBER 1885

CHAPTER TWENTY ONE

For a fortnight after the train arrived, the town went mad. There were balls, banquets and race meetings, cricket matches, picnics at Alexanderfontein and excursions to Riverton. and every time we turned a corner we seemed to run into the Scots band. There was not a beggar to be seen, they had all been locked away in jail, for fear of giving a bad impression to the Governor, and whereas I did not give the matter any thought, Amelia confronted Fanny.

"It's not right to deprive people of their freedom just to give a good impression."

"Lovin it, they are. Three square meals a day and a blanket to sleep on. What more could they want?" Fanny replied, which was pretty much what I would have said, had I been asked. In those days I was happy to keep my opinions to myself as long as Fanny funded my lavish lifestyle.

It was a fortnight I would remember for the rest of my life, but not for the picnics and cricket matches.

Breakfast was a lively affair. Amelia's father never stopped talking and I had not seen Fanny so animated since Martin disappeared. The usual scrambled eggs and kidneys were augmented by muffins and toast and an assortment of cold meats, and Johnson's face became a mask of mild irritation.

I overheard him grumbling in Zulu to the cook.

"What the matter with the madam? Gone mad since that man came. Johnson, the tea is cold, Johnson the eggs are overcooked, Johnson there is a mark on this knife."

Amelia had a camera, it was a beauty, with a mahogany body and a cherrywood base and bore a brass plate with the words American Optical Company engraved on it. One afternoon we had Johnson carry out a chair and put it under the wild fig tree next to the verandah and Amelia arranged me in a pose, folding my hands on my lap and tilting my head slightly to one side.

"You must not move at all, not even an eyelid, until I tell you to."

She put her head under the black cloth and just as she was about to take the picture Asjas dropped out of the tree onto my lap. Amelia threw back the cloth.

"He has ruined it," she shouted, "Get Johnson to lock him away and I will take another.

I laughed at that. Not long after I moved into Number Five, while Fanny and I were having afternoon tea, Asjas had run in through the French doors leading to the garden and snatched a cake from the plate. He leapt up on top of the armoire and sat picking out the currants and throwing them onto the floor, while Fanny backed into a corner, holding her handbag in front of her. This turned out to be the wrong thing to do because Asjas jumped down, seized it from her outstretched hand and ran away. I found him sitting in the tree pulling out the contents of Fanny's bag and tossing them onto the ground, ignoring Johnson's pleas to come down. Only when the bag was empty and he had tipped it upside down and shaken it thoroughly did he climb down the tree trunk, lie on the ground in front of me and cover his eyes, an old trick which he thought would save him from a hiding. Johnson had stepped forward, hit him with a stick and received a nasty bite on the arm in the ensuing scuffle. It was unlikely Johnson would agree to take him on again.

"He won't go with Johnson. Why don't you put him in the picture?"

"Will he stay still?"

"Yes, he will."

I held him next to me and pinched the back of his neck so tightly that he bared his teeth and later, when Amelia developed the photograph, he looked as if he were smiling. I kept that photograph next to my bed for years.

At night the Kimberley Mine was lit up with a chain of lights, like a necklace of gold with a diamond pendant suspended from the middle, and the night before Amelia and her father were due to return to the Cape I took Amelia there and we climbed up onto one of the hauling engines. I was doing the things I used to do before Fanny made me into a lady.

We sat on top of the rig, staring down into the blackness and I thought how empty my life would be once Amelia and her father went back to Cape Town. I helped her down from the rig and we walked back to Number Five hand in hand. I did not realise it, at the time, but I had fallen in love.

That night Amelia came to my room to talk, as she always did, and we fell asleep together. I felt her breasts against my back and pulled her hand against my stomach. She turned me over to face her and we lay, only inches away from each other, saying nothing. I could barely make out her nose and lips and I could not see her eyes at all. Her arm rested across my waist and her fingers traced a triangle on my back. I could not help myself, I moved closer until we were touching, the whole length of our bodies, and when she kissed me I did not pull away.

At breakfast I avoided Amelia's eyes, fiddling with my eggs until Fanny snapped at me.

"For heaven's sake, Jacoba, either eat those eggs or ask Johnson to take them away."

"Amelia and I have been thinking it would be a capital idea if Jacoba came back with us," said Charles.

Later I would wonder whether they had been planning this all along. The forkful of egg I was about to eat hung suspended between my plate and my mouth as I waited to see what Fanny would say.

She took a bite of toast before she replied.

"Do you know, Charles, that would suit me very well. I need some documents dropped off at the bank. Save me the journey. And Jacoba deserves a holiday. Sea air will do her good."

She beamed at me.

"What do you say, ducks? Fancy a trip to the seaside?"

I could hardly believe my ears.

"Oh yes, that would be lovely."

I caught Amelia's eye and when she smiled at me my stomach lurched.

"And of course you must bring the baboon with you. He will be the toast of Cape Town," Charles added.

"That goes without saying. He ain't staying here with me," said Fanny.

The train was something of a disappointment. The Pullman sleeping car in which we travelled was hardly deserving of the name. On one side of the gangway was seating for one person and on the other a row of seats for two. Suspended overhead was a piece of canvas on which lay a thin, dirty mattress. I eyed it with distaste wondering how I would get up to it. Earlier in the week, Amelia's father had made Asjas a little doll out of scraps of material, a miniature soldier complete with red jacket and blue trousers and yellow piping down the sides and he sat by the window, clutching it to his chest.

"A skill I learned in the army," said Charles.

"More likely in prison," Amelia muttered.

If I had spoken to my father like that he would have taken the strap to me but Charles just laughed and patted Amelia's hand.

Asjas would not part with that doll for a minute and carried it everywhere with him. I hoped it would keep him quiet all the way to Cape Town.

The train was pulling into Oranjerivierstasie and I was studying the way the cut of Amelia's dress revealed her breasts so daringly, when I saw Baas Fox standing on the platform with half a dozen detectives. We were made to step off the train and into the waiting room where everyone was searched, even two Anglican bishops on their way back to England. Asjas was running around with his new doll, making a complete nuisance of himself, showing it to anyone who would look.

"Ah, Miss Rawlings, off to the seaside for a holiday are you?" Baas Fox enquired.

"I expect so, Mr Fox, since that is the train's sole destination. How long are you going to delay us?"

I kept quiet while he went through my baggage. I had nothing to hide and only wished he would hurry up so that we could get on our way again. I had never been to the Cape, and until I travelled across the Orange Free State to Kimberley I had never been further than sixty miles away from our farm in Zululand.

When he found Fanny's documents he made to open them but I was quick to snatch them away.

"Those are Mrs Yudelman's private papers," I snapped.

The detective department was a law unto itself, they even had a woman to search the female passengers, but in the time it took for half a dozen ladies to get in and out of their corsets Asjas became very restless. The long delay combined with the heat and the loud protestations of the Bishops were too much for him and he sat down on the platform, tore the head off his little doll and poured out a stream of uncut diamonds at the feet of Baas Fox.

"Oh dear," said Charles.

I stared at the diamonds, unable to conceal my shock. Baas Fox bent down to gather up the scattered stones while I tried to gather my wits. When he was done he walked over to me, smiling.

"He must have had a good night at the tables, your baboon?"

"I swear I do not know how he got those," I replied, but even as I said it I knew how ridiculous I sounded.

"Well, he has hardly stitched them in himself unless he has added seamstress to his list of accomplishments."

Asjas was screaming his head off, trying to snatch the doll out of Baas Fox's hand and two detectives rushed to restrain him but he bit one of them and launched himself at Baas Fox. It took all my strength to pull him off and while I was doing it I looked up and caught a glimpse of Charles Spalding's face and I knew.

"You did this," I said.

Charles shrugged his shoulders but before he could answer me Baas Fox called the porter over.

"I believe we have found what we were looking for, you are free to go."

I turned to look at Amelia but there was no look of shock on her face, only anger.

"Papa, how could you?"

"Come Amelia, not time for standing around," he replied grasping her firmly by the elbow and propelling her into the carriage. I stood on the platform, watching the train recede into the distance, its hooter wailing across the veld, until Baas Fox tried to put handcuffs on me and I slapped him across the face.

I returned to town in the back of the police wagon with Asjas sitting beside me trying to put the head back on his doll. Someone had obviously gone ahead because I was met by a crowd almost as big as the one which had welcomed the Governor two weeks before. Fanny was waiting outside the jail.

"You'll be sorry about this. I have friends. I'll have you run out of town, you son of a pox ridden whore!" she shouted poking her parasol in Baas Fox's face.

"Calm down, Mrs Yudelman, or I'll have you arrested for assault," he replied. The look of triumph on his face was plain for all to see.

They led me off to the special court and charged me with Illicit Diamond Buying. Baas Fox kept up a constant gloating in my ear but I knew enough to keep quiet and said nothing whilst he escorted me to the cells.

They let Fanny in to see me that evening.

"Did you know?" I asked her.

"Course I didn't. I knew he was carrying diamonds, they're my bloody diamonds, ain't they? But I didn't know he'd put them in the monkey's doll. Do you really think I would have allowed that?"

"I suppose not," I replied, desperately wanting to believe her.

"Look ducks, everything will be alright. I have Winslett on it and he says since it's a first offence the judge will let you off lightly if you plead guilty."

" I won't. Why should I plead guilty to a crime I have not committed?" I replied, feeling my temper start to rise.

Fanny leaned forward. The smell of her perfume was quite overpowering and on that day it sickened me.

"Because if you don't you'll be going away for a very long time."

"But I didn't do it. That *skelm* Charles Spalding put those diamonds in the doll."

"And who's going to believe you?"

She was right. Who was going to believe me? I had made enemies over the past few years with my highhanded behaviour. More than one person would enjoy seeing me fall from my perch. And thanks to Martin Cooper I would get no bail.

I had been there three days when the guard shouted "Visitor!" and Mary O'Hara walked in. I felt ashamed when I saw her.

"Oh Mary. How did you know?"

"Bad news always travels fast, dearie. It's all over the newspapers. People are talking of nothing else. Don't say I didn't warn you."

"I know, Mary. You were right and I should have listened to you."

Mary smiled and put her hand through the bars to comfort me.

"You were always stubborn, Jacoba. That's what I liked about you. You never gave up. But I haven't come to tell you off. There's a rumour you're going to get a harsh sentence. They want to make an example of you."

"Fanny says Geoffrey will get me off if I plead guilty"

Mary shook her head and I saw anger in her face.

"Are you going to?"

"I think so. Fanny says its the best thing to do."

"The best thing for Fanny,"

"How so? Fanny is not on trial."

She leaned forward so that the guard could not hear her.

"No, but she will be if you plead not guilty."

"I don't understand."

"If you plead guilty that will be the end of it. You'll go down and it will all be over in five minutes. If you plead not guilty there will be questions asked and those questions will lead right back to Fanny. Fox has been waiting a long time to catch Mrs Yudelman. She's the one he really wants."

I knew she was right but I was full of confidence that Fanny and Winslett would get me off. I thought I was invincible and so, for the third time, I ignored Mary's advice.

CHAPTER TWENTY TWO

The courtroom was packed and I knew that most of them had come to take pleasure in my downfall. Fanny had brought me clean clothes and I sat behind a table, in a dress that would have cost many of them half a year's wages, with Geoffrey Winslett beside me, shuffling through a sheaf of papers. I could hear them whispering and murmuring behind me but I kept my head high and my eyes fixed on the wooden panelling behind the judge's desk. My palms were sweating and when I took my hands off the table they left a damp mark there.

The judge came in and I breathed a small sigh of relief when I saw who it was. I knew him well and only the week before I had watched him lose a frightening amount of money at the tables and spent half an hour commiserating with him over his bad luck. I was sure he would never send me to jail.

After everyone had stood up and sat down again he addressed Geoffrey.

"How do you plead?"

"Guilty, my Lord."

The judge adjusted his pince nez.

"Very well. Since it is your first offence, and there seems to be some confusion as to how the diamonds got into the monkey's doll, I will let you off with a caution, while we track down Mr Charles Spalding."

This is was far better than I had expected and I smiled triumphantly at Baas Fox. The court erupted and the judge banged his gavel.

"Silence! Silence in the court!" the judge shouted, barely able to make himself heard above the calls of "Shame on you," and "Not fair," and "Different rules for the rich."

Baas Fox did not look particularly bothered. He smiled back at me and folded his arms across his chest and suddenly I felt uneasy

"Thankyou, your honour," I said, once everyone had stopped talking. People were already starting to leave and I lifted my skirts and stepped down from the dock but the judge motioned me to stay where I was.

"However, there is another matter before me," he said, holding up a sheaf of papers. "I have here a number of letters between you and a diamond dealer in London who is known to deal in stolen diamonds."

"Your honour! This is highly irregular," Geoffrey protested

"Be quiet, Geoffrey." the judge snapped.

He leaned forward and handed one of the letters to me.

"Did you write this letter, Miss Rawlings?"

I looked at the letter I had written to Freddie Atherstone's parents.

"Yes, your honour, I did."

"And did you ever meet this Freddie Atherstone? Because to my knowledge he does not exist."

"Of course he exists. Why else would I have written to him, your honour?"

"That is precisely what we are here to find out. Tell me again, Miss Rawlings.have you ever met Mr Atherstone?"

"No, your honour, he.....he is in Mashonaland on business for Mr Rhodes."

"Indeed. Would it interest you to know that Mr Rhodes says he has never heard of him."

"That's not possible, your honour."

"I expect you know, by now, that anything is possible in this town, Miss Rawlings."

I glanced at Fanny. The colour had drained from her face.

"Mr Fox alleges that you used the names of flowers as a kind of code to let this diamond merchant know when shipments would arrive in England"

Suddenly, I felt dizzy, my heart pounding so hard against my ribcage that I could hardly breathe. I became dimly aware of the noise level rising in the room and when the judge banged his gavel again I almost jumped out of my shoes.

"Are you quite alright, Miss Rawlings? Would you like a glass of water?

"No. Thankyou."

The judge continued and as he talked everything became clear to me.

"Mr Fox suggests that perhaps it was Mrs Yudelman who

persuaded you to write these letters and that you, an uneducated young farm girl from a country background, had no understanding of what you were doing. Is that the case Miss Rawlings? Did Mrs Yudelman ask you to write these letters?"

There was only twenty feet between the dock and where Fanny was sitting and I could see Geoffrey supporting her elbow. I had never seen her lose her composure like this. Baas Fox sat with a smirk on his ginger face. I might have given Fanny up then, had it not been for the surge of fury which overwhelmed me at the veiled insult to my Boer heritage.

I turned to face the judge.

"No. That is not the case, I wrote the letters myself without any instruction from Mrs Yudelman. I understood perfectly what I was doing."

Baas Fox's face twisted with fury as he leapt up from his seat.

"She's lying!" he shouted, banging his fist down on the table in front of him.

"Mr Fox, if she says she did it then she did it. Now sit down and be quiet before I hold you in contempt."

He turned back to me and I thought I heard pity in his voice.

"Miss Rawlings, are you quite sure? You do understand the consequences of your statement?"

"I do, your honour."

But I didn't.

"Stand up Mr Winslett."

Baas Fox subsided into his seat and Geoffrey let go off Fanny's arm and straightened his tie and I could see by the look on his face that something very bad was about to happen. The judge banged his gavel and sentenced me to five years at hard labour, three months of which would be on a spare diet.

I was so shocked I could not move. Geoffrey was jumping up and down waving papers and shouting at the judge, Fanny had collapsed into her seat, and the entire courtroom was in uproar. Amidst all this commotion I was hurried off to the cells, shortly to be joined by Mrs Ventura from DuToitspan, who must have been at at least seventy years old, and got ten years. She was a lot more philosophical than me.

"Could have been worse. In the Free State we'd be looking at a hundred lashes and twenty years," she said.

All I could think of was that, two weeks ago, I had been sitting on a train admiring Amelia's cleavage and now I was going to prison for five years and might never see her again.

Three days went by before Fanny came to see me, three days during which I had nothing to do except think about how Fanny had used me so skilfully. I could have told the judge the truth but then we would both be in jail and what purpose would that serve. There was still a small part of me that believed that Fanny could make all of this go away, she always had before, but there was a bigger part of me that was furious and frightened.

Fanny walked in wearing a black dress and hat, looking as if she was in mourning.

She offered her hand through the prison bars but I ignored it. I must have looked terrible, my eyes were on fire from crying.

"How could you do it?" I burst out.

"I'm so sorry."

"I trusted you."

"I don't know how they got hold of those letters. Did you tell anyone about them?"

"Only Martin Cooper."

Fanny gave me a sharp look.

"You told Martin you were writing letters for me?"

"Yes. I didn't see the harm in it."

She nodded her head slowly up and down.

"Well, I'm sure you've seen the harm in it now."

"I don't understand. Martin told me he loved me. He said he wanted to marry me. He would never do anything to harm me."

"Martin Cooper would do anything to save his own skin. Did you not think it strange that he so easily skipped the country? He must have told Fox about the letters."

The look of pity in Fanny's eyes was more than I could bear and I turned my back to her. Minutes passed before she spoke again.

"There is a way out. "

"And what would that be?"

"I've spoken to Mr Rhodes and he'll talk to the judge and get your sentence reduced. But there's a condition."

"What is the condition?"

"Remember that diamond we spoke about when you first came to stay with me? The one you didn't know anything about? Cecil wants it back."

"I told you I don't have it!"

Fanny leaned back in her chair and stared at me.

"Do you have any idea what it's like at the Breakwater? You will not survive it."

I remembered Mary's stories about the treadmill and shuddered.

"Have you a pair of scissors?" I said

"Yes. Why?"

"Give them to me."

Fanny hesitated

"You're not going to do something stupid?"

"I think I have already been stupid enough. Give me the scissors," I snapped.

I lifted up my skirt and cut open the waistband of my drawers. John Corcoran's diamond popped out into my hand and I held it for a moment, feeling its warmth, before I passed it through the bars.

CHAPTER TWENTY THREE

I got my holiday in the Cape but not where I had intended. My sentence was reduced to two years and they sent me to Robben Island where the lepers and lunatics were kept. The sea was calm that day and the island sat like a plate upon the ocean. It was not always like that. Most of the time the surf crashed continuously upon its shores, washing up planks and flotsam from the ships which lay scattered around it on the seabed, but the island wasn't only a graveyard for ships, I buried a part of myself there. I felt humiliated by both Fanny and Amelia. Humiliation is a terrible thing, it burns your heart like a branding iron.

The prison boat moored at a small stone jetty and a warder met me and removed my shackles. I didn't need them any more, no one but a complete fool would attempt to swim the five miles of shark infested water back to the mainland.

I got to know every inch of that island, it was only one mile across and two miles long, covered in yellow flowered *hotnotsvye*, and you could easily walk from one side of it to the other and back in a morning. The gales and tides that battered the northwestern shores made that side of the island a cruel place and all the buildings were on the eastern and southern shores. All along the coast were submerged rocks, except for Murray's Bay where they had built the harbour. South of the harbour was a sandy, dune covered beach, and one of the mental patients, an old coloured boy called Platjes, walked the strand every day collecting planks to make a boat. The attendants left him undisturbed until the boat was finished and then they burned it and he would start all over again. He collected brass, too, and hammered it flat into coins and carved Queen Victoria's head on it for the day he would escape and row himself across the five miles to Cape Town.

There was a large colony of wild cats, descendants of the ship's cats that had swum ashore and I made a friend of one of them. He followed me everywhere until one of the warders shot him, mistaking him for a rabbit. Rabbits. They were everywhere and we ate them with rice at almost every meal.

I took the loss of the cat very badly and cried over him for months afterwards.

Twelve months after I arrived on the island a ship, on her way from Boston to Calcutta, ran aground in Murray's Bay during a South Easter. She broke up rapidly and her cargo was mostly salvaged and taken to Cape Town to be sold but I found a keg of brandy and a box of tobacco, which had been carried further down the coast and wedged amongst the rocks. The tobacco was no use to me but I hid the brandy and drank it every day for the rest of my sentence. It helped to ease my loneliness.

While the men worked in Jan se Gat, hacking out blue slate for the *stoeps*, kitchens and gravestones of Cape Town, the women sewed pieces of torn blanket together and cut shirt pockets out of thick material until our fingers were blistered and raw. We made *veldskoene* out of bullock's faces. You could make two out of one face and sell them for a shilling a pair.

At first we sewed by hand but later on five sewing machines arrived from the mainland and I learned to sew properly. If anyone had told me then that, in later years, it would prove to be a very useful skill I would have laughed at them. When we weren't sewing we were scrubbing the floors of the warders' houses and digging paths ready for the crushed limestone, which the men brought from the quarry.

The island was a damp, cold lonely place. We lived in little whitewashed stone cottages, underneath the blinking light of the white and red lighthouse on the top of Minto Hill. So many drowned, so many hanged themselves, so many cut their own throats. We found the hanged man, his tongue sticking out of his mouth, the shit and piss dried on his trouser legs.

The lepers and lunatics were mostly kept away from us but one day, while I was walking with my cat, a *kaffirgirl*, dressed in men's clothes, accosted me and said she was a king, and another day a man from St Helena told me he was Jesus and when I told him he wasn't he tried to take my eye out with a piece of driftwood. After that I agreed with everything anyone said.

The lepers lived in wooden cottages, further up the coast, separated from the village by a road. Their skins looked like elephant hide, their fingers and toes shortened and twisted. There were hundreds and hundreds of graves in the leper cemetery, most of them unmarked or topped with little shale headstones with nothing written on them and I thought what a terrible thing it must be to know that once you stepped on the boat to be shipped across to the island, you were never going back to the mainland.

   I stayed angry for a very long time. I waited for the letters from Amelia which never came and I vowed I would never forgive Fanny, for what she had done but in the end I did, because I was going back and I could see no way forward without her.

MARCH 1888

CHAPTER TWENTY FOUR

Amelia stared across the pleasure gardens, watching the snow flakes float past the window. The boughs of the enormous redwood cedars, which overhung the avenue, scraped the ground under the weight of the snow and she saw a little fox cross the haw haw, a duck hanging limply from its mouth. She remembered her father telling her you should never harm a fox, and if you did a fox a good turn good luck would come to you.

The police had been waiting when Charles Spalding stepped out of the carriage at Cape Town station. and started running down the platform. He emerged from the station entrance, his pockets stuffed with illicit diamonds, and stepped off the pavement into the path of an oncoming cab. Only a man like Charles would have had the presence of mind to press those diamonds into his daughter's hand as he lay dying in the middle of Adderley Street.

"Can't be buried as a scoundrel, my dear, what would the relatives think?" were his last words to her. And only a girl as sensible as Amelia had the presence of mind to hand over the diamonds to the police and obtain, in return, a passage back to Southampton on the same boat on which they had travelled to South Africa seven years before. From Southampton she had made her way to Ireland, where it had all begun and fallen on the mercy of her father's relatives. She had spent the past three years running the affairs of this cold, miserable mansion, serving the needs of her aunt, who remained in her cups from morning till night. So far, the old cow had shown a remarkable ability to survive her daily bottle of gin but she had lately taken a turn for the worse and there was talk of committing her to an asylum and if they did Amelia would have no choice but to marry her cousin if she wanted to keep a roof over her head.

Her thoughts wandered back to the day they had sat in this very room in this ugly house, waiting for Herbert to arrive home after a six month tour of Italy, full of plans to study art at the Slade. She had seen the look on his face when his stepfather had handed him his commission and told him to report to Aldershot in three weeks time and heard the awful row that later ensued. She had also seen the shock written across her father's face when the Earl announced that his wife had surrendered control of her inheritance to him. If his sister was no longer in charge of her own money, where would they obtain their living?

But Charles Spalding had years of experience sponging off his relatives and the next morning when they were alone at breakfast, helping themselves to devilled mushrooms, poached eggs and kippers he had announced, with a broad smile on his face, that his brother in law had agreed to pay him an annual allowance if he would only go to South Africa and never come back. Amelia had not been pleased to go to Africa but surely anything was better than continuing to stay in this dreadful house where even the kitchen maids looked down on them.

They had arrived in Zululand in 1878 where, her father assured her, a fortune was to be made out of supplying the needs of the two armies which were presently preparing to kill each other. Charles Spalding's definition of neutrality was to deal with both sides but to favour neither one over the other. His plan was to trade guns to the Zulus in exchange for cattle which he would sell to the British. To this end they had disembarked at East London where Charles had .bought an old grain delivery wagon and two horses, as well as fifty Westley Richards falling block, single action, breech loading rifles, and tagged onto the back of a military supply column marching to Zululand. He had paid £32 each for the guns and the Zulus had given five oxen for one rifle. On his way back he had sold the oxen to the army for £61 each. After a brief visit to Kimberley, they were on their way back to East London to buy more rifles when Charles was arrested by the military police for gun running. Amelia had spent the next three years at the home of Bishop Colenso, while her father sat in jail in Pietermaritzburg.

Herbert's six months furlough was almost at an end and he continued to press his suit, promising a generous allowance in return for playing the part of the dutiful wife.He knew his prospects of advancement were poor so long as he remained unmarried. He was charming and witty and she had been almost tempted to accept him until this morning, when she had entered the gallery above the kitchen just as the coachman marched in, bursting with self importance and something about his manner had made her hesitate. He seated himself at the kitchen table, took out his pipe and carefully tamped the tobacco into the bowl.

"I hear," he said, as he struck a match against his boot, "that there was trouble in India."

Amelia shrank back behind the pillar.

"And what might that be?" Cook enquired.

"They say that himself is after doing the bold thing with an Indian gossoon and when the family found out, didn't they burn the poor lad alive and wasn't there every class of a riot and the whole village nearly burned to the ground."

Cook's eyes widened and the soup ladle hung suspended in mid air. The coachman, clearly delighted with her response, took some time to empty and refill his pipe, whilst the kitchen girls stopped their chatter and glanced surreptitiously over their shoulders.

 "Wasn't it the worst kind of luck, now, that a young lad came forward to the missionary society and reported the whole sorry business. And isn't it a fact that one of them missionary fellows is on his way here at this very minute to make his complaint."

There was a collective gasp from the maids.

"Wouldn't be the first time would it? Don't you remember that young blacksmith's apprentice? Gave the young master a right clattering, so he did. Waited for him near the summer house and knocked him down. Hit his head on the plinth of the sundial. Young feller stole himself's best hunter and ran away. Joined the army and went abroad so we heard later. Young master lay unconscious for a week, they thought he might die. Pity he didn't."

Amelia had hurried from the gallery, forgetting to toss down the dinner menu in her haste to get away.

As she turned back to the window, a carriage clattered up the avenue and Mabel Hudson, the Earl's sister, stepped down from the driver's seat. Mabel was much younger than her brother, only a few years older than Amelia, and she smoked cigars and drank brandy and drove her own carriage. Mabel was a member of the Land League and there was invariably a row whenever she came to visit. Amelia decided to confide in her.

Mabel did not seem surprised.

"Herbert was never a good boy," she said. "But he became worse when my brother made him join the army. Herbert wanted to be a painter, but William put a stop to that. It twisted him, he's never been the same."

"Herbert, a painter?"

"Oh yes. He was all ready to go to the Slade when he came back from Italy. Did you not know?"

"I'm afraid I didn't."

Mabel poured herself a glass of brandy and lit a cigar.

"How is Sophie?" she asked.

"She is confused most of the time. She wanders about the house, looking into all the rooms and tormenting the servants. Yesterday I found her down by the ice house, without a hat or coat. It's a wonder she didn't freeze to death. I am at my wits end with her."

The snow had melted overnight and grey clouds promised a downpour. The horses' breath froze on the cold air and gusts of wind lifted the flaps of the huntsmen's jackets as they laughed and joked and took glasses of sherry from the butler's tray. Amelia stood on the lawn with Mabel.

"You are not tempted to go with them, Mabel?" she said.

"Certainly not. Wretched horses throwing mud everywhere and even more wretched guests. Perish the thought!"

Herbert smiled and lifted his glass of sherry to Amelia and she shuddered. His black man stood a little distance away and for the first time she noticed a terrible air of sadness about him. He spoke to no one and no one spoke to him.

Suddenly the front door opened and the countess appeared on the steps, dressed for hunting, and all conversation ceased as the black mare was brought around and she was helped into the saddle.

"What on earth is Mama doing here? Why, she can hardly sit the horse," said Herbert.

"She insists, Mister Herbert," replied the butler.

"I'll go and get her," Amelia said, but before she could move the Countess had set off towards the first ditch.

"For God's sake, blow the horn, man!" Herbert shouted at the Master.

The hounds found early and the hunt romped across country, like a thing demented, the countess galloping full tilt, with only one hand on the reins, the other waving her hat wildly above her head.

Spectators, in the form of local farm lads, added to the general confusion as they popped up from behind banks and hedges to shout encouragement. Suddenly three heads rose, like flushed grouse, from the far side of a ditch. The vigorous shouting startled the black mare and it stumbled and somersaulted, tossing the countess into the air. She landed on the other side of the ditch, and the horse came down hard on top of her. She lay in the muck, her habit flung up around her thighs and then the big black clouds loosed their load and the rain came pelting down.

Where should have been a hunt ball was now a hastily cobbled together buffet, while groups of guests, still in hunting dress, spoke in hushed whispers. Down by the chapel next to the graveyard, the sound of shovels on frozen ground echoed across the pleasure gardens. In the workshops, the estate's carpenters hurried to make the coffin and a great, melancholy hush descended on the house. The servants tiptoed around the house and spoke in whispers, but Amelia was only thinking of her own bleak future.

Aunt Mabel found her standing at the morning room window and went to stand beside her, slipping her arm around Amelia's waist.

"Why don't you come and live with me, my dear? I am in need of a companion and you will find life in Dublin quite delightful after this dreadful old pile."

"Really, Mabel? You would have me come and live with you?"

"Yes, really. I have already spoken to William and told the maid to pack your bags. We shall leave tomorrow after the funeral."

"Herbert will not be pleased," Amelia replied.

"No, he won't but we don't care do we?"

"No, we don't."

Her aunt's accident had disrupted the hunt and the fox had got away and Amelia felt only a small twinge of guilt as she wondered whether this was the good luck she had longed for the previous day.

CHAPTER TWENTY FIVE

I stepped off the boat onto the fishing jetty at the Roggebaai, still dressed in my prison garb and paused to look around me. I don't know why I expected to find Amelia waiting for me, I had never received a single letter from her. The smell of the fish smokers on the beach and the screeching of seagulls as they squabbled over the offal, competed with the shouting hawkers and fishcarts as they clattered away towards the suburbs and it took me a while to adjust to the colour and noise after the windswept drabness of the island. Wagons piled high with wool bales stood on the quayside, waiting to be hoisted aboard ship and as I stood there a fishwife thrust a piece of paperwrapped smoked snoek into my hand.

"Welcome back, lovey!" she said. and watched me pull off a piece of the oily fish. I had never tasted anything as wonderful as that first bite of fish on my first day of freedom.

Johnson appeared from behind the wool bales, holding Asjas by the hand. The baboon's little black eyes sought me out and then Johnson let go of him and he ran chattering towards me, clutching the *verdomde pop* that had caused all the trouble.

"*Haai*, Miss Jacoba. So thin. Look like a *veldkaffir*, can't get on the train looking like that," Johnson said, shaking his head. "The madam sent money to buy clothes."

People turned their heads to watch us as we walked up Adderley

Street, what a strange sight we must have made, a convict woman, a black man dressed like a church minister and a baboon holding a doll.

Kimberley had not changed much during my time in prison. Its streets were still unpaved, it still had no trees and most of its houses were still built of corrugated iron. Only the very rich could afford the turrets which rose, here and there, above groves of gum trees. But there had been one big change which would decide the future, not only of the diamond industry, but of the the entire country. The battle for control of the mines was over and the whole lot was now amalgamated into one big company called De Beers Consolidated Mines, at the head of which sat Cecil Rhodes.

Fanny did not meet me at the station and she was not at home when Johnson brought me into the kitchen for the cook and the Griekwa cleaning girl to cluck and fuss over.

My room had been redecorated in shades of white and green, striped curtains hung at the windows and a matching eiderdown lay on the brass bed. Three new dresses lay on top of the eiderdown. There was a new bathroom, all porcelain and gold, with a gas burner which erupted into life when I turned a tap and I lay in the water for half an hour, twiddling the taps on and off with my toes.

Fanny appeared at supper time, embracing me as if I had never been away.

"Prison don't seem to have treated you too badly," she said, as she sat down at the opposite end of the table. But I was not so easily mollified.

Dinner was a strained affair as one by one, Johnson set down my favourite foods before me and one by one I ate two mouthfuls and pushed my plate away. Salmon mousse and roast beef were too rich for my stomach and the smell of the lamb cutlets made me nauseous. Even a dessert of fruits and almonds suspended in berry coloured aspic could not tempt me. My stomach rebelled, unused to such rich food.

After supper we retired to the parlour.

"Well, ducks, now you can tell me all about the island," Fanny said, as if I had just returned from a holiday.

"I don't want to talk about it," I replied.

Fanny sat back in her chair, pursing her lips, and a cat jumped onto her lap.

"Won't do any good adopting this bullish attitude, Jacoba. I said I'd look after you and I will."

"You should have looked after me three years ago."

"Well, I didn't and I'm sorry for that but what's done is done and best left in the past where it belongs."

She rang the bell and Johnson came in carrying a leather valise. After he had left Fanny opened it and tipped onto the table more money than I had ever seen in my life. During the final battle for the mines, while I had been making bullocks heads into shoes, Fanny had gone on a spending spree, buying shares in the Kimberley Mine at £14 each. Once the battle was over and the price of the shares rose to £49 she had sold them all and what I was looking at was half the proceeds of that sale and it was all mine. I forgave Fanny for her treachery then, the money was too much to resist, but I did not give in completely. Gold had been discovered in the Transvaaal while I was in prison and when she told me I was going to invest my money in gold shares the following day I refused. I did invest half of it, I had a great deal of respect for Fanny's business acumen but the rest I put in the bank. It wouldn't have mattered what I did, eventually I lost it all anyway.

Some things stayed the same. We took breakfast every morning and tea every afternoon at four. I bought myself new clothes and played chemmy in the Privee. I went to concerts and dinners. But I could not settle. I still woke up every morning at four o'clock and I could not get used to sleeping without the lighthouse flashing through my window every seven seconds. I bought a horse and rode, in the cool of the morning, for miles, in every direction until I was exhausted. And I drank. Brandy mostly. Two years in prison had taught me the comfort that could be found in the bottom of a bottle of Hennessy. When Fanny locked it away I sent Bloody Fool to buy squarefaces of gin and when she found out and put a stop to it, I drank whatever I could lay my hands on. Fanny had rewarded me for my silence but nobody could give me back the years I had spent on the island. Nothing she did improved my mood and I could find no peace in my head.

One morning I found myself riding back the way I came to Kimberley. I told myself I wanted to see if there was any trace of the wagon I had left in the *veld* almost ten years before. I reached the *donga* where we had left Oupa's wagon but there was nothing left of it, not even a spoke of a wagon wheel. I sat for a while in the shade of a prickly pear tree my knees pulled up under my chin while Asjas pulled down the fruits, stripped them of their thorns and stuffed his mouth until his cheeks were bulging. And then, amidst the tall turpentine grass, I spotted the little cairn of rocks I had piled on my baby's grave. Delicate yellow *botterblom* flowers had grown on it and I reached out to pick one. I pulled off the petals, one by one and dropped them on the grave. I should give the baby a name, it wasn't right that she should lie out here nameless and forgotten, but I couldn't bring myself to do it. I had made a mess of my life.

I got back on my horse and looked back across the plains and for one brief moment I thought I might keep on going and ride back to Zululand.

On my way back I saw a large hill and I urged the horse towards it. There was a dam on top of it, a disused quarry of some kind and I dismounted and sat on the rim, with a square face of gin beside me, staring down into the green depths. I drank the gin and tossed the empty bottle into the dam, watching it twist over and over before it splashed into the water, startling a flock of ducks. A family of meerkats popped up from the grass and stared at me, their front paws hanging neatly in front of their upright chests, until Asjas chased them back to their burrow, screeching in alarm.

It was late afternoon when I came across the farmhouse, partially hidden behind a grove of eucalyptus trees and I was almost upon it before I saw it. The paint was peeling from its gables and the roof was half gone, revealing stinkwood beams as thick as a man's waist. Broad steps led up to a stone flagged verandah and strands of thickstemmed bougainvillea entwined themselves around its fluted pillars, their purple flowers cascading onto the ground. At one end was an old *riempie* bench in need of repair and wooden shutters were nailed over the windows. I walked up the steps and pushed open the heavy door, disturbing a squeaking colony of fruitbats, clustered beneath the roof beams. A portion of the reed ceiling had fallen onto the great planks of roughly hewn yellowwood which covered the floor. The long, low building reeked of decay and neglect.

Two rooms led off to the right. One was empty but the other contained an iron bedstead, its brass fittings tarnished by age, the striped ticking of the mattress torn in places, its feathers lying on the floor. I could hear the scrabbling of rats in what was left of the ceiling and the smell of the onions that were once stored there filled the room. A jacket hung from a wooden peg on the wall. There was a Dover stove in the kitchen, surrounded by black and white tiles and a row of dust covered paraffin lamps stood on a shelf next to the back door.

Darkness came quickly, a terrific whirring heralding the departure of the bats and I watched them stream out of the open roof before wandering out onto the *stoep* to sit down on the *riempie* bench. There were no clouds in the sky and the moon cast ghostly shadows amongst the eucalyptus trees as I waited for the night sounds to begin. The whistling rats were first, a thin, high pitched screech followed by a question mark. An early hunting owl whooped and I caught a brief glimpse of a white face. A civet cat, carrying a kitten in its mouth, leapt up onto *stoep* and stopped in surprise when it saw me, its yellow eyes holding my gaze for a moment before it vanished into the night. A jackal screamed close by and then there was silence except for the chirruping of a million crickets in the grass. I had missed the sounds of the *veld* so much and I was almost overwhelmed by sadness. My Oupa must be turning in his grave to see what I had become for the sake of money. I slept on the old *katel*, in the only room which had a roof on it and when I woke up I had decided what I was going to do.

I strode into Number Five, ignoring Fanny's histrionics and told her I was going to buy the farm.

"What?"

"I've had enough of Kimberley, Fanny, I want some peace and quiet."

"Well, you'll certainly get that if you go and live there. It must be over thirty miles away."

"It's what I want."

"And how are you going to make a living?"

"I don't know, Fanny, I haven't thought that far yet. But one thing's for sure, I am not making it out of diamonds again."

Fanny stared out of the window for a few minutes before turning back to me.

"There was never any changing you once your mind was made up, ducks. We'd better go down and see Winslett."

Geoffrey had been avoiding me since I came back from prison and he looked nervous as he came out of his office. His clerk, a new man, stared at me curiously. Everyone stared at me since I returned from the island. I was used to it by then.

"Tea for Miss Rawlings and Mrs Yudelman, Albert," he said, as he ushered us into his office. I had never had much time for Geoffrey's fussy ways and I had even less time since his dismal performance at my trial. I suppose I was unfair to him, he could only work with the information Fanny gave him and he had had no idea about the Freddie Atherstone letters.

"And what can I do for you today, Mrs Yudelman?"

"Not Mrs Yudelman, it's me who wants to see you," I interrupted.

He fiddled with his bowtie and forced a smile.

"Bring Miss Rawlings's file, please, Albert."

Geoffrey frowned when I told him I wanted to buy the farm.

"You must mean Nooitgedacht. That farm has quite a history. I believe the present owner won it at a game of cards. He never actually lived on it."

" In that case surely he would be willing to sell it?"

" I'm sure he would but there is a problem."

"And that is?"

"He's dead. Died in the De Beers fire last July and left no will. It could be years before the estate is finalised."

The De Beers fire had been the worst mining disaster in South African history. It had started, nobody knew how, at six thirty one evening and by the next morning over two hundred miners had died underground. It was the worst luck that the farm's owner had been one of them.

"How many years?"

"That all depends on how long it takes to trace any living relatives. It has to be advertised in all the newspapers both here and in England.It is a very sad case. He was due to retire from the mines the day after the accident."

When he told me the man's name I almost fell off my chair and nobody missed my sharp intake of breath.

"Jacoba? Are you alright?" said Fanny

"Yes. Yes. I'm just tired. And the heat. I think I need to lie down."

"Very well. Let us know as soon as you hear anything, Geoffrey. Even if you do find any relatives they might want to sell it themselves."

I could feel my pulse racing as we walked home. Now I was in trouble.

Three days passed before I made up my mind to confide in Fanny. I waited until Johnson had served tea and left the room. Fanny stared at the *Statenbijbel* I held in my hand.

"We're going to have a prayer meeting are we?" she said.

"That man. The one Geoffrey said owned the farm. He was my uncle."

Fanny nearly dropped her teacup.

"Your what?"

"My uncle. Wynand Swanepoel was my father's brother."

"Well, ain't you just full of surprises. Better get Johnson to bring us more tea."

"Rawlings was my mother's maiden name. I took it when I came to Kimberley because someone was looking for me."

I opened the bible.

"Look. Here are the names of my family since 1652. They are all here in this bible."

"And you have your birth certificate?"

I pulled out a piece of paper from between the pages.

"What am I going to do Fanny?"

"It's obvious, ain't it, ducks? If you want that farm you'll have to tell Geoffrey your real name."

"And if he asks me why I changed it? What do I tell him?"

Fanny laughed.

"He won't ask. Do you think you're the only person in this town going under a name different to the one they were born with? Do you think my real name is Yudelman?"

"I.....I don't know. I suppose I do."

"Well, ducks, maybe it is and maybe it ain't. Point is, Geoffrey won't care. And I don't care either. That's your own business."

"What if they come looking for me?"

"How long has it been? Ten years? Nobody's been asking about for a Jacoba Swanepoel have they?"

"No."

"Mind you, it was lucky you weren't going under your own name when you got sent down. That was all over the papers for weeks.

They would have found you then."

It would be many years before I discovered that the reason my Transvaal cousins did not come forward to claim Oom Wynand's farm was that while I was crossing the river at Laing's Nek, they were being murdered by the Pedi. All of them except Etienne, and I would only discover his fate when Conor returned and brought more trouble into my life.

It hardly seemed possible that I would once again own a farm and more importantly I would regain my name. I only realised then how much I had missed it.

PART THREE - JACOBSDAL

JANUARY 1889

CHAPTER TWENTY SIX

The ostriches were Fanny's idea. I should have known better than to think she would stay out of my business and if I am honest with myself I did not want her to. I had no experience of keeping books or making a profit and. I did not even know how to operate a bank account and I was more than happy to leave my affairs in Fanny's hands. It was a decision I would later come to regret.

"Ostriches is what you want to put on that farm of yours, ducks. Big money in ostrich feathers, these days, £12 a pound. All the rage in New York and London."

She produced a small grey velvet cap on which an arrangement of pale pink feathers sprayed upwards and outwards, cascading down its sides.

"I know nothing about ostriches."

"Well, I happen to know someone who does."

"Oh? And who might that be?"

"Bloody Fool. Used to work on an ostrich farm. Says he knows all about ostriches. I'll lend him to you for six months."

"He also said he knew all about gardening."

"Look ducks, truth is he was arrested for public drunkenness last week. Peelers say if they catch him again they'll send him to the

Breakwater. I need him somewhere he can dry out. And even if he don't know anything about ostriches, he's bound to be useful for something."

"I don't know. I'll think about it."

I examined the cap again. It was quite beautiful. I was seduced by that cap.

The next morning I was woken up by Asjas shrieking and when I went outside I found Lukas waiting on my verandah. Seven years with Mary had not changed him much, only a front tooth missing which he told me he had lost in a fight.

"*Missies* Harry sent me. The *missies* going to need a good boy, this place very broken," he said, looking up at the hole in the roof.

The ostriches arrived two weeks later, young birds, only six months old, wearing rough, black and grey plumage, and the place was in uproar as they were offloaded and set loose. Asjas went crazy and had to be chained to a eucalyptus tree where he screamed his head off all morning. Bloody Fool had made sure to fill himself with liquor on his last night of freedom and had to be dragged to safety when he fell under the feet of an angry cock. Lukas scratched his head and kept up a constant muttering under his breath.

"Birds, *fokken* stupid birds. What we going to do with them?"

"Shut your mouth, Lukas," I replied.

"Horses better. Even goats better."

"Ostriches are what we have and ostriches are what we will farm," I snapped. I was sweaty and dirty. It had been a very long time since I had dealt with unruly livestock and I had grown soft in Kimberley.

I was not in the mood for an argument with Lukas.

In the midst of this chaos I saw a lone horseman riding down the long avenue leading up to the house. He still sat his horse the same way and I recognised him immediately. I felt my heart beating faster as he rode towards me, hardly able to believe my eyes. His skin was darkened by the sun but his jaw was a bright pink where he had recently shaved off his beard and as he pulled up his horse in front of the verandah, he took off his hat and the lock of white hair fell over his eyes. I removed my leather gloves and wiped the sweat off my face with my sleeve.

"Well, *rooinek*, I never expected to see you again," I said.

"Nor I you. They told me at Majuba you were dead."

"Get off your horse, then, if it is yours, and I will make us coffee,"

My hands trembled as I ground the coffee beans and threw them into the coffee pot and as I reached up to fetch down two mugs I dropped one on the tiled floor and it shattered. He came into the kitchen, wearing the cheeky grin I remembered so well.

"Get out. I have not yet invited you into my house," I said and he backed away, holding his hands up in front of him. When I came out onto the *stoep* he was settled in a chair as if he had sat there all his life. I put two cups of coffee and a plate of *beskuit* on the table in front of us.

"How did you find me?"

"Be impossible not to. You are famous all over the Cape. Is it true that you used the baboon to transport stolen diamonds?"

"Not me. Someone else put them there and I did two years on

Robben Island for it."

"Doesn't seem to have done you any harm. You look very well."

"Who told you I was dead?"

I saw him hesitate.

"Well? Who was it?"

"A man I met at Majuba. Etienne Swanepoel was his name. Said he was your cousin."

"Etienne was at Majuba?"

"He was. Fought like a tiger."

It was Etienne who first put me up on a pony, when I could barely walk, seating me on the saddle in front of him. Etienne teased me and threw me in the air until I got sick and his father thrashed him. Of all my cousins, I loved Etienne the most, so when Conor went on to tell me that he had died at Majuba, avenging my death, I put my head in my hands and cried.

"I'm so sorry, Jacoba, I didn't want to tell you."

"You promised you would come back once the soldiers left. If you had, you could have told him I was alive and perhaps he wouldn't have put himself at such great risk."

And perhaps the other thing would never have happened either and set in motion the chain of events which had landed me in prison. But I could hear my oupa's voice telling me the story of Lot's wife. There was nothing to be gained by looking back at what might have been. I brought myself back to the present and went inside to make more coffee. Conor followed me, looking around at the exposed beams and dirty walls and the sheet of canvas covering the hole in my roof.

"I could stay and help you," he said.

"I seem to remember that the last time you offered to help me my life was left in ruins,"

"True. But lightning won't strike twice in the same place, will it?"

He could not have been more wrong.

Bloody Fool, it turned out, was not lying about his experience and when plucking time came and we gathered the ostriches into the kraal, stamping their two-toed feet, hissing savagely, and nipping the heads of their neighbours every time a feather was cut from its tail, it was Bloody Fool who got the idea to throw a cloth over their heads to calm them down and Bloody Fool who graded the feathers and packed into cases. I think he would have gone with them all the way to London had he been allowed and I decided I was never giving him back to Fanny.

We worked hard, that first year, building dams and kraals and putting acres under crops of cabbages and corn which we sold to the mines. I treated my *plaasvolk* well, as my grandfather had taught me and by the middle of the following year I had twelve families living on my farm and my hills were dotted with sheep and goats. Every evening when the herdboys brought them into the kraal I took the tally and wrote it down in my ledger. I might not have had a clue about book keeping but I knew how to keep track of my animals.

Under Conor's guidance a team of labourers pulled down the remains of the *rietdak* and replaced it with a solid ceiling of yellowwood planks brought up from the Cape. The shutters were repainted green and a new red zinc roof extended over the verandah. I spared no expense.

I could not keep up with the demand for feathers, the value of my gold shares was soaring and once a quarter I rode into town and Fanny laid out my dividend statements in front of me and guided me through my bank accounts. I never paid much attention to anything except the black figure at the bottom of the page, which grew bigger and bigger, as time went by.

I had furniture sent up from the Cape and revelled in my good fortune and the power that money gave me. I was no more popular in Kimberley than I had been in my diamond stealing days but I didn't care. I had a farm and a good man and that was all I needed. Conor made me forget about prison and Amelia and everything that went before. We were married on my twenty sixth birthday, my only condition being that he take my name, to which he had no objection.

"O'Reilly-Swanepoel? Sounds like a good name to me and you never know when a Dutch name might come in useful."

That was the way he was, always seeing ways to turn everything to his own advantage.

It wasn't a marriage that Fanny approved of but, like my mother so many years before, I went ahead and did it anyway.

Conor was a constant source of moneymaking ideas which never came to anything, but he amused me and I did not care that he sometimes disappeared for days on end in pursuit of his schemes. I had a scheme of my own which was proving hard to bring to fruition. The ostriches were my livelihood but horses were my passion and I was determined to revive my grandfather's bloodlines. I made a trip to Molteno to buy mares but even the mention of my grandfather's name could not persuade Oom Cloete to part with any of his stallions for any amount of money. I decided to import a Flemish stallion from the Netherlands.

In May, Rhodes posted recruitment notices all over Kimberley offering three thousand acres of land and fifteen mining claims to anyone who joined a column he was raising to go to Mashonaland and Conor came skipping in the door, threw his hat at the hatrack and announced that he was going with them.

"I won't be gone for long. Perhaps six months. And the money is good. The papers say they will pay me £3 a page to send back reports."

"We don't need the money. I have more than enough for both of us."

"I don't want to live off you, Jacoba."

"You've been doing it for the past year and it hasn't bothered you."

His face flushed then and I realised I had said the wrong thing. It sounded like a complaint. I didn't mean for it to come out like that. He worked hard around the farm and I was more than happy to support him.

He turned on his heel and strode out the door, not even bothering to take his hat.

"Conor!" I shouted but it did no good. I watched him galloping down the avenue, beneath Bloody Fool's beloved jacaranda trees and was immediately back in Zululand, watching him gallop into the hills, with the British troopers galloping behind him.

I sat for a while on the *stoep*, before calling Lukas to saddle up my mare.

"Six months? Be lucky if you see him in six years. Don't say I didn't warn you," said Fanny

"I should never have said what I did."

"You were never one to think before you speak, ducks. Or think before you act, for that matter."

"What if he never comes back?"

"Employ a foreman, " Fanny replied. I should have known better than to expect any sympathy from her and I stormed back to the farm in a temper.

He was hardly gone a month when I woke up one morning and started vomiting. It wasn't possible. The doctor had told me that I would never be able to have children. I put it down to a bad piece of beef I had eaten the day before, but after three days I knew I was pregnant. At first I was angry. I had never expected to have children and my pregnancy was an inconvenience I could ill afford. As the months went by and there was no word from Conor, my anger gave way to resentment, as my life became circumscribed by the limits my increasing immobility and nausea placed upon me. At Fanny's insistence I went to stay with her when my time was near and the doctor was very surprised when he was called out in the middle of the night to deliver Quartus and even more surprised when Elizabeth popped out behind him.

"I never thought you would be able to bear children," he said.

"Neither did I, or I mightn't have been so careless."

The Griekwa cleaning girl had just weaned her own baby and was elevated to wetnurse, a job at which she was much better than cleaning. She brought my babies to see me first thing in the morning and last thing at night and I patted them on the head and let them wind their tiny hands around my forefinger and considered my job done. Fanny, on the other hand, was quite besotted with them and bought a special pram so that she could parade them around town every day, so that everyone could admire them. You would have thought she had given birth to them herself.

MAY 1895

CHAPTER TWENTY SEVEN

I met Olive Schreiner on my childrens' fourth birthday.

At Fanny's request I had brought my twins into into town to treat them to a day at the funfair and that evening Fanny and I were to attend a farce by Miss Florence Miller at the Theatre Royal, which was intended as a treat for me. The children were sick with tiredness and excitement by the time we took our usual table on the Grand Hotel verandah and we were about to order tea when a short, dumpy woman mounted the steps, pale faced and breathing heavily. She seemed a little unsteady on her feet and I jumped up to help her. I later discovered that she had recently had a baby, which had lived for only a few hours.

"Olive! Will you join us for tea?" said Fanny.

Fanny and Olive could not have been more different. Fanny, the brothelkeeper and illicit diamond buyer and Olive, the principled supporter of unfashionable causes and passionate enemy of Mr Rhodes ,appeared to have nothing in common. Olive had no interest in Kimberley's high society, the carriage folk, as she called them and she had no interest in money either. I wondered how she got along with Fanny whose only interest was money.

"Mama, may we go into the square?" Elizabeth asked.

"You may. Johnson will go with you."

They were so different from each other, my twins. Elizabeth, with her father's black hair and stocky build, and Quartus, tall and blond like me, with his almost girlish good looks. Like me, he had inherited my father's odd coloured eyes, one blue, one green. Life came easily to Elizabeth. Or perhaps it was that she went out to meet it where her brother hung back and everything was a struggle for him. One day it would be Elizabeth who ran the farm, I had no doubt of that.

Tea arrived, accompanied by lemon buns and almond cakes and it soon became clear that there was no love lost between Olive and Cecil Rhodes. Olive was incensed by his support of the Strop Bill, which was currently before the Cape Parliament and, if passed, would allow us to legally thrash our servants. Fanny would never go up against Rhodes, but it was clear that she didn't want to lose Olive's friendship either. Myself, I had no opinion either way, my family had never beaten our *kaffirs* and I wasn't about to start now.

"They'll never pass it, anyway. Why get yourself so exercised? It can't be good for your health," Fanny said

"That is not the point. It is the principle of the thing that matters. One should be seen to stand up against injustice wherever it is found," Olive replied.

Principles were not commonly found in Kimberley and I immediately began to pay more attention. There was something compelling about the way Olive spoke and as I listened to her talking to Fanny, I knew I wanted to get to know her better. She must have felt the same way because as she got up to leave, she handed me her card.

"Perhaps you might call on me before you go back to your farm, Mrs Swanepoel?"

"Well you certainly made an impression on Mrs Schreiner, ducks. Not often she invites people to her house," said Fanny.

At the theatre, that evening, we found ourselves seated next to Lou Cohen, a diamond buyer friend of Fanny's who fancied himself as a drama critic. His stony silence throughout the performance promised a damning review and the following morning we were treated to the sight of the tall and muscular Miss Miller taking a running jump at Cohen with a gingham umbrella, outside the theatre. He only managed to escape by dashing into the auditorium and leaving by the back door. Such encounters were not uncommon. You needed to have your fists ready and your wits about you to be a drama critic in Kimberley.

Olive's house in Otto street was quite small, no more than a little cottage set on three acres of land. The kitchen was separate from the house and it reminded me of our kitchen in Zululand, although I could not imagine why it was set apart since there was hardly any danger of the tin roof of this house going on fire. It was a pretty little house and very neat, so quiet you could hear the cat walk across the floor. Olive showed me into her study, from which big glass doors led onto a verandah, and a young black boy brought tea. Olive was the person who first aroused my interest in politics and made me start thinking of myself as a Boer again. I had not spoken Dutch for years and my children spoke nothing but English.

She had come to Kimberley to seek relief from the asthma which had plagued her all her life. Olive did not depend on her husband for support and, like me, she had insisted he change his name to Schreiner when she married him. Like mine, he was often away for long periods of time, although never as long as Conor, who had, by then, been gone for almost five years. There was something very attractive about Olive, not for her looks, which were uninspiring, but for her character. Perhaps she saw something of herself in me, too, for we took an instant liking to each other.

Her dislike of Rhodes bordered on hatred and she was convinced he was fomenting trouble amongst the *Uitlanders* in the Transvaal and intended to spark a rebellion. I knew about the rumours, of course, Fanny made it her business to know about everything that might affect her finances. The foreigners who controlled the mines had been engaged, for years, in an ongoing battle with President Kruger and his government over his refusal to grant them the franchise, but, like Fanny, I was only interested in how it affected my shares in the gold mines and so far I had seen no reduction in the amount of quarterly dividends which flowed into my bank account. I didn't believe that anything would come of the *Uitlanders*' plot and I didn't believe that, as Olive alleged, Rhodes was behind it, so when, early in the New Year we received the news that Dr Jameson had invaded the Transvaal, I was as shocked as everyone else.

JANUARY 1896

CHAPTER TWENTY EIGHT

A couple of hundred miles to the north of Kimberley, at Pitsani, just three miles from the Transvaal border, Leander Starr Jameson paced up and down in the hot sun outside his tent. He had just received a message from the *Uitlanders* in Johannesburg telling him to call off his invasion. Jameson had four hundred Rhodesian mounted police belonging to the Cecil Rhodes's Chartered Company and one hundred and twenty volunteers with him. It wasn't a lot to take on the entire Boer army but Jameson and the Rhodesian troopers had faced hopeless odds before. They had crushed Lobengula in 1892, six hundred against six thousand Matabele and Rhodes had assured him that this new expedition would be easier than Matabeleland.

Jameson had managed to scrape together six Maxim guns, two seven pounder mountain guns and a twelve and a half pounder field piece, as well as a cask of Cape Brandy for the men and crates of champagne for the officers. He planned to make a three day dash to Johannesburg before the Boer commandos could mobilise.

He read the message once more, before setting it alight. A short, slight man, with nervous brown eyes, dressed in a fawn coloured coat, he stepped onto the dusty parade ground, climbed on top of a barrel, took out of his pocket a crumpled piece of paper and began to read aloud an invitation from the British and foreign business community in Johannesburg. The *Uitlanders*, he said, would be waiting to join them when they reached Krugersdorp. Whilst everyone's attention was occupied Conor slipped into the telegraph tent and sent a telegram to the Advertiser saying :He means to go on.

In the gathering dusk, the troopers trotted down the rutted wagon road towards the Transvaal border, the moonlight glinting off the brass mountings of the Maxims and Conor tucked himself in at the rear of the column of polished boots and white helmets and patted his horse on the neck.

"Well, Nick, we're off on a jaunt to visit Mr Kruger, what do you think of that?" he said.

"Remember Majuba!" they shouted as they crossed the border.

You be remembering it, alright, Conor thought, especially when you see yourselves raising the white flag again.

Conor had to concede that Leander Starr Jameson was an extraordinary man, He had led the pioneer column to Mashonaland and Conor had witnessed first hand how he had established a government and beaten Lobengula in his stronghold of Bulawayo. But you've bitten off more than you can chew this time, boyo.

They rode for four days, with hardly a halt for sleep and by the time they arrived at Doornkop, Conor was exhausted, slipping from side to side in his saddle. As dawn broke he got his first sight of the endless lines of tall iron chimneys, the gigantic wheels above the mine shafts and the gleam of the golden slag heaps in the distance, but the *Uitlanders* had made their peace with Kruger and no one was waiting to join them. Johannesburg had not risen, as promised.

For two days they fought a running battle with invisible commandos before, at a farm called Vlakfontein, crouching behind ambulance wagons and ammunition carts while the Boers rained fire down on them, someone raised a white flag made from a servant girl's apron. The Boers rose from the surrounding veld, dressed in their Sunday best, straight from their New Year festivities, and took them all prisoner. They had lost sixty five dead and wounded and Jameson was led away, weeping, to jail.

Conor was standing with the other prisoners when he spotted the short, black bearded figure of Piet Cronje amongst the Boers.

"Commandant Cronje! Do you remember me?" he shouted.

Cronje's face split into a smile.

"*Rooinek*!" he said, clapping Conor on the back." What are you doing with this crowd of ruffians? You are still telling war stories for the newspapers?"

"Indeed I am. And a fine story I will have to tell as soon as you give me the use of your telegraph wires."

"Certainly. But let us first put these mongrels in the *tronk*, and then you will come to my house and we will eat our New Year's dinner. You must be hungry by now."

The food reminded him of Jacoba's cooking. A lamb and chicken pie, rich with the flavour of butter and eggs, wrapped in golden pastry and a plate of fat, roasted sausages. Boiled pumpkin with cinnamon and sugar and butter. And when he thought he could eat no more, Cronje's wife put down a whole *melktert* in front of him.

"So, *Engelsman*, it is a long time since we last met at Majuba. You must be a father of sons by now?"

"Not yet," Conor replied, " but I do have a wife."

"Ah, *Engelsman*, a man needs sons. I myself have only daughters, it is a sorrow to me. Tomorrow, I will give you back the horse we took from you so that you may go home and do your duty but but first I have something to show you.

He called out and a man brought in a black tin box and put it on the table.

"Do you know what this is *rooinek*?"

"It looks like an officer's trunk."

"That's exactly what it is. Do you know what is inside it?"

Conor shook his head.

Cronje opened the box and took out a pile of papers.

"These are the coded letters between Rhodes and the plotters. And this is the code book that goes with them, my man has already decoded them. Here, read them for yourself. As you can see, the *verdomde* British are determined to get their hands on the goldfields and we are equally determined that they will not. There will be more trouble soon, mark my words."

As Conor read each letter he could feel his pulse racing. This was the scoop he had been waiting for. It might even save him from Jacoba's temper when he got home.

"Well these will put the cat amongst the pigeons. May I have the use of your telegraph now?"

CHAPTER TWENTY NINE

Olive had been right. Rhodes was in it up to his neck and when we read in the newspapers that some of the officers accompanying Dr Jameson held Imperial commissions and that, for months, shipments of arms and ammunition had been sent to Johannesburg via Kimberley, concealed in the false bottoms of oildrums and bags of coke stored in the diamond mines, there was uproar.

"Oh, there'll be a fine howdidoo now, Cecil won't get away with this," Fanny remarked.

Below the article was a picture of a group of prisoners, in handcuffs, flanked by Boers brandishing rifles. They looked as if they had been on a hunt and were showing off their bag and in the middle of the picture was Conor. He was the only one smiling.

"At least he's alive," said Fanny. I did not know whether to be relieved or angry.

And I had more important things to worry about than Cecil Rhodes and Dr Jim and the whereabouts of my husband.

For more than a year, there had been no rain worth mentioning and the dams were empty. A haze rose off the sunscorched *veld* and, as the drought worsened, my land was turned into an oven. The river was no more than a stream and soon it would be dry. Every animal on the farm was congregated about the house and I had to fight my way through them when I went out the front door. The cattle bawled day and night for water and the ostriches tapped their bills on the windows and looked in at me, gasping for breath, their wings held away from their bodies. Once every bush and shrub and plant had died they survived on the *spekboom* trees which grew like weeds up the sides of the *koppies*.

Hot winds swept across the country, and everybody was tired, and head-achy and bad tempered. The dust which the winds brought with them drove us all half-mad. You could attack the house with a bunch of ostrich feathers and ten minutes later the children were writing their names on every flat surface. The wind carried the dust high up into the air, in columns, like a water-spout. We ate and breathed dust from morning till night. It was worse than anything I had ever experienced in the miners' camp. We were tormented by snakes, and Lukas nailed narrow strips of horse hide along the threshold of each outer door but nothing could keep my son and daughter from bringing in a succession of dead puffadders, cobras and *skaapstekers* to show me. Only the horses seemed to suffer no ill effects.

Every day I rode up to the top of Bleskop and prayed for a miracle and when, one afternoon, I saw the storm clouds gathering on the horizon I thought God had heard me at last. I galloped back down the hill, driving the horse forward, with Asjas clinging, sodden and miserable, to the cantle of my saddle, as the thunder rolled and great sheets of lightning cracked across the sky. But the storm came faster than I had calculated, overtaking me in minutes and then the heavens opened and rain lashed down.

The *sluits* which crisscrossed my land filled and overflowed within the hour and we watched, helplessly, as sheep drowned and ostrich nests were washed away. The wind-mill pump was whirled aloft and blown apart to land in pieces scattered across two square miles of *veld* and even Lukas, who was good at such things, could not put it back together again and so it lay abandoned beside the sheep kraal.

It rained all night and all of the next day and then the sun came out and the sweet smell of freshly watered dry earth filled my nostrils. Within a few days, even before the perennial karroo bushes had recovered, all the spaces between its isolated tufts were covered with *opslaag*, the softest and most delicate looking plants with tiny, pretty flowers, and the new crop of ostrich chicks, which I had despaired of saving, were let out to eat.

But my relief did not last long.

The next day I rode the Flemish stallion along the river, where the grass was longer and the midges rose in a dense cloud around my head. The horse tossed his head in irritation and I pulled my hat lower over my face, but it made no difference. The insects crawled into my ears and nostrils and up the sleeves of my shirt.

A very young foal stood motionless, in the long grass, next to her dead mother and as I walked closer my heart sank. Her head was swollen to nearly double its size and the swelling continued along her neck and down her back. Horse sickness.I shot her and she crumpled to her knees.

I did not have far to ride before I found others, lying in an obscene circle under a thorn tree and by mid afternoon I had shot twenty five.

Day after day I rode out into the veld with the herd boys, shooting those that were too far gone and walking the others home. It was exhausting, heartbreaking work and I thought I might collapse when I had to shoot my childrens' ponies. It was a long time before they forgave me for that.

The farmhands gathered manure and packed it around the walls of the kraal and every night, for the rest of the summer, we lit bonfires. The stench was awful and when the wind changed direction the smoke forced its way into every corner of the house but no more horses took sick and when the first frosts came I called a halt to the fires and let the horses back out on the *veld* again. Almost my entire herd was gone and, worst of all, I had lost my Flemish stallion. I sat down on the *stoep* and wept.

When I looked up I saw Conor riding down the avenue.

"Where the hell have you been, God damn you? You said six months. It's been almost five years."

He smiled that irresistible smile but this time I was not won over.

"I'm sorry Jacoba, I got held up."

"Held up? Is that all you can say? Held up?"

Before he could answer me I slapped him across the face but as he put up his hands to ward off another attack the children came running from behind the shearing shed. Conor stared at them.

"And who are these?"

"Who do you think they are? They are your children," I snapped.

"Both of them?"

"Of course both of them. Can you not see they are twins?"

"In fairness, they don't look very alike," he replied and I wondered how long we were going to stand there having this stupid conversation before I hit him again.

Quartus and Elizabeth were studying him carefully.

"Is he our father, mama?" Elizabeth said.

"Yes, he is," I replied.

Conor went down on his haunches and held out his arms.

"Come here you little rascals."

"What's a rascal, mama?" Elizabeth said

"It's what your father is."

They ran to him without any hesitation and he scooped them up, one under each arm, and marched up the steps into the house, leaving me overcome by resentment. They had never even met him and yet they took to him like ducks to water.

"Where will I put them?"

"Wherever you like, and when you are done you will find me outside and I will tell you about all the things you should have been here to do instead of gallivanting around Mashonaland."

I was pleased to see him, I had almost given up hope, but I had learned to do everything on my own and things were not the same. The Conor who had enchanted me now only irritated me and it took a long time before I softened towards him.. But he loved his children and they kept him at home until the war which would change us all forever.

Olive was delighted at the failure of what she called Rhodes's murderous attack on the Transvaal.

"Serves him right. Who does he think hes is to go around taking other peoples' countries at will?"

"He is a powerful man, Olive. It's not wise to make an enemy of him."

"He is not powerful. It is only his money that is powerful. Without money he could do nothing. Rhodes will never rise again in South Africa. His career here is ended. It is a terrible thing to those of us who once admired his talent and personality."

She was only partially right. Rhodes did resign as Prime Minister of the Cape and sail to England in disgrace, but it would not be very long before he returned to help start another war.

JUNE 1899

CHAPTER THIRTY

Four years passed before the Raid came back to haunt us. In 1897, the British had appointed Sir Alfred Milner as Governor of the Cape. Now he was on his way to Bloemfontein for a meeting with President Kruger, ostensibly to hammer out an agreement on the *Uitlander* franchise. His real plan was to annex the Transvaal again and rule it as a Crown Colony but this I would only find out much later. On the morning that I said goodbye to Conor for the last time I had no inkling of what was to come.

I had ridden to to the top of Bleskop, as I often did, to look at my lands. To the west lay the meeting place of the Modder and Riet rivers, the dam at Rosmead just beyond, rowing boats moored to its banks. The red steel latticework of the railway bridge over the Orange River stood out against dry, brown veld and I could see a large crowd gathered on the station platform It had been a long time since Baas Fox took me off the train and he was dead now, his heart broken by the merciless persecution of Barney Barnato, who never forgave him for the arrest of his nephew on IDB charges. Poor Fox had lost his job and died of facial cancer the year after I was released and I had attended his funeral. I could not have wished him such a sad end, no matter what pain he had caused me. He was, as Fanny had pointed out, only doing his job. Besides which, without his intervention, I might never have abandoned my life as a diamond thief and become what I was now, the wealthiest farmer in the district. I had installed a pump and water now flowed down from the dam onto the fields of cabbages which the mines gobbled up at a rate faster than I could produce them and I was planning to expand my citrus orchards. The ostrich feather market had slumped but the mines could not get enough mutton and my flock numbered over two thousand. To the east, the blue grey hills were dotted with horses, and people came from all over South Africa to buy them. Even the Griekwa cleaning girl had turned out to be less stupid than I thought and my children adored her.

I pulled up the collar of my jacket against the winter chill and watched Conor come out of the front door, where the children waited on their ponies. Since his return from the Raid, he had never once failed to take them riding every morning, but this time he was dressed in his suit and I saw him lift them off their ponies and speak to them for a few minutes before kissing them both and mounting his horse. As I watched him gallop towards me I wondered what scheme he had thought up now.

"You are in a hurry today. And dressed up for the theatre," I said.

"I am going to Bloemfontein. Milner and Kruger are meeting to try and sort out their differences and the paper has asked me to report on it."

"Will you ride there?"

"Not a bit of it. I am stealing a ride on Milner's train."

I could already see the plume of smoke from the engine in the far distance, where it had stopped to let a herd of cattle cross the line.

"You'd better hurry up then," I said, as I heard the screech of the wheels starting to move again. He leaned over and kissed me and then he was gone, whipping his horse into a gallop as he flew down the hill towards the station, his jacket tails flapping in the wind.

I was halfway down the hill when I saw Quartus waving a mimosa branch at one of the male ostriches. That ostrich had lately been coming to stand outside the kitchen door and he had already bitten the Griekwa cleaning girl twice. She was threating to leave if I did not do something about him and I had planned to have him slaughtered that morning while the children were out riding with their father. They were too far away for me to hear what they were saying but I could see that Elizabeth egging her brother on. He looked uncertain, as he always did when his sister was about to get them into trouble.

She snatched the tackey out of his hand and began to dodge about, waving it around her head, inviting the ostrich to charge her. The enraged bird squatted down, flapping its wings and throwing its head from side to side and as Elizabeth gave the stick back to Quartus, I felt the panic rush through my body.

"No, Quartus, no!" I shouted as I urged my horse into a gallop, but I did not get there in time. As Quartus raised the stick above his head the bird got up, ran past him and struck Elizabeth on the head with its foot. My horse was still galloping as I leapt from his back and rushed to my daughter's side.

I don't think I will ever forget that nightmare journey, Lukas lashing the horses along the bumpy road to Kimberley as I sat cradling Elizabeth on my lap. There was a lump the size of a duck egg on the back of her head, her breathing was shallow and irregular and I was convinced she was going to die. When she regained consciousness in the doctor's surgery I cried with relief and swore to beat the living daylights out of Quartus when I got home.

But my relief was shortlived. When the doctor finished his examination he told me she was blind.

His words fell to the floor like stones and I stared at him in disbelief.

"Blind?"

"I'm sorry, Jacoba."

I walked to the window. It was market day and the square was crammed with huge tent-covered wagons filled with hides, and wool. Elegant ladies and rough miners jostled shoulders with farmers in broad felt hats and Malays in muslin skirts and embroidered vests, bearing trays of fruit, hurried past rows of stalls piled with butter and vegetables. Elizabeth loved market day. It wasn't possible that she would never see it again. I straightened my shoulders and turned back to face the doctor.

"We can send her to America, there are surgeons there. I can pay, Oliver, you know that."

He took the stethoscope from around his neck and laid it on his desk.

"There are some things money cannot buy, Jacoba. Perhaps her sight may come back, we can only wait and see. I will give her a draft to make her sleep and admit her to the hospital."

I shook my head.

"No."

"You cannot take her back to the farm. She needs to be kept still and the journey could make things worse."

"And what could be worse than being blind?"

"Being dead," the doctor replied.

I could not find Quartus when I got back to the farm and perhaps that was a good thing for I would surely have beaten him half to death. It was almost midnight before Lukas found him at the *plaasvolk's* compound and brought him to me.

He stood in the doorway, his face tearstained and dirty.

"Is she dead, mama?"

"No, Quartus, she is not dead. It is worse than that. She is blind."

"I am sorry, mama."

"How many times have I told you not to torment the ostriches?"

"It was not me, mama."

"What do you mean, it wasn't you? I saw you with the tackey."

"It wasn't my fault, mama, Elizabeth made me do it."

I had seen Elizabeth's reckless behaviour myself, but still I blamed him. It was the beginning of a rift which would never heal.

"Where is she, mama? Can I go to her?"

"Not unless you plan to ride into Kimberley, she is with Olive, the doctor said she could not stand the journey back to the farm."

CHAPTER THIRTY ONE

Conor stood in the shade of the water tower and waited as the locomotive and its two wooden carriages, flying two Union Jacks beside the cowcatcher, pulled into the station. As the passengers tumbled out onto the platform, while fresh coal and water was loaded, he inserted himself amongst them. Nobody raised an eyebrow when the whistle blew and he climbed on board and positioned himself where he could see into the first carriage and watch the High Commissioner. With his long, thin face and downcast, grey- brown eyes, Milner looked so gentle and detached that Conor found it hard to believe that this was the man chosen by the British to cut the Transvaal down to size.

The train arrived at the Free State capital at five o'clock to a welcome by President Steyn, a twenty one gun salute of detonators under the rails, and a rendering of God Save the Queen. A great white banner draped the station with the words May God direct your counsels emblazoned upon it. As he took out his notebook and sharpened his pencils, Conor thought it would take more than God to bring a successful resolution to the conference and he was right.

Seven hours earlier another special train, flying the green and orange flags of the Transvaal and the Free State, had steamed into the station from the opposite direction, carrying the aging President

Kruger, blinking painfully at his young State Attorney, Jan Smuts, through small gold spectacles. The president was like an old warhorse scenting battle. Although he had accepted President Steyn's invitation to the conference, he was suspicious of Milner and he was pessimistic about its outcome.

The conference was held in a room beside the railway station and the two men were introduced to each other by their host. Kruger, seventy three years old, dressed in a baggy black suit, and Milner, only forty four, in a morning suit and grey topper. Despite the good humoured exchanges, Conor felt a deep foreboding. He had heard the rumours that Milner had no intention of reaching an agreement, and was determined to force the Transvaal into a war.

Five days later, the conference ended in a stalemate, with Kruger standing for the last time saying "It is our country you want", and Conor slipped aboard the president's train, stood on the back platform of the carriage holding the railings and watched Bloemfontein recede into the distance.

Milner returned to the Cape and wrote to the War Office requesting ten thousand troops be sent to South Africa. Kruger made a gift of half a million Mauser cartridges to the Free State.

CHAPTER THIRTY TWO

News of the failed conference reached us very quickly and there was no more speculation about whether war could be avoided, only about when the fighting would start. Five hundred miles from the nearest port, bounded on one side by the Transvaal and on the other by the Free State, Kimberley was defenceless and Rhodes and his fortune would be a rich prize. Kruger was already talking about parading him around the Transvaal in a cage. And yet life went on amidst the anxiety.In September the new Town Hall was completed and Fanny and I attended a masked fancy dress ball to celebrate the official opening. It would be the last time we celebrated anything together.

By the time of Elizabeth's accident, Olive had had three miscarriages. The last one had nearly killed her and she had, at last, accepted that she would never bear a child. It upset me to see her so sad and brought back all the memories of my mother's suffering. Perhaps that was why I let Elizabeth stay with her as long as I did, and why I agreed so readily to allow her to take her to Johannesburg.More likely it was that I did not want to admit that Elizabeth was now a disappointment to me, but I was nowhere near ready to admit such a scandalous feeling. We were sitting in Olive's little study, one afternoon, watching Elizabeth making clay models in the garden when Olive told me she was moving to Johannesburg to join her husband.

"Would you let me take her with me, my dear? She is such a lovely child. She never complains and despite her infirmity she is doing so well at her schoolwork. I have grown very fond of her and I think she is fond of me."

Olive had worked for many years as a governess and she had thrown herself body and soul into Elizabeth's education. I knew I could not have done better. I would have asked Conor what he thought but he had written to me from Pretoria to say that the newspaper had asked him to stay on in the Transvaal until hostilities broke out. I might have taken longer to think about it had Elizabeth not come inside to play with the cat. She picked her way around the furniture as if she had lived with Olive all her life.

"Mama! Olive is going to take me to Johannesburg and put me in a school for the blind. There will be other children like me and when I come back I will be able to do everything, just like I did before."

Even at eight years old, Elizabeth had a strong sense of her own abilities.

"You will still not be able to see, Elizabeth," I replied.

"I know that, mama. but Olive says it won't matter if I can do everything else. She says there is a girl in America called Helen Keller who is blind and deaf and she can do everything. Olive says I should count my blessings."

"Olive is right. We should all count our blessings, " I replied. I would remember those words in the not too distant future when all my blessings had been taken away from me.

"So can I go, mama? Can I?"

There was no school for the blind in Kimberley, nor even in the Cape. What future would she have here on a farm where danger lurked around every corner for a blind child? I smiled at Olive.

"Yes you can."

Quartus burst into tears when I told him his sister was going away and nothing I said could convince him it was for the best.

"Don't send her away, mama, please don't send her away."

"I am not sending her away, Quartus, she wants to go herself. And there are too many ways she can hurt herself on the farm. Do you not remember when she fell off the *stoep* the last time she was here?"

"I will look after her. I will go everywhere with her. No harm will come to her. Please, mama, let her stay."

"Stop now. She is going to Johannesburg and that's the end of it."

"Fuck you," he screamed, his face contorted with rage.

"I beg your pardon? What did you just say?"

"Fuck you, fuck you," he shouted as he ran out of the house, leaving me wondering where he learned such bad language. Only from Bloody Fool, I was sure.

Although I didn't know it at the time, giving Elizabeth into Olive's care was probably the first unselfish act of my life.

When I next went into town for my quarterly meeting with Fanny, the place was hardly recognisable. Forts had been built and trenches dug, and every building in Main Street, including the Grand Hotel, was stacked with sandbags. The streets were full of soldiers, half a battalion of Loyal North Lancashires had arrived the week before, and I had the greatest difficulty driving my carriage to Number Five.

President Kruger not been idle either. He now had an army of forty thousand men, including his Free State allies, which could be mobilized within a week, armed with the most modern guns and rifles. It was four times the size of the British garrisons in the two colonies of Natal and the Cape.

Olive wrote to say that Elizabeth had settled into her new school and was already top of her class. She also said that the burghers had gone quite mad, the women telling their men that in the event of war they must shoot every *Uitlander*. She was still convinced that Rhodes was behind it all and some perverse part of me could not help but admire a man who was so powerful he could send an Empire to war.

It was hard for me to reconcile all this activity with the peace at Nooitgedacht where everything looked so normal. Except for the stream of black people crossing my lands, bundles on their heads, small children tied to the women's backs, and the heavily laden ox wagons and Scotch carts lumbering down the Cape road, you would never have thought we were on the brink of disaster and I almost believed that war might yet be averted.

I didn't have long to wait before I found out I was wrong.

Fanny and I were sitting on the sandbagged verandah of the Grand Hotel, drinking tea, when the Town Hall clock struck five and a paper boy ran past, shouting at the top of his lungs.

"Boer ultimatum! Read all about it! Boer ultimatum!"

I snatched a paper from him and stared at the headline.

President Kruger had delivered an ultimatum to the British Agent in Pretoria. The terms were simple and unequivocal: withdraw all your troops stationed on the borders of the two Republics, withdraw all reinforcements that arrived after the first of June and do not land, in any South African port, the troops which are currently on the High Seas. He had given them forty eight hours to comply. I handed the paper to Fanny.

"That's it then, we may as well brace ourselves, ducks. Going to be war now," she said. and I was immediately plunged into my own personal war. Fanny supported the annexation of the Transvaal. It was, she said, the only way we would keep our money. I, on the other hand, was ambivalent. Years of listening to Olive had reignited my Boer heritage, but the price of patriotism would be high and I was not prepared to lose everything I had worked so hard for. It would be a while before I decided whose side I was on. Fanny folded the paper, put it on the table and sent a waiter to call Johnson with the carriage.

"They are bound to attack Kimberley. Will you not come to the farm? You will be safer there, " I said

She shook her head.

"No, ducks, I'm too old to be shifting from here, and who knows what those girls would get up to while I'm gone.?"

I stared across the street. Geoffrey Winslett's office was right opposite with the new haberdashery store beside it. Red letters spelled out the words A.P. Jones and Son in red on a dark blue background. Behind it, the tops of the mine dumps bristled with soldiers and artillery, all overlooked by the conning tower which had been built on the De Beers headgear. It was an image that would stay with me for the rest of my life.

"I have to get back to the farm," I said, resting my hand on Fanny's shoulder.

She smiled and offered her cheek and as I stooped to kiss her, I noticed for the first time how frail she had become. Lately, her hands shook when she lifted her teacup but she had lost none of her stubbornness. In that we were alike.

I had not gone far when I was stopped by a British Patrol.

"I'm sorry, Mrs Swanepoel, you'll have to turn back," the soldier said.

"Why? I am on my way to my farm," I replied.

"The Boers are advancing from Jacobsdal. It's not safe."

"I hardly think they will have any quarrel with me, Sergeant, they are my neighbours. Now let me through, please."

"I'm sorry, I can't, I have orders not to let anyone through."

"Get out of my way."

"Madam. Please. If you do not turn back I shall be forced to arrest you."

"Well, you will have to catch me first."

And with that I raised my whip and brought it down hard on his hand. He let go of the horse's bridle with a yelp and I was gone. I did not think they would shoot at a woman but I was wrong and I had to loop across country and get behind the *koppies* before I was out of range.

The sun was just beginning to rise behind the *koppie* when a small group of armed men trotted up to my verandah, led by my neighbour, Retief Smit. They were all wearing black jackets and felt hats, with two bandoliers of ammunition across their chests, one rifle in its saddle holster and another one across the pommel. Each one had a black *agterryer* leading two spare horses.

Retief lifted his hat.

"*Mevrou*, we are about to besiege the town. We are sorry for the inconvenience," he said.

I watched them canter away, just as I had watched my father and grandfather canter away twenty years before. All day long I watched hundreds of riders loping across my farm towards Kimberley. I could hear them laughing amongst themselves and I wondered how many of them would still be laughing by Christmas. A short time later, a British armoured train steamed through Orange River Station towards Kimberley and it was not long before I heard an explosion and saw, in the distance, a cloud of brown dust and debris thrown up into the air. The war had begun and before it was over eighty thousand would die, half of them in British concentration camps.

In those early days it was no more than an inconvenience to me, my main concern was what I was going to do with the surplus vegetables which would rot in my fields if Kimberley was still under siege by harvest time. Surely not. The green shoots were only just starting to push their way through the soil. It would be another six months before we had a crop and it would surely be all over by then.

CHAPTER THIRTY THREE

On top of Majuba, ten miles from the Natal border, Conor looked at the low stone wall surrounding the small cemetery, its white crosses and plain headstones weathered with age. Beside it stood a plain stone monument engraved with the names of the men of the 58th Regiment who lay there and a little distance away a small stone cairn topped by a wooden cross marked the place where General Colley had fallen but there was no grave for Jacoba's cousin. He reached into his pocket, drew out a pencil, wrote "Etienne Swanepoel" on a scrap of paper and pushed it into a crack between two rocks. It was a desolate place and he turned and began to make his way down the rough path to rejoin the fifteen thousand Boers sitting around their campfires at the base of the hill.

Two weeks earlier he had left the offices of the Pretoria News, popped a letter to Jacoba into the post office, and made his way to the railway station, where the first batch of Pretoria commandos were preparing to entrain for Natal. Fighting his way through the crowds who had come to see them off, he managed to throw his belongings through a carriage window and clamber aboard, just as the he train pulled out and the first blood of the war was spilt as, during the volleys of farewell shots, a bullet rebounded from the rocks, broke a carriage window and mortally wounded one of the men. But even this unfortunate incident failed to dampen their high spirits, they were like schoolboys let off for the summer holidays as they clanked along towards the border.

On arrival at Sandspruit, he had bought the little chestnut pony, left ownerless by the man shot at the railway station, for fifteen pounds, and struck up a friendship with the teenage sons of the Secretary of State of the Transvaal, Denys and Joubert Reitz and they had invited him to share their campfire. Tomorrow, issued with five days rations of biltong and meal, they would cross the river and head for the coast to stop the British before they had a chance to disembark their troopships.

He spent an unhappy night in the rain, sitting on an antheap, before, at daybreak, the downpour stopped and he heard the shouts to *opsaal*. Their route lay between high mountains along a road parallel to the border and they jingled along in high spirits, before spending another uncomfortable night at a dismal spot, churned into a quagmire by the horses. In addition to the rain, a cold wind blew off the Drakensberg mountains, chilling Conor to the bone until, towards sunrise, the weather lifted and they got on their way again. After a long ride they emerged into open country and there before them wound the Buffalo River. The long files of horsemen reined in and gazed silently at the green hills and valleys of Natal beyond. It took nearly an hour to ford the river and as soon as they were across they spread out on a front of several miles and Conor who had not felt the camaraderie of war in almost twenty years, looked about him and felt pride for the first time in his life.

A week later they laid siege to Ladysmith and when tents arrived, they settled down to a life of ease, amusing themselves by sniping at the English outposts and riding around visiting neighbouring *laagers*. Things were so quiet around Ladysmith that some of the burghers had ox wagons brought from their farms with their families. Conor could only imagine what Jacoba's response would be, had he asked her to bring the children to visit him. After a month of this inactivity he grew bored and restless and decided to go in search of excitement. He found it at Colenso, where General Buller was assembling his troops to attempt the relief of Ladysmith.

The Boers dug into the hills above Colenso soon put a stop to that. It was a nasty, brutal battle, fought in ferocious heat. When it was over there were almost a thousand English soldiers lying dead or wounded on the plains, amongst them Freddie Roberts, son of Lord Roberts, Commander in Chief of the British forces in South Africa. The British had brought twenty thousand troops and thirty six guns to the meeting, but they were no match for the three thousand Boers and five guns entrenched in the hills above the river. Whether by chance or intention, a native guide led the Irish Brigade into a bend in the river, where earlier in the week the burghers had stretched barbed wire along and built a dyke which dammed the water back. Trapped in the loop and marching in close order, like a parade at Aldershot, the leading battalion of Dublin Fusiliers stood no chance against the massed magazine-fed Mauser fire which the Boers unleashed on them, and those that were not shot were snared by the wire and fell headlong into the river where they drowned, finding eight feet of water where they expected only two. They lost five hundred men in less than an hour and from there things went from bad to worse until at three o'clock in the afternoon the British withdrew, leaving their dead and wounded on the field, some of whom had lain in the baking sun for five hours, their moans and cries carrying up to Conor, whenever the firing ceased.

He had woken at dawn to the sound of the older burghers standing, rifle in hand, singing the morning hymn, a sound like peals of muffled thunder rolling down from the hills, and echoing along the river, before it died away to leave a deathlike stillness in the morning air. Right after that the British naval guns on the hill opposite had started to pepper the sunlit koppies with lyddite shells and shrapnel and he had taken cover in a trench, where he had a perfect view of the battlefield, and spent the morning scribbling in his notebook.

The previous day he had been dragged into camp by a Boer patrol, accused of being a spy, and only narrowly escaped being shot by the intervention of Isaac Malherbe, whom he had met twenty years before at Majuba. Now Isaac tapped him on the shoulder and jerked his head in the direction of the carnage below.

"Come. We must go down and tend to those poor devils until their own doctors can come back to help them."

After they had walked amongst the men, bandaging their wounds and giving them water, urging them to have courage, their own ambulances were on the way from Chievely, they turned their attention to the wounded horses and Conor had just shot the last one when he found Herbert Webster, lying in a *donga*, shot in through both shoulders and bleeding heavily. He didn't look as if he had long to live.

"I think I'll put you out of your misery," he said, raising his pistol.

"I don't think you will," Herbert replied.

Conor felt a hand on his shoulder.

"Hey man, what are you doing?"

"I have old business with this man," Conor replied, tightening his finger on the trigger.

Isaac grabbed his wrist.

"You will have new business with General Botha if he finds out you have killed a wounded man. He will surely have you shot."

"And who's going to tell him?"

Isaac gestured to some men, nearby, who were busy hitching a team of horses up to an abandoned gun.

"Any one of these. Don't be a hothead," he replied.

Conor reluctantly put his pistol back in his waistband and took Herbert's Webley and a sporting Lee Metford rifle from him.

"Pray you never meet me again," he said, as he walked away.

He thought he might go home for Christmas now. He had presents for the twins in his saddlebags, a box of six tin soldiers for Quartus and a doll for Elizabeth with a porcelain face and eyes that opened and shut.

DECEMBER 1899

CHAPTER THIRTY FOUR

My first experience of the realities of war came when the wounded from both sides came flooding into my house after the Battle of Magersfontein. Nothing could have prepared me for what I saw.

General de la Rey had passed by earlier in the week, riding his famous little white faced pony, carrying no arms, only a pocket bible and a *sjambok*. He was a formidable looking man, this Koos de la Rey with a high forehead, aquiline nose and deepset eyes. They called him the Lion of the Western Transvaal. It was de la Rey who had fired the first shots of the war, derailing the British armoured train at Kraaipan and it was de la Rey who was overseeing the siege of Kimberley. The General was morose, his son, Adriaan had died in his arms two hours before at the base hospital in Jacobsdal. All I could do was serve him coffee and beskuit, there are no words to comfort someone who has lost a child.

"Do you think we will win this war, General?" I asked.

"Probably not. I was against it all along, we ought to have given the *Uitlanders* the vote. But I shall obey the decision of the government and I assure you I will still be fighting long after Kruger and his friends have given up and fled for safety. And now I must go to join Cronje at Magersfontein. Thankyou for your hospitality, *mevrou*. God willing we shall meet again once this war is over."

It was not the answer I was expecting and I did not understand it. It was not in my nature to enter into a conflict I did not think I could win and it would be a while before I went to fight for a cause which was already lost.

A few days later an enormous gun drawn by thirty two oxen crossed my land, accompanied by eighty British sailors, and that night the sailors were followed by soldiers. It was raining heavily and they were so close I could hear them shouting to each other as they marched past the house.

It was still black and raining when I heard gunshots in the distance and at daybreak, when I rode to the top of Bleskop, I saw great gouts of earth flying up into the air and soon there was a cloud of smoke hanging above the Magersfontein hills. The shooting went on all day and in the pauses between, the sound of bagpipes carried across the veld. It was the most mournful sound I had ever heard and I was pleased when, late in the afternoon the wailing stopped and all was silent, but I did not stay pleased for long. An hour later the first casualties began to trickle in.

They came to my door, some holding each other up, others carrying their comrades on stretchers made of poles and blankets and some they needn't have bothered bringing, they were already dead. Wounded and dying men from both sides lay in every room

During the first weeks of the war, they had turned the schoolhouse in Jacobsdal into a hospital, and a matron, six nurses, and several ambulance men had been sent from the Bloemfontein Hospital to run it. The Germans sent an ambulance with three surgeons, and four nurses, and an x ray machine. When Dr Ramsbottom, the Principal Medical Officer of the Free State forces, arrived we knew we were in for it. Now the ambulance arrived, with three nurses from Jacobsdal, and we turned my house into a dressing station. .The floor of my *voorkamer* was awash with blood and mud and the Griekwa cleaning girl soon gave up trying to clean it.

The wounds were terrible. Expanding lead bullets left holes I could put my fist into and tore stomachs and intestines to pieces. Broken bones stuck out of legs and arms and chests were torn apart. There was nothing we could do but pack the wounds and wait for the overworked ambulance to take them to Jacobsdal. We worked late into the night, and when, around midnight, I walked outside to get some air I found Hannes Vosloo lying in the middle of a row of six bodies on the veranda, a neat hole in the middle of his forehead. Hannes, who seemed so indestructible to me when I was a child was dead, his blue eyes staring up at the bougainvillea. I could not take it in. I closed his eyes and covered him with my best blanket. When I went back inside I found a young Highlander lying face down in my kitchen, his legs flayed and blistered below his kilt. He was unconscious, he would not last long and I sat by him on the floor and held his hand until he died, while my memories of Hannes resurfaced to torture me. They told me later that the Highlander had lain on the veld below Magersfontein Hill all day, pinned down by the magazine fire from the Boer trenches.

I had never witnessed such carnage, never seen men die in front of me. Up until then the war had been fought on the pages of the newspapers but now it had come into my sitting room and I was dazed by the suffering I saw all around me. If this was how it began, how would it end?

The gravediggers came to ask me where the cemetery was and I stared at them uncomprehendingly. I was so exhausted they had to ask me twice.

"The cemetery, *mevrou*. We need to bury the dead, before morning. They are already starting to stink."

"I....I have no cemetery."

"Well, you are going to get one now, only show us where you want it."

They dug sixteen graves altogether, each one with a cross and a number carved on it and when they were finished they gave me the list of numbers with names next to each one.

"Perhaps you can keep this in a safe place, *mevrou*, until the families come."

There would be families, but not until many years later, and nobody would come for Hannes.

Quartus came to tell me that the British had lost nine hundred men dead and wounded and another seventy six they didn't know where they were and it was only much later that I found out that he had got his information by riding his pony over to the British camp and pretending to be an English orphan and I gave him the thrashing of his life.

On our own side we lost two hundred and fifty and I did not need my son to tell me this for I counted them as they were driven past, loaded in piles on oxwagons, and taken into Jacobsdal for burial. The British bodies lay piled alongside the railway track for days until an armoured train puffed out to collect them. The stench was overpowering.

Soon news arrived of other battles at Stormberg in the Cape and Colenso, where we had inflicted resounding defeats on the British. They were calling it Black Week, we were calling it victory. The Boers passing to and fro on their way to Kimberley were full of hope and I was swept along by their optimism.

A letter arrived from Conor. Do not fear for my safety, for I am a non combatant, here only to report on the progress of the war. It is very jolly here, the men are in good spirits after the victory at Stormberg and I expect I shall be home in time for Christmas.

I put the letter down on my table and stared out of the window at my labourers, building a stone wall around my new cemetery. I only half believed he would be back for Christmas and jolly was not a word I would have used to describe what I had just seen. Often when we removed a bandage, an even layer of dust moistened by perspiration covered the skin with a coating of mud. The flies were dreadful, the house swarmed with them, and it was impossible to keep them from settling, when we were dressing the wounds. By the time the last of the wounded were removed to the hospital, a week later, I was shattered. Every sheet in the house had been torn into bandages and I thought I would surely never be able to wash away the bloodstains from my yellowwood floors.

FEBRUARY 1900

CHAPTER THIRTY FIVE

Fanny sat on the hotel verandah, cradling the bandaged Pearl on her lap. As the clock struck noon Johnson appeared, carrying a large metal trunk and she scooped the cat off her lap and thrust him at a waiter.

"Hold onto this cat, and don't let him go, he's a wily devil. I'll be back in half an hour."

She marched across the street with Johnson behind her and disappeared into the solicitor's office.

The previous day, while she was having her afternoon nap, a shell had passed through the roof of the house, flown above her bed and exploded against the wall. One of the splinters had cut off the tip of Pearl's tail.

Kimberley had, by then, endured a daily barrage of hundreds of shells from the nine guns scattered on the surrounding hilltops and the heat and flies and boredom were killing her. Hopes of an early relief had been dashed when the mangled remains of the Highland Brigade had marched into Kimberley from Magersfontein and by now they had almost run out of food. The big lights on top of the mine dumps sent out signals every night but no answer came back. The mine dumps were full of soldiers, covered from head to toe in the brown dust which blew in continuously from the Kalahari Desert, while outside on the *veld* ten thousand Boers waged a patient war of attrition on the town. Rationing had been introduced and rich and poor alike queued for hours on end at the Town Hall. Eggs which had cost three shillings a dozen at the beginning of the siege now sold for fourteen shillings and almost three thousand people queued for two hours every day at the soup kitchen in the Market Square. To add to her discomfort the Boers had captured the sanitary wagons' oxen and Johnson came every day to complain at having to bury the household waste in the garden. A few days earlier a Chinaman had come to the door looking to buy cats to eat. He said he would pay five and six for a small one and twelve and six for a big one and Fanny had chased him down the street with the umbrella, holding Pearl under her arm.

"Should have sold that cheeky cat, what the good of a cat if we can get twelve and six and buy eggs to eat instead?" Johnson had remarked to the cook.

The incident with the bomb had proved the final straw and Fanny had taken the cat and moved into the Grand Hotel.

Geoffrey Winslett was a dapper little man in his sixties with brilliantined hair and a thin pencil moustache. Even in the stifling heat, he wore a starched white shirt and dark suit. A fan whirred lazily in the middle of the high ceiling and a thick pile, ruby red carpet muffled his footsteps as he crossed the floor to greet them.

"Mrs Yudelman. How nice to see you," he said, taking both of Fanny's hands in his.

"Got any tea, Geoffrey? We've run out at home," Fanny replied as she squeezed herself into the chair in front of his desk.

"I'm afraid I haven't, we used our last teaspoon yesterday. Ghastly business, this siege, isn't it?"

"You can say that again. Never thought I'd see the day I was eating horse meat. You'd want to be getting more comfortable chairs, Geoffrey. How's a body supposed to do business when she can hardly breathe?"

"I heard a rumour that the cavalry are at Ramdam, awaiting orders to advance," Geoffrey replied.

"Well, they'd want to be getting a move on. I can't take much more of this."

She pointed at the trunk, which Johnson had placed on the floor next to her.

"I want you to put this trunk in that underground vault of yours."

Winslett frowned. Nobody was supposed to know about the vault. He had had all the work done at night for that very reason. Damn that woman, she knew everything.

Access to the vault was through a trapdoor beneath Geoffrey's desk. The relentless shelling by the Boers had made him nervous and it was prudent to have somewhere to keep important items safe. He pulled back the carpet and lifted the heavy trapdoor, picked up the box and walked down the steps into the cavern below. The smell of paint was overpowering in the airless space. Nevertheless, the sight of it pleased him, the neat rows of cabinets lined against the walls, the small desk in the centre with its banker's lamp and padded chair appealed to his sense of order. A yellow legal pad and box of freshly sharpened pencils lay obediently on the desk. Even a decanter of sherry and a small tumbler. He put the trunk on the floor and sat down to catch his breath, and then the building shuddered and he heard a thud as the trapdoor slammed shut. Bugger! Now he'd have the bother of pushing it open from below. Geoffrey sighed and poured himself a glass of sherry. He studied the swirling, rich brown liquid. It had been a good buy, this last shipment he had managed to obtain before those damned Boers cut the railway line to the Cape, he had a full dozen cases stashed away in the end filing cabinet. After a while, the bombardment ceased and Geoffrey climbed up the steps and pushed against the trapdoor but it was stuck. He put his shoulder against it and heaved but it wouldn't budge.

"Johnson!" he shouted, but there was no answer.

"Mrs Yudelman? Are you there?"

Above ground the scene was one of total destruction. The blast had blown out the windows of the hotel and knocked the waiter to the ground. He could only watch as the cat fled up the road as fast as its legs would carry it. When the dust and smoke cleared all that was left of Winslett's was bricks and twisted corrugated iron, but the explosion had happened minutes before five thousand British cavalrymen galloped into town and some time elapsed before the workmen returned to Winslett's offices to dig through the debris. They found Johnson's legs, cut off from his body and Fanny's body with no legs at all. Of Geoffrey Winslett there was no sign at all.

CHAPTER THIRTY SIX

I woke up to find Quartus standing at the foot of my bed, hopping from one leg to the other.

"What is it, Quartus?"

"There is a *kaffirgirl* at the door."

"What does she want?"

"I don't know. She didn't say."

"So give her something to eat and send her away. It is not a reason to wake me up."

"She has a cat."

"Then give the cat something to eat, too, and send them both away."

" I think it's one of Auntie Fanny's cats."

"What?"

"It looks like Pearl."

I jumped out of bed, pulled on my clothes and ran quickly across the entrance hall. The front door was open and Fanny's cook stood in the doorway, carrying Pearl in her arms. Tears were flowing down her cheeks.

"Nandi? What's wrong?"

"They are dead."

"What are you talking about? Who's dead?"

"Miss Fanny, Johnson, Baas Winslett, all dead."

"No," I said, as my stomach knotted and my heart began to race. In the distance a flock of angora goats made their way up the side of a hill, a long line of snowy white against the red and green of the aloes and spekboom, their soft wavy coats almost brushing the ground and I watched them until they vanished over the ridge.

The scene which met me when I rode down Main Street reminded me of the day the railway - and Amelia - had arrived fifteen years before. The retreating Boers had left seventy two food wagons behind and their contents had been emptied out for everyone to help themselves. People were dancing in Main Street and tables, set up in Market Square, groaned under the weight of food and drink. As I watched, Long Cecil, the big gun they had manufactured in the De Beers workshops during the siege, was drawn into the centre of town preceded by the Mounted Militia marching band. The hotel was full of soldiers, some with Emu feathers in their soft hats, others with a strip of cheetah skin round the crown, and a short tail holding up the side of the hat, and I recognised Hendrik van Rensburg amongst them. He stepped down from the verandah, smiling.

"Jacoba? Good Lord. This is the last place I expected to see you."

"And the last place I expected to see you. You are fighting for the British?"

"I am. Most of the Natal Afrikaners are fighting on the British side."

"I'm sorry to hear it. You have cousins in the Transvaal, do you not? Tell me. What will you do if you meet them in a fight?"

I did not wait for his answer. It came as a shock to me that Boers were fighting against their own people but I had no time to think about it, I was desperate to get to Number Five. After letting myself in I stood for a moment in the hallway, before I climbed the stairs to Fanny's bedroom, half expecting Johnson to appear in his officious way, and offer me a cup of tea. Except for the gaping hole in the wall above the bed it was exactly as it was when I had first arrived in Kimberley almost twenty years previously and I lay down on the big featherbed and closed my eyes. It was mid afternoon when I woke up not knowing, for a moment, where I was, and went into the sitting room. The bureau where I had sat to write the letters to the fictitious Freddie Atherstone's non existent parents had been moved to make way for a new sofa which had arrived from the Cape just before the siege. In the left hand drawer of the bureau I found a pile of unopened letters, neatly tied with blue ribbon and every one of them was addressed to me. I sat down in Fanny's armchair, took the silver letter opener and opened the first one. It was dated June 1886 and it was signed by Amelia. The last one was dated January 1890. It was dark by the time I finished reading them all and went back upstairs to sleep in my old room.

The following morning my world, already shaken by Fanny's death and Amelia's letters, began to fall apart, when the bank manager told me that, a few days before, Fanny had withdrawn all the money, closed all the bank accounts, and emptied the safety deposit box where we kept our shares.

"All of it?"

"I'm afraid so. She was worried about the shelling. I believe she was taking everything to Mr Winslett for safekeeping," he replied.

I rode out to the Jewish cemetery. There was no headstone on the grave but someone had put a simple metal plaque, made, surely in the De Beers workshops. Frances Ellen Yudelman. I had not known she had a middle name and I wondered who did, who put the plaque on the grave. I sat on the ground next to the fresh mound. I felt numb, I could not cry, I simply could not believe that she was gone. And with her had gone all my money.

That night the I stood on my verandah and watched the silhouettes of hundreds of ox wagons moving silently across the veld as the five thousand Boers who had been guarding the Magersfontein hill for the past two and a half months retreated in the direction of Bloemfontein.

JUNE 1900

CHAPTER THIRTY SEVEN

In June the news came that President Kruger had fled by train to the Eastern Transvaal and the *Uitlanders* were singing God Save the Queen on the streets of Pretoria. The war was over and, with mixed feelings, I sat in my *voorkamer* and began to plan my recovery. Most of my money might have been blown up with Fanny but I had £250 in cash and I still had my stock and my *plaasvolk*. Horses, sheep and ostriches still dotted the hills and the siege had ended just in time for me to reap my harvest of cabbages and sell them to the mines. More importantly, the goldmines in Johannesburg were now in the hands of the British and all I had to do for the dividends to resume was write to the mines and give them my new bank details. Or so I thought.

I also had Asjas, who had lately developed a fondness for gin and ginger beer and often returned from Bloody Fool's hut, walking upright, clutching an empty bottle. He stole soda water from the kitchen cupboard to alleviate his hangovers and lay in the eucalyptus trees throwing stones at anyone who walked within range. On more than one occasion I had found him asleep on my bed, soaking wet, having pulled the string on my showerbath and drenched himself from head to foot. He was finally banished from the house when I discovered my watch in pieces all over the floor and every rifle cartridge in my gun cabinet pulled to pieces.

But the war was not over. The President had taken with him all the reserve ammunition from the Pretoria magazine and all the gold and coin from the Mint and Botha and Smuts start to gather a new army. In Jacobsdal the women held a meeting, which I did not attend, where they vowed to bar their doors against their returning men. Soon the men who had come home in droves, demoralised after the fall of Bloemfontein, were heading back to the field, the curses of their wives ringing in their ears. A different sort of war was about to begin, the brunt of which would be borne by women and children. I thought the neutrality I had maintained since the beginning would protect me but I was wrong.

Lord Roberts issued a proclamation to the Orange Free State burghers, telling us that if we did not assist our men in the field we would be left undisturbed on our farms. He ordered us to supply British troops with forage, water, food and whatever else they required, for which we would be paid. If we did not comply it would be taken from us by force.

At the same time our own General Botha issued a warning of punishment for those who laid down their arms or offered assistance to the enemy. What were we to do, caught between the two of them?

Late one afternoon there was a loud banging on my door and when I opened it I was looking straight into the face of Hendrik van Rensburg and I don't know which of us was more shocked.

"What are you doing, Hendrik?"

"We are here to search the house for rebels," he replied. Half a dozen armed soldiers stood behind him.

"I cannot believe this of you, Hendrik. What has happened to you?"

His face flushed and I saw the shame in his eyes.

"I....I did not know this was your farm."

"And would it have made any difference if you had?"

He had no answer for me.

They poured into every room in the house, taking whatever they wanted and I gripped the railing of my verandah until my knuckles were white, as I watched them load my carriage with my bed-linen, my forage and my poultry.

"Why do you not stop them, mama?" Quartus said.

Something began to turn in me then.

"Come inside. I am going to tell you a story," I replied.

Quartus clapped his hands.

"What story?" he asked, his eyes bright with excitement.

"It is a story my grandfather used to tell me."

I told him the story of Blood River, word for word, in Afrikaans, the way my *oupa* told it to me every 16th of December, like a catechism. Which is what it was. Until I was six and went to church for the first time, I thought Blood River the name of our religion and when I lay in my bed at night and tried to imagine what God looked like, it was always my grandfather's face I saw.

"On the 27th November 1838 when your *oupagrootje* was 12 years old he left the *laager* on the Little Tugela with four hundred and sixty eight trekkers and sixty four oxwagons under Commandant

Andries Pretorius. The *sanna* in the gun cabinet and the h*erneuter* knife I use to cut *biltong* are the very same ones that o*upagrootjie* took with him to Blood River. They had with them two cannons, one they called Ou Grietjie."

"Why did they go, Mama?" said Quartus.

"They went because your *oupagrootjie's* mother and father and four hundred others were murdered by the *kaffirs* at Weenen. They went to pay them back."

"On the 15th of December they made their *laager* on the bank of Blood river between a *donga* and a hippopotamus hole They arranged the *laager* big enough to hold all their oxen and horses inside and tied them all together with ropes. Then they made two narrow gates for the riders to go through. That night they gathered together and made the Vow that if God gave them victory the next day they would forevermore keep that day as a Sunday."

"Your *oupagrootjie* went to sleep that night fully armed like all the men. Two hours before dawn they went to their posts and when the mist cleared they saw the Zulu army sitting only forty yards away surrounding the *laager*. The Zulus stormed the laager but the *trekkers* drove them off with rifle and cannon. Then Bart Pretorius led three charges through the gates."

"And was *oupagrootjie* with them?"

"No, Quartus, he was too young. He stayed behind, his job was to open and close the *veghekke*. On the last charge they broke through and hunted the Zulus from behind and into the canons. They broke in two and ran and this time your *oupagrootje* took his chance and disobeyed orders and rode out with them and they chased them for three hours until the river ran red with their blood. Then Andries Pretorius' horse jumped backwards and he had to dismount and a Zulu stuck him through the hand with his spear. That was when your o*upagrootjie* rode up and saved him."

"Oh! Greatgrandfather was a hero! Did they give him a big party?"

"No they did not. When they returned to the *laager* he got five smacks with a *sjambok* for disobeying orders and leaving the *laager*."

"But he saved Pretorius!" Quartus protested.

"He did, Quartus, but he did not do as he was told and that's why he was punished."

I finished the story exactly as my *oupa* used to finish it.

"In a thousand years time they will still remember Blood River and how God gave us this land for our children and our children's children."

I could hear myself solemnly promising Oupa that I would remember Blood River every year and I was conscious of the fact that I had broken my promise every year since his death.

Later, after Quartus had gone to bed, I took the *Statenbijbel* out of the trunk where it had lain, unread, for the past twenty years. It fell open at the Book of Joshua and as I read the High Dutch I could, once again, hear my grandfather's voice at morning *godsdiens*.

Wees sterk en heb goeden moed! want gij zult dit volk dat land erfelijk doen bezitten, dat Ik hun vaderen heb gezworen hun te geven.

Be strong and of a good courage! for unto this people shalt thou divide for an inheritance the land, which I sware unto their fathers to give them.

When I closed the bible I knew whose side I was on.

As the war entered its second year, my kitchen, together with every other kitchen and oven in the Free State, became a bakery, in which we converted the one hundred and fifty pound sacks of wheat provided by our government, into twenty five pound bags of *boerebeskuit*, which we sent out to our men in the field. We filled our great three legged cauldrons with brown vinegar and spices and slaughtered ostriches and cattle to make *biltong*. Lines were strung from the outhouses to the house and you could not walk anywhere without bumping your head into the strips of dripping meat. It was becoming dangerous, for all of us, for the men to come to the house and I put the sticks of *biltong* into old coffee tins and sent Lukas and Bloody Fool to hide it in crevices in the rocks on top of Bleskop. As winter approached I became tailor and cobbler as well as baker, making overcoats and jackets and shoes. Who would have thought that the skills I learned in prison would prove so useful. I took Nandi and the Griekwa cleaning girl into Jacobsdal for first aid classes at the hospital. I went more for the camaraderie of my neighbours, I did not think I would ever witness anything worse than what I had seen after Magersfontein but I was wrong about that too.

The British had recalled Lord Roberts and a new man had taken over as Commander in Chief, Kitchener of Khartoum they called him. It soon became clear that we were now in real trouble as

Kitchener gave the order to burn our farms and destroy our crops. No one was safe except the Colony Boers who sided with the British. Soldiers came regularly to camp on my land. They took my wagon and all the harness, even the dried fruit stored in the loft, and the servants' clothes. The Griekwa cleaning girl cried for an entire day over her rags, until I gave her one of my dresses, which was far too long and trailed along the ground behind her. They asked me the same questions over and over again, where was my husband and whether the Boers came to the house and did I let them inside and what were their names. I gave them the same answer every time.

"My husband is a war correspondent and I have not seen him since the beginning of the war. Yes, the Boers come to the house and I let them in, how can I keep them out when I cannot keep you out? I do not ask them their names. Do I ask you your names?"

Day by day my fury grew and I knew it would not be long before I lost my temper and got us all arrested.

Conor had not come home for Christmas as promised and as the months went by I noticed a subtle change in the tone of his letters. I saw no articles in the newspapers and I began to suspect that he, too, had chosen sides and when I heard that a Boer commando, led by an Irishman had blown up every bridge and culvert between Bloemfontein and Pretoria I knew it was him. I prayed they did not start blowing up the line which ran past the farm because Kitchener had issued orders that whenever a railway line or a telegraph wire was damaged all the houses in the vicinity would be destroyed and its residents taken as prisoners of war. More than that we were now expected to hunt out our own men on our own farms and report them to the British or we would be assumed complicit.

The winter of 1901 was the coldest in living memory and I was horrified when I saw open cattle trucks of women and children offloaded at Orange River Station and turned onto the bare *veld* without tents or blankets, but what horrified me more was our own General Botha's letter to Lord Kitchener declaring that nothing they might do to the women and children would stop his men from continuing to fight. It was becoming a women's war and the women of the Cape Colony, Dutch and British alike held a protest meeting in Paarl against the treatment of the women of the two republics, appealing to the rest of the world for aid, but nobody believed them.

Except for one Englishwoman.

In November 1900 a letter had appeared in The Times of London which sent a wave of revulsion around the British Isles. In it, the daughter of one of the Boer generals described in vivid detail how her father's farm had been burned, the livestock confiscated and she and her mother sent to a camp in Bloemfontein, without food or clothing. This had prompted Emily Hobhouse, the daughter of an Anglican rector from Cornwall, to found the South African Women and Childrens Distress Fund but no one of influence would support it. The newspapers were suppressing news about the farm burnings, saying the claims were exaggerated. So early in 1901, Emily Hobhouse had come to South Africa to see for herself. She travelled to Bloemfontein where she found almost two thousand women and children living at the camp in appalling conditions but I knew nothing of this when O'Brien was sent to spy on us.

SEPTEMBER 1901

CHAPTER THIRTY EIGHT

He was very young, his beard just a little fluff on his jaws and he reminded me of Conor when I had first met him, although he later told me he had never set foot in Ireland in his life. He stood on the *stoep*. holding his cap in his hands.

"Yes?"

"I am sent from the blockhouse, ma'am."

"Blockhouse? What blockhouse?

"At Jacobsdal. I am sent to guard you."

"Guard me? Guard me from whom?"

"From the Boers, ma'am."

"The Boers are my own people, I do not need to be guarded from them."

"I'm sorry, ma'am. Them's my orders.I have my own rations, ma'am. If you could only show me where I must sleep."

"Wait here."

The blockhouse was three storeys high, made out of stone under a timber and corrugated iron roof with a corrugated iron observation tower on the top. There were two loopholes on the ground floor and four on the top. The entrance door was on the first floor and I got there just as they were lowering the ladder to carry up their food and ammunition.

"Who is in charge here?"

A soldier put down the bag of coal he was carrying.

"I am."

"One of your soldiers is at my farm. I want him removed."

"Oh? Is that right?"

He turned to his men, who had stopped offloading the wagons to watch us.

"Do you hear that, boys? She wants young O'Brien removed? And I suppose you'd like all of us removed, too?"

The soldiers started to laugh.

"We'd like nothing better than to be removed, wouldn't we, boys? We'd like to be gone away from this godforsaken country but as it is, we have a job to do."

"If you don't remove him, then I will," I replied

The man walked over to stand a few feet away from my horse.

"I wouldn't try that if I were you, missus. Woman on her own with a child be in need of protection. Our men been away from their home comforts for a long time. If O'Brien doesn't suit I can send Raleigh instead. Come over here Raleigh, missus might fancy you more."

A burly soldier put down the sack of flour he was carrying and walked towards us.

"Been in a few scrapes, has Raleigh. Wouldn't take no for an answer would you, Raleigh?"

Raleigh's eyes were too close together and his eyebrows met in the middle and when he smiled at me I saw that half his teeth were missing.

"No sergeant."

"What do you think then, missus? O'Brien or Raleigh?"

I saw that I was beaten, turned my horse and galloped back to the farm. I could hear them laughing as I left.

O'Brien kept to himself, sleeping in the outhouse and cooking his own meals and once a week he marched to the blockhouse to get his rations. During the day he sat cleaning his rifle and writing letters to his mother and at night he patrolled around the house. He told me he was only seventeen and he missed his mother. One day, when I saw him sitting alone by his cooking fire I invited him to eat with us. He looked as if he would burst into tears and I felt ashamed that I had not asked him before.

Food had become very scarce, by then, as Kitchener burned up the country, and we were living on maize meal and whatever small game I managed to shoot. The days when we made bread and *biltong* were long gone. The next time O'Brien joined us for supper he brought a three pound tin of stew with him and when we had finished eating he broke open the metal tube which contained his emergency rations. The tube was partitioned in the middle, one end contained Bovril Paste, which he gave to me and the other a chocolate bar, which he shared with Quartus. At least, after O'Brien came to stay we were no longer troubled by marauding soldiers.

O'Brien told us that Kitchener was building blockhouses up and down the country and putting barbed wire fences between them to trap our fighters.

"He's a right royal bastard, is Kitchener, they say he allowed 'em lop off hands and legs in the Sudan. He had the Mahdi's tomb opened and his bones thrown into the Nile and said he was goin to make an inkstand out of his skull. Caused a right furore in England, it did."

O'Brien made little soldiers for Quartus out of the empty bully beef tins and soon he had two armies and pestered the soldier all day long, to play with him.

One night I caught him leaving the house after dark.

"Quartus! Where are you going?"

"Nowhere, mama."

"And where exactly is this nowhere?"

He scuffled his feet and would not look me in the eye.

"I am waiting, Quartus."

"Our men, mama, they come to the dam in the night sometimes."

"And?"

"I go there, mama, to bring them food."

"What? Do you know how dangerous that is? What if O'Brien catches you?"

"O'Brien knows about them, mama, he tells me what to say to them."

"What does he tell you to say?"

"I can't tell you mama, it is a secret."

I shook him then, harder than I intended, and he started to cry.

"You will tell me everything. Now."

"O'Brien tells me where the British soldiers are and I tell it to the commandos. Please mama, you can't tell him I told you. He said it was to be our secret."

I was shocked, I did not know what to make of this at all.

"What if it is a trap for our men, Quartus? Did you think of that?"

He looked at me then, squarely in the eye.

"If it was a trap why would our men keep coming back, mama? Wouldn't they all be dead by now?"

I turned to look out of the window where I could see O'Brien making his nightly circuit of the house.

"You won't tell him, mama? He won't play with me any more if you do."

"No, Quartus, I won't tell him."

It made me uneasy, this blurring of the lines. I felt more comfortable when O'Brien was the enemy.

By September things were very bad, the dams were full of rotting animals, the *veld* covered with slaughtered herds of sheep, goats and cattle, every farm for miles around had been burned and yet, by some miracle, we had ,so far, been left in peace. By the time my neighbour, Anna Smit arrived at my door in a Scotchcart, loaded with furniture I had started to hope we might get through it unscathed.

Anna's cart was pulled by a very large, ancient, coal-black mule, called Swart Lawaai, because of his endless braying, so loud that on a still night his voice easily carried over the twenty miles between our two farms and he chose that moment to open his mouth. It was a full five minutes before we could hear ourselves speak.

I stared at Anna's dirty face and torn clothing. The children's bare feet were covered in ash.

"Take Frikkie and Mouton to the kitchen and give them something to eat and drink," I said to Quartus.

I did not need her to tell me what had happened because I had seen the pillar of smoke rising into the air above Zoetwater early that morning.

The previous night the residents of Jacobsdal had let forty burghers into the houses around the square where some British soldiers were sleeping and at sunrise, the burghers had opened fire and eighteen of the soldiers had not woken up. In retaliation, the British had burned twenty houses and taken all the women and children and when they passed Anna's farm on their way to the camp, they had burned that, too. They were coming back later to take Anna and the children, they said, and Anna had decided not to wait.

My house was bigger than most in the district. I had six bedrooms, a drawing room and a dining room as well as my big kitchen and pantries. I could easily accommodate Anna and her family but how was I going to feed them when we could barely feed ourselves?

CHAPTER THIRTY NINE

Up in the hills Conor, sat amongst the rocks and stared down at Nooitgedacht. He was thinner now, his gaunt, bearded features seemed chiselled from the stony outcrop itself, and his tattered clothes hung from his limbs. His companions were no better off. Emaciated, dressed in skins, their beards grown long and matted, they sat between the boulders, cleaning their rifles. The laughing Boers who had cantered gaily off to war with three horses each and a black servant to tend to their needs were reduced to a pitiful band of scarecrows. As the farms had burned so had they starved until they were by now in very poor condition, the lucky ones mounted on donkeys, the rest of them on foot, carrying the saddles of their dead horses until they could capture another.

Sarel de Kock put a hand on Conor's shoulder.

"That is your farm, *rooinek*?"

"It is," Conor replied.

"Your wife and children are there?"

"They are."

"You could ride down and warn them."

"I could. And if I am shot along the way who will make the bomb?"

Karel studied him for a moment.

"You are a brave man, *rooinek*."

Conor sawed at the stock of a rifle until all that remained was an exposed trigger and a six inch stub of barrel. To this he carefully fixed a package of fifty sticks of dynamite before loading the gun with a black powder cartridge. As the shadows lengthened and the chill of the Karoo night began to seep into his bones he stood up.

"Come, Sarel, let's go and start the hooley," he said, and began to walk down the hill, towards the railway line. Jacoba would pay the price for what he was about to do but what choice did he have? There wasn't a man among them who had not seen his farm reduced to rubble.

"Shit!" he said as his trousers tore on a length of barbed wire at the side of the track. Together they stepped onto the rails, holding hands for balance. They walked a hundred yards and then, kneeling on a sleeper, Conor carefully buried the bomb just beneath the gravel surface, its trigger pointing upwards. They retraced their steps to a grove of scrubby thorn trees on the hillside, and settled down to wait. First the patrol came. Two foot soldiers shining torches along the length of the lines looking for footsteps in the gravel. As they drew level with the bomb and paused, Conor's pulse quickened a fraction and then one of them lit a cigarette and they moved on. By now the lines were beginning to sing, heralding the approach of the train and then he heard the huff and chuff of the engine in the distance. On that train lay the survival of thousands of men still fighting in the hills. Maize meal, bully beef, clothing, medical supplies, wine and spirits, tobacco, newspapers and dynamite for the next train. It was a rich prize. It would also be armed to the teeth with artillery and soldiers and Conor wondered whether his luck would hold tonight. The searchlight appeared, illuminating the line for almost a mile ahead and then the train was over the bomb, the explosion threw her into the air and the sky was lit up like daylight. The engine fell back and ploughed into the ground for another two hundred yards next to the tracks before slowly toppling over and Conor and his men rushed down from the hill, rifles blazing.

The explosion woke us all up. It was what I had been dreading for months and the next morning I found O'Brien kneeling on the verandah, wiping Quartus's eyes with his handkerchief.

"They will come for you now, Mrs Swanepoel," he said, choking back his tears.

"I know."

We stared at each other for a moment and then I stepped forward and put my arms around him. When he went off to collect his rations I knew he would not return. Quartus knew it too.

"Make him stay, mama, make him stay," Quartus sobbed. He ran after O'Brien and I saw the soldier bend down to talk to him, before going on his way. I hope he got back safely to his mother for I never saw him again.

We buried everything I had managed to hide from the soldiers over the past twelve months under the floor of the shearing shed. My trunk, the Sharps, my Oupa's sanna and the best linen and crockery. My good saddle and bridle, wrapped in a blanket, were the last things to go in.

"Make sure you cover the floor with dung once you are finished. The soldiers must see no sign of digging," I told Lukas.

I walked from room to room, adjusting the furniture and straightening the curtains. God knows why, it would surely all be charcoal by evening. I stood in my high ceilinged *voorkamer*, looking up at the stinkwood beams, inhaling the smell of the reed mats and cured sheepskins which lay on my yellowwood floors, still stained with the blood of the wounded who came back from Magersfontein. It had taken me over ten years to restore this house to its former beauty and by tomorrow it would all be gone.

And then we sat together on the stoep to wait. Me, Quartus, Anna and her little boys. A stillness hung over the veld as if the very earth itself were holding its breath and soon black plumes of smoke broke the hard, blue horizon. They must be burning van Vuuren's.

CHAPTER FORTY

Herbert Webster rode his horse up to my verandah, as he had done in Zululand twenty two years before and we rose from our chairs.

"Keep quiet now," I warned my son. He had inherited my volatile temper as well as my looks and I knew it would be hard to keep him quiet.

Herbert was heavier now, and he no longer wore a scarlet jacket, but his khaki uniform was still perfectly tailored and he had lost none of his arrogance.

"You are Mrs Swanepoel, I believe?"

"I am sure you know very well who I am."

"Your husband is a British Army deserter, now fighting for the Boers, is he not?"

"I don't think so. My husband is a reporter for the Pretoria News."

"Well, Mrs Swanepoel, your reporter husband and his friends are blowing up trains the length and breadth of the country. If you tell me where he is, I may spare your farm."

"I cannot tell you where he is because I do not know myself," I replied, trying to conceal my shock. Conor was fighting? He was the trainwrecker everyone was talking about? One thing was clear. I was going to lose my farm for the second time because of him. I heard Quartus shifting his feet beside me and pulled him closer.

"Pa is the trainwrecker?" he said.

"Apparently," I replied, squeezing his hand.

"Move aside please, madam."

I wondered how long I could keep him there, staring down at me from the back of his horse.

"You will have to shoot me first."

It was an empty gesture, I could do nothing to stop them doing what they had come to do but I must seem to put up a fight if only to show my son that we did not just roll over and give up. He dismounted and walked towards me, smiling, and then his gaze shifted to a point behind my right shoulder and when I turned around I saw Nandi standing there, dressed as I had never seen her before. A thick cowhide skirt covered her from waist to ankles, over it an apron of red material, her breasts concealed by a bead decorated cloth. A strip of twisted leopardskin circled one arm and a porcupine quill stuck out of her hair. Holding Herbert's gaze, she produced a small bone from beneath her apron and threw it at his feet. One of the black soldiers recognised her.

"It's her," he whispered, "the one we left in Zululand."

"What's that? Speak up, man!"

"The woman. She's the one we left in Zululand, sir."

Nandi extended two fingers and pointed them at him It was then that I noticed the thumb was missing from that hand and I wondered how I had never seen it before.

"What is she doing?" said Herbert.

"She has cursed you," replied the man, his eyes rolling wildly, "you should not touch that thing!"

"Bloody savages," Herbert sneered. He bent down, picked up the piece of bone and threw it into the flowerbed below my verandah. I knew those bones from my childhood, monkey bones used by the Zulu witchdoctors. We were told never to touch them and we never did. I wondered if their magic would work on a white man. If it did, Herbert Webster was a dead man, as surely as if I had shot him. It was only a matter of time.

Herbert's black soldiers had scattered across the *veld* as soon as they saw Nandi but the white ones had no fear. They clattered up the steps and into the house, tearing down curtains and carrying tables and chairs outside. They went into every room, pulling drawers out of chests and strewing the contents all over the floor, laughing while they did it. They loaded my piano onto a wagon and punched their rifles through the windows. Then they piled everything in front of the house and set fire to it and when it did not burn quickly enough they brought out my clothes and threw them onto it. They even took the washing off the line.

They took the little food we had out of the kitchen and stamped it into the ground and then they went to the stockyard behind the stables and killed every sheep and cow that stood there, shooting the cattle and stabbing the sheep to death with their bayonets. They caught the chickens and cut off their heads. Then one of them got up on the wagon and began to play the piano and the others stopped what they were doing and gathered around him to sing a song. Once they had finished they got down from the wagon and set fire to the house. I saw a man in civilian clothes setting up a camera on a tripod to photograph the great sheets of flame as they rose into the air.

They left then and before long I saw smoke rising from the direction of the Kannemeyer's. I looked for Nandi and the Griekwa cleaning girl but they had both disappeared. I stood, looking at the bodies of my dead sheep and cattle, until my whole body began to shake.

"What are we going to do, mama?" Quartus asked.

I looked at Anna Smit and her two boys. The eldest one, Frikkie, was holding his little brother Mouton's hand. I could see by the look on their faces that they were ready to give up, but I was not.

"We are going to run, Quartus," I replied.

"Where to, mama?"

"I don't know, but we are not staying here for them to come back for us."

"God will help us," said Anna and she was right. God helped us by sending the first summer rains, which put out the fire raging through my house but I remember thinking that he could have made more of an effort and stopped the soldiers burning it in the first place.

Swart Lawaai had taken off into the hills with a speed which belied his age, as soon as he saw the soldiers, but Lukas had hidden four oxen behind a *koppie* and we hitched them to his cart. The soldiers had missed a wooden box of kaffircorn which lay under the ruins of the veranda and we threw it into the cart and I set the children to gather up the goose feathers which lay scattered in the house and fill two mattress covers. The dough I had prepared that morning was still in its pot in what was left of my kitchen and I made *vetkoek* on the burning embers of my stinkwood ceiling and gave it to Anna to carry. Anna could not have been more than eighteen years old, less than half the age of her husband and she looked to me to make every decision. It was a new experience for me and I did not settle into it easily. We left after dark, Anna driving the cart, while the rest of us walked to keep the oxen straight. Lukas and Bloody Fool begged to come with us but I told them to stay behind and guard the farm. I was not planning to stay away too long, I intended only to hide in the *veld* until the soldiers had left the district, which I was sure they would do, once there were no more farms left to burn. A light rain still fell but lasted only long enough to wet our clothes and and I was grateful for the clouds which obscured our departure. At each farm we passed, more women and children joined us and soon we were over a hundred, travelling on foot with a collection of carts and wagons pulled by an assortment of donkeys, mules and oxen. At one farm a woman stood holding six sheep which she had tied together. At least now we would have mutton. We had milk, too. One of the refugees had managed to hide a cow and her calf and we brought them with us. We ground the kaffircorn in a coffee grinder. It took a long time to grind enough to feed us all but nobody complained, not even the children. We believed we were suffering for our freedom and everyone except me still believed we would win the war. From time to time men from the commandos came in and warned us of British patrols and we moved off in another direction. We shared whatever we had and Anna cooked one big pot of *mielie* porridge every afternoon and divided it in three, one for midday, one warmed up for evening and one for the next day's breakfast. We were careful to keep our clothes clean and when the soap ran out we burned *asbossies*, boiling the ash until it sank and a kind of fat rose to the surface which eventually turned into soap if we left it boiling long enough. It was black but it was first class soap. It had been a very long time since I had washed my own clothes, let alone made soap. Wherever we went we passed hundreds of slaughtered sheep and cattle, left to rot on the *veld* and the pillars of smoke rising into the air marked the route of Lord Kitchener's troops. I learned the power and comfort of women working together during that time and it was a lesson I would never forget.

It was three months before the khakis caught us. We were camped beside the river when a commando galloped in to tell us that fifteen hundred horsemen were heading in our direction and we should move across the river immediately. There was a ford close by and we pushed our wagons into it, standing in the icy water, tugging at the wheels and urging our oxen on, but we were only halfway across when the soldiers arrived and turned us back. They drove us to a railway station, took our wagons and left us to wait by the tracks in the hot sun for the train that would take us to the camp. I will never forgive myself for abandoning Anna Smit and her boys at that station.

That night I saw lights twinkling on the *koppies* and I woke Quartus, putting my finger to my lips to shush him. There were only two guards and they were both asleep, I suppose they thought we were only women and children and old men, and we had nowhere else to go. They had left their horses hobbled in the *veld*, saddled up, and it only took a minute before my son and I were riding quietly away.

"Where are we going, mama?"

"We are going to find your father," I replied, without thinking, for I had not the vaguest notion where Conor might be.

We rode towards the lights in the *koppies* but by the time we got there they were gone and all we found were the remains of campfires and a dead horse. Nothing to do but keep riding away from the railway line.

"Do you think Pa will let me help him blow up trains?" Quartus asked as we rode along the crest of yet another ridge.

"I hope not," I replied.

We would be in trouble if we did not find a commando soon for we had no water and only a few sticks of *biltong*. In the event, they found us.

The commando was on its way to invade the Cape, sixty men led by a man called van Ryneveld, when they came across us, resting in the shade of some rocks, roasting a *dassie* which Quartus had managed to catch in a snare.

At first they were reluctant to bring us with them.

"A woman and a child? You will only hold us back."

"Where else are we to go? My farm is burned and my husband is fighting god knows where."

"I do not know, *mevrou*, but you cannot come with us."

They were turning their horses around to leave when Quartus spoke.

"My Pa is the trainwrecker," he said.

Van Ryneveld pulled up his horse.

"Indeed. And what is your pa's name, boy?"

"Conor O'Reilly- Swanepoel."

There was a moment of silence then, which Quartus hastened to fill.

"And my ma can shoot the head off a *skaapsteker* at two hundred yards"

"Is this true, *mevrou*?"

"What? That my husband is Conor Swanepoel or that I can shoot the heads off snakes?"

"Both."

"It's true."

The other men had started to murmur among themselves and then one of them rode forward. He was small and thin and one of his arms was missing and I could see by the faces of the others that he was held in great respect. Much later, I would know why that was when I saw him shoot his rifle with one arm and bring down six British soldiers who had ambushed us.

"Let them come with us, Tjaart. Swanepoel saved my life once."

"Very well. We will bring you with us but you will have to pull your weight. You will get no special favours because you are a woman."

And when have we ever had that, I thought.

I fought with that commando for almost five months. I rode the length and breadth of the Free State and even crossed the border into the Cape at one time. I had my horse shot out from under me and was forced to ride a Shetland pony which had wandered up to us from a British camp, until we ambushed a patrol and I got myself another horse. I froze and I starved and I watched my son grow thinner and thinner. One morning I woke up covered in clotted blood, having slept unawares under a wagon loaded with our dead awaiting burial. I shot scores of British soldiers, before a rock I was using to smash a log for firewood came back at me like a shot from a catapult and broke my left leg between knee and ankle. I lay for three weeks in great pain while splinters of bone worked their way out through a suppurating wound.before they carried me from our camp to the British hospital. And in all that time I heard hardly a word about the suffering of the women and children. In their own eyes these men were all heroes, fighting to save their country. I listened to them boasting around the campfire every night, oblivious to the suffering of their families, with a growing sense of outrage. Soon there would be no country left to save and no wives and children either. We did not know it then, but an entire generation would perish in Kitchener's camps.

The British field hospital was a large marquee flying the Geneva Cross and they took me in and put me on a bed, with screens around it. It was the first time I had lain in a bed since leaving the farm. My legs and stomach were covered in veld sores and I was suffering from malnutrition and they said they could not operate on my leg until my strength was built up.

Not long after my operation they found out who I was and two officers with red tabs on their collars came to ask me where my husband was and when I could not tell them they put me under arrest and left me in the care of four soldiers. The officers were gentlemen but the soldiers were not and as soon as I could get about on crutches they put me on a train to Bloemfontein. I thought I had lost everything when they burned the farm but soon I was to find out what it was like when your very dignity is stripped from you.

MARCH 1901

CHAPTER FORTY ONE

I stepped off the train and felt my heart collapse into my stomach. The camp was a cluster of grubby white tents, thrown down on the slope of a *koppie* on the bare brown *veld* a few miles from Bloemfontein. There was nothing to see for miles around except the long snaking ribbon of railway line which had brought me there, only the hundreds of wooden crosses which divided up the hillside. My guards marched me through the gates to the superintendent's office, the only brick building in the camp. A Union Jack fluttered at half mast outside the building and it was then that I discovered that Queen Victoria had died in January and there was now a king on the throne. I spat on the ground as I walked past.

"I hope you are going to behave yourself, Mrs Swanepoel," he said, as he pushed a ration card towards me. "But just in case you aren't, I have arranged special accommodation for you.

There was a big welcome awaiting me when I stepped outside, my reputation had preceded me and everyone wanted to touch me and kiss me and tell me how proud of me they were, but I was not proud of me. I had seen the bodies of the soldiers I had shot. Looked into the sightless eyes of young men and thought only of the women in England, waiting for letters from their sons and husbands. What they would get was a letter from the War Office telling them where they could pick up their things and any outstanding pay due to them. No, I was not proud.

The soldiers took me to a tent surrounded by a barbed wire fence. There was not even a gate and they had to lift the wire for me to crawl under. Inside the tent I found one rough blanket and a slop bucket. During the night a storm came up and broke the tentpole, collapsing the tent on me, and drenching me with water and in the morning I had to squat over the bucket in full view of everyone and that was what finally broke me. I sat down on the ground beside the ruins of the tent and pulled the blanket over my head.

For the second time in my life it was Mary O'Hara who saved me. I heard her calling my name and when I lifted my blanket she was standing next to the fence with Frikkie and Mouton Smit. I had not seen nor heard of her for over fifteen years and at first I thought I was imagining it.

"Mary? Is that you?"

"It's me alright. God would never have made another one as ugly," she replied. She was smiling, but she looked old and tired, and thinner than I remembered. Frikkie and Mouton started to cry, pushing their hands through the barbed wire to touch me.

"These little ones' mother died, they say they know you."

"Anna is dead?"

"Last week. Of the typhoid."

Poor Anna, only eighteen years old, who had thought herself fortunate to marry a man old enough to be her father and produce a son for him every year, now lying under one of those crosses on the hillside above the camp. We had all lost so much. How much more could we take? I turned away to hide my tears.

"You've got to pull yourself together, Jacoba," Mary said.

"What for? I have lost everything."

She gestured towards the tents.

"Do you think you are the only one?"

I looked at the tearstained faces of Frikkie and Mouton. I wanted to pull myself together but I hadn't the strength.

Mary continued.

"If you won't do it for yourself, do it for these others. You are the sniper wife of the Irish trainwrecker, it's not a small thing. Show these women that you can't be broken. It's your responsibility."

If there was one word I hated above all others it was that one. All my life I had managed to find someone else to do things for me, so that I could be free to do and say exactly as I pleased. I had given my daughter to another woman to take care of. I had left my son with the commandos. I had allowed Fanny to manage my money and lost it all as a result. I had left my servants without a backward glance when I ran away from the farm. Even Asjas was left to fend for himself that day.

When the soldiers came to give me a new tent they laughed at me but they did not laugh for long. During the night, something happened to me, I still cannot say what, but the next morning I brought my bucket outside, lifted my skirts, and pissed in it. Then I stood beside it and started to sing God Save the King. On the second day I heard voices joining me and by the third day everybody had brought out a bucket and the entire camp was urinating and singing. On the fourth day the guards let me out. Over the years I forgot many things about the camp, but I never forgot those three days when we pissed on the new King of England.

We were crammed together, twelve of us to a tent, like sardines in a tin. It was like an oven in the day and an ice box at night. Our rations were half a pound of fresh meat, half a pound of meal, one and a half ounces of coffee, one ounce each of sugar and salt and one eighth of a tin of condensed milk. No butter, no jam, no vegetables, no fresh milk. Wood for the cooking fires had to be collected from the green bushes on the slopes of the *koppies*. The children, gaunt and filthy, wearing garments made from flour sacks, roamed the camp in search of any tiny scrap of food , hanging around the guards' cooking fires and foraging in the dustbins for bully beef tins to scrape a taste of fat from the inside. By the time we discovered the tins were lined with lead, many had died an agonizing death. The wind and flies and dust were everywhere and over everything hung the putrid stench of the latrines.

I met Tibbie Steyn, our President's wife in that camp. Tibbie was the granddaughter of a Scottish minister who had come to the Free State to relieve the shortage of ministers in the Dutch reformed church. I might not have had Tibbie's strong Christian principles but it did not stop us forming a lifelong friendship. Tibbie set us all an example of courage, endurance and patience. I had plenty of the first two qualities but almost none of the third.

At the beginning of April a measles epidemic broke out and the mournful call of the morgue whistle woke us every morning, summoning us to collect our dead. Mothers wrapped their babies in flour sacks and walked to the cemetery to bury them in communal graves. All the talk was of death, of who died yesterday and who lay dying and who would be dead tomorrow. Only the Sunday Church services relieved the stultifying, soul destroying agony of nothing to do except watch people die.

During the day, we walked around the camp and visited each other and at night we sang hymns together and praised God, although what we were praising him for, I could not fathom. More were dying in the camps than on the battlefields. The war which should have ended by Christmas had now dragged on for almost three years and Lord Kitchener had burned the entire country to the ground.

Mary's sons had joined John McBride's Irish Brigade and were fighting with the Boers. It was the first time I had heard his name but it would not be the last. Many years later I would meet him in very different circumstances and he would tell me he had felt privileged to fight alongside my husband.

APRIL 1902

CHAPTER FORTY TWO

Amelia stood on the deck of the ship as the pilot guided them into Cape Town harbour. It was autumn, the air was chilly and damp and the mountain was covered by its tablecloth, the mist spilling gently down its sides. She had hardly slept a wink, blaming it on the nightlong banging and clattering in the hold below their cabin but the real reason for her insomnia had nothing to do with mailbags and luggage and everything to do with the thoughts of Jacoba which had tormented her ever since they had shipped anchor in Southampton.

On arriving in Dublin some fourteen years before, she had soon discovered that whilst Aunt Mabel was wealthy she did not live an idle life. Mabel was always looking for a cause and she found it in the Boer women and children.

Just before Christmas Amelia had been sitting in the glassed in porch watching the waves crash over the lighthouse at the end of the East Pier when Mabel rushed in brandishing the newspaper.

"Have you seen this?"

"Hardly, Mabel, since you have only brought it in the door."

"Read it," said Mabel, thrusting the paper in front of her.

The article was quite small, tucked away where very few people were likely to see it. Emily Hobhouse had been refused permission to visit the women's camps again. In fact she had been refused permission to land in South Africa and had just arrived back in England.

"Pack a bag, we are going to South Africa," said Mabel." And be sure to bring your camera."

"What? On Christmas Eve?"

But Mabel was already gone and Amelia could hear her banging around upstairs.

Two things happened that night which disrupted Mabel's plans. First, a ship foundered in the bay and one of the lifeboats sent out to her capsized in the heavy seas, drowning the cook's husband. Second, a loud banging jolted Amelia out of a nightmare and when she ran downstairs she found Aunt Mabel at the front door, with a poker in her hand.

"Go away! Go away before I call the constables!"

Standing on the porch, clearly visible through the glass doorpane, was Herbert's black man.

These events delayed their departure until the beginning of April.

They had stepped off the nine o'clock train from Waterloo onto the wharf at Southampton eighteen days before and after shivering in a continuous heavy downpour, waiting for their luggage, had boarded a steam tender and plunged and tossed down the Water until they found themselves alongside the Union ship which was to take them to South Africa. Once up the swaying gangway Amelia had watched the donkey engine lower her camera trunk into the hold and then gone below to join Mabel in the ship's saloon.

The voyage had been pleasant enough until the previous evening, after dinner, when Mabel had lit up a cigar, taken a sip of brandy and asked her about Jacoba.

"This girl you are in love with. Does she reciprocate your feelings, my dear?"

"What girl?"

"The one you have not stopped talking about since we came on board. Jacoba. That's her name isn't it?"

Amelia's face turned scarlet.

"Yes. Jacoba. She is a girl I met in Kimberley just before Papa died. We became friends. I am not in love with her."

Mabel continued to sip her brandy.

"Whatever you say, my dear."

Mrs Koopmans de Wet met them at the door of her house in Strand Street.

"I am so sorry I could not come down to the harbour to meet you, my dears, but the British have put me under house arrest because of the protest meetings," she said.

Maria Koopmans de Wet had fought long and hard on behalf of the women and children in the concentration camps. Once a close friend of Cecil Rhodes she was now one of his most bitter opponents and a passionate supporter of the two Boer Republics. By that time support in the form of clothing and other essentials was flowing into South Africa from all over Europe and most of it made its way to Maria's drawing room. Her last two protest meetings together with a petition she had intended to send to Queen Victoria had proved the last straw for the authorities and now she was confined to her house. She was a great friend of both Olive Schreiner and Emily Hobhouse and it was Emily who had persuaded Mabel to undertake the distribution of the donations which were stacked floor to ceiling in Mrs Koopmans de Wet's front room.

As they chugged up the Touws River Pass and through the Hex River valley, with its green pastures and mohair goats, Amelia could see no difference from the last time she had travelled on this very same train on its inaugural journey to Kimberley, seventeen years before, and she began to wonder whether it was true that the reports of atrocities were exaggerated. But the acres of trees, heavy with apricots and plums, soon gave way to an arid, windswept wasteland and where there had been flocks of sheep grazing peacefully alongside the railway track there was nothing but miles of burnt grass and the ruins of farmhouses, their blackened shells deserted and stark against the landscape.

Mabel soon fell asleep, lulled by the motion of the train but Amelia was not so easily soothed. Hours passed before she stopped wondering where Jacoba was in all of this desolation. They woke up to a hot, unsympathetic day, the landscape parched, brown winter grass stretching for miles across the open *veld*.

Their first stop was Orange River Station. It was just as it was the day Jacoba was arrested, a corrugated iron shop on the platform, a small hotel nearby and eleven little whitewashed labourer's houses with flat fronts and small wooden windows. The camp was a mile away across the flat sandy expanse and they had to get up on a mule cart to reach it.

A small flock of ostriches stared at them and one ran forward stretching his wings and was shooed away by the driver.

"Do you think they really put their heads in the sand?" Mabel asked.

"I don't know. Perhaps. I've never seen them do it," Amelia replied.

Painfully thin old men and women and young children stand against the barbed wire fence, barefoot, dressed in rags, their faces dull with the resignation of the defeated.

The superintendent of the camp met them at the gate. He was a Dutchman who had chosen not to fight and he was at great pains to tell them that he was previously a magistrate and had to flee to Basutoland to avoid conscription into the Boer forces. The camp was thrown down against a hillside. There were three smaller camps on the other side of the railway line and when Mabel enquired she was told that one was for the isolation of people with infectious diseases, one was for new arrivals and the third one was a punishment camp.

"Punishment camp?" Mabel said," why would they need to be punished? Have they not been punished enough?" and Amelia could see by the superintendent's face that they had made a bad start.

The camp was full of measles and dysentery and typhoid. The hospital was a big marquee tent without beds and the patients, mostly children and old women, lay on the ground with only a few flimsy blankets. The smell was appalling. Patients suffering from diarrhoea had not been properly cleaned, if at all.

While they were in the superintendent's office a woman came in asking for medicine for her child.

"I'm sorry, *mevrou*, we have no more medicines."

Behind him was a glass fronted cabinet on the wall, full of rows of bottles.

"Then what is that behind you?" said the woman.

"Those are kept for inspections."

Amelia could not believe her ears.

"Inspections? What inspections?" the woman replied.

"Government inspections. The regulations say that we must always have medicines on hand."

"Of what use are medicines if they are not used?" the woman screamed.

He shrugged his shoulders.

"I'm sorry *mevrou*. Those are the rules. They are not of my making"

"Please, " she pleaded " I beg you. For the child's sake."

But he remained adamant and the woman left emptyhanded.

The women told them the superintendent made offers to buy their farms for a pittance.

"I expect he thinks that most of us and our husbands will be dead by the end of the war," said one of them.

It soon became clear that what they had brought was totally inadequate. They had come intending to give them an extra garment or comfort but these people had not even the bare necessities. The clothes and mattresses allocated to this camp were not enough to go around and they left feeling completely hopeless.

"What are we going to do?" said Amelia.

"We shall simply do the best we can," Mabel replied, as they got back on the train. " And if needs be we shall return to England and start all over again."

As they crossed the border into the Orange Free State they passed families huddled up close to the railway line and and people, old and young, bundled in open coal trucks under a scorching sun left near a station building. Crowds of them along railway lines, hungry, sick, dying and dead. Beside her on the seat lay the new Brownie camera she had bought in Dublin and when they stopped to take on coal and water she got off the train and began to take pictures. In years to come she would credit that moment as the one which launched her career as a war photographer.

CHAPTER FORTY THREE

I was helping to wash the children in the hospital tent when I heard the hooter howling across the *veld* and at first I thought it was the morgue whistle but when I stepped outside I saw a train with a single carriage and five closed trucks screeching to a halt. Two women stepped out of the carriage, wearing black dresses, and hats with wide brims to protect their faces from the sun. One of them was carrying a parasol. The other one was Amelia.

I watched as the woman with the parasol supervised the offloading, and women ran down and clustered around the train. Some came away, their arms full of blankets and soap and candles, with tears streaming down their faces. Amelia was taking pictures of everything, the tents, the women, the children.

"Come on. There'll be nothing left if we don't hurry up," said Mary, but I shook my head. Behind me dying children moaned in agony.

"I can't, I must go in to the children."

"Don't be daft. It'll only take a minute."

My dress stank of vomit and diarrhoea, and my armpits were rank with sweat. I could not let Amelia see me like this.

"I can't," I repeated.

I walked away, weaving between the tents until I thought I was out of sight.

That night I sat outside my tent, staring at the train, still parked in the siding. A light burned inside the carriage and I could see Amelia standing at the window, silhouetted against the lamplight.

I started as a hand touched my shoulder.

"What's wrong, dear?" said Mary.

"Nothing, Nothing at all."

"I think I've known you long enough, Jacoba."

I sighed and pulled my knees up under my chin.

"I don't want to talk about it, Mary. I'm sorry."

I watched the carriage, fighting the impulse to walk down there, until the light went out and the curtains were drawn.

That night I fell into a fever and I thought I would die. I tossed and turned on my straw pallet and when, after three days, I woke up, the train was gone. A spider had made a web on the centre pole of the tent and I watched as it descended on an invisible thread until it was inches away from my face. So busy. Why are you working so hard? Perhaps tomorrow they will take down the tent and all your efforts will be for nothing.

Three weeks later, joy shots cracked along the thousands of miles of blockhouses and twenty one thousand *bitter-einders* emerged from their hiding places, threw down their rifles and trekked off to the concentration camps to look for their families. The two republics had ceased to exist and from now on King Edward VII would be regarded as our lawful sovereign. Others in the camp were numb with shock and despair but it came as no surprise to me. These women had not seen the conditions in the field and believed to the very end the letters they received from their men. I had seen it coming three months before. What did surprise me was that I had actually survived it.

"Are we going home now, Tannie?" asked Mouton.

"Yes, we are," I replied

The signing of the peace brought us no immediate relief and life in camp went on much as it had before. We might as well still have been at war for all the difference it made. I soon found out they were not just going to open the gates and let us out. We were told we would have to wait for our men to come and fetch us before we could leave. We, who had suffered more than anyone, were not thought capable of taking care of ourselves without a man. Twenty six thousand of our men were scattered in prisoner of war camps across the British Empire, some as far away as Bermuda and Ceylon and all of these had to be brought home. The railways were hopelessly blocked and it was nearly the end of June before they began to arrive at the camp, looking for their families. I saw men break down and cry when they found a wife with no children, children with no mother and sometimes neither. Frikkie and Mouton stood at the fence every day waiting for their father and I hadn't the heart to tell them that he lay buried in a camp in Bermuda.

We were told that there were forty three thousand of us in the Free State camps and another sixty six thousand in the Transvaal and Natal and we must be patient and await our turn. Those who had no land, the poor whites and *bywoners* who had no home to go to, were sent to relief camps at Kroonstad and Senekal, where they were employed building dams and such, on Government Farms. Mary fell into this category.

"I asked if I could go to my cousin in Johannesburg but they said no," she told me.

"Then you will come home with us. I will speak to the superintendent."

I could see he did not believe me when I told him that Mary was my sister but I think he was so glad to see the back of us that he did not argue with me.

Finally, when it became clear that no man was coming for us, our turn came and we joined the long snake of ox and mule wagons, raising great clouds of dust as we set off across the *veld*. I was surprised by how much we had to transport. I arrived with nothing but the clothes I stood up in but I left with bits of old broken furniture and cooking items inherited, out of kindness or lack of space on their wagons, from those who left before me I also inherited Frikkie and Mouton after a stand up row with the camp superintendent who wanted to send them to an orphanage in Pretoria.

I left the camp with mixed feelings. The friendships formed through shared grief and adversity were harder to let go of than I expected. We would be scattered now, all over the Free State and the Transvaal, and it was unlikely we would ever see each other again. Frikkie and Mouton were very upset to leave their friends, indeed most of the children were crying.

They gave us the tent we had been living in, a month's rations and bedding. Frikkie and Mouton clutched their schoolbooks and the little toys they had made from scraps of wire and tin. We drove for five days past *mielie* and cornfields overgrown with weeds, along a road almost impassable from neglect. Every farmhouse we passed was in the same condition, windowless, roofless, water furrows choked, dams broken and orchards devastated. Lines of blockhouses joined to each other by an entanglement of barbed wire, cut the veld into squares.

Four blackened, roofless walls and the kitchen chimney were all that remained of my house. What was not reduced to ashes by the soldiers had long since been used as firewood by one side or the other. The bones of the dead sheep and cattle, picked clean and bleached by the sun still lay in the *kraal*. No dogs bickered with each other, no cats sneaked along the walls of the barn, no chickens chattered noisily amongst themselves.It was eerie to listen to the silence.

The wagon driver watched us offload, telling us to hurry up, he had to go back to the camp to take others home. He did not lift a finger to help us and I knew then that Olive had been wrong when she said that in fifty years time we would be facing a big problem with our blacks. We would be facing it far sooner than that.

I walked up the steps into the ruins and the only thing remaining was a mirror leaning against a wall. It was the first time I had seen myself in over a year and I could hardly recognise my own face looking back at me. I was so thin and the beautiful skin I inherited from my mother was burnt and dry. My dress was no more than a rag.

I was still standing there when Asjas ran at me, chattering and screaming, clutching an empty gin bottle under his arm. He leapt at me and knocked me down and I sat in the rubble, laughing and crying by turns, until my ribs ached. Frikkie and Mouton danced about like puppies and the tears rolled down Mary's face. None of us had laughed like that in a very long time and I felt my spirits begin to lift.

"We'll pitch the tent, shall we?" said Mary, pointing to the bare patch where Bloody Fool's flowerbeds used to be..

"No we won't. We'll take it apart and make a roof out of it and live in the house. I've lived in a tent for long enough"

We were busy all day, clearing rubble out of what was left of the kitchen until finally we saw the black and white tiles. The Dover stove was buckled and bent but we could light a fire under the chimney if only we could find the wood to burn in it. Our rations for the month consisted of a fifty pound sack of mielie meal, fifty pounds of flour, ninety pounds of tinned meat, eight tins of condensed milk and twenty pounds of sugar. That night I made *putu pap*, the way my Oupa had taught me. I watched the meal simmering in the three legged pot and as it began to steam and the outer layer caramelised against the sides of the pot the smell of it made my mouth water. Frikkie and Mouton had caught a guineafowl in a snare and we roasted it over the fire. I found one of O'Brien's metal tubes and the bar of chocolate inside it was enough to make a hot drink and as we sat around the stove, warming our hands, Frikkie turned to me.

"Will we go to our farm tomorrow, *tannie*? We must be there to welcome our father when he returns."

Mary caught my eye and shook her head. I would have to tell them soon, but not tonight, not after we had just eaten our first meal of freedom.

The shearing shed was gone, but its floor was still there and the next day I dug it up and everything was just as I had left it.

"Sheets, Mary," I said, holding up my linen. "Real sheets."

We rubbed the fabric against our cheeks, our eyes closed.

I unwrapped the Sharp's and felt its smooth contours under my hands.

A week passed before Lukas and Bloody Fool came back, followed three days later by Nandi, guiding an old pram, pulled by two goats, in which sat Fanny's cat on top of a bag of *mieliemeel*. She said the Griekwa cleaning girl had died in the camp at Heilbron and we said prayers for her and put up a little cross in the cemetery with her name on it.

AUGUST 1902

CHAPTER FORTY FOUR

A month after we got back Frikkie and Mouton found Swart Lawaai grazing on the veld and their joy was pitiful to see. So happy to see an old mule. But not as happy as me. For I was now going to step across the border into the Cape Colony and go to Kimberley to see if there was any post for me. I had not heard from Olive for over a year and I had no idea where my daughter was.

How different was the landscape. No burned out farms here. No vast tracts of wasteland. No poorly dressed *bywoners* walking the roads in search of a place to settle. Only a few miles from my farm and I was in a different world. The Cape Afrikaners had remained loyal to Great Britain and reaped the rewards.

There was a pile of letters waiting for me, all postmarked Johannesburg, and a small parcel.

I opened the parcel first. Inside it was a small sculpture of my head and a letter from Olive.

Dear Jacoba

I do not know what to do any more. I have had no replies to my letters since the middle of 1901. Nobody can tell me where you are or if you are even alive I pray you have not died in the camps. I am sending you this sculpture in the hope that you have now been released safe and well. Elizabeth made it for you. I am saddened to have to tell you that even the specialist in Johannesburg could do nothing for her. But she continues to excel at her studies and spends all her spare time producing these beautiful sculptures. I have her under the tutelage of a dear friend of mine, Wouter Mouton. He says she is sublimely talented. My health has deteriorated badly I fear I shall soon be unable to take proper care of Elizabeth. Wouter has expressed a willingness to foster her.

If you receive this letter please write and tell me what I must do now.

Olive

The sculpture was exquisite. Every detail of my face was perfect and I wondered how a blind child could create such beauty. I wrote back to Olive immediately and told her to do what she thought best for Elizabeth, for the time being, because I could surely offer her nothing here.

They had rebuilt Geoffrey's offices and his son Peter had taken over his practice.

I was pleasantly surprised by Peter. He had been a young boy of fourteen when I last saw him, before Geoffrey sent him away to school in England. Now he was a tall young man of twenty five, with untidy fair hair flopping over his ears, he did not look like a solicitor at all.

"Mrs Swanepoel," he said, jumping up from his desk to embrace me.

"I think you may call me Jacoba now, Peter,"

"Terrible thing, Fanny and Johnson,"

"Yes. And your father, too. Did they ever find his body?"

He shook his head.

"Not a thing, not even a shoelace. I was at Balliol at the time. By the time I got back it had all been cleared away. But what about you? I heard you were in the camps. Was it very bad?"

"Worse than anything you can imagine," I replied.

He called for tea.

"And your family?"

"My daughter is in Johannesburg. She was blinded by an ostrich just before the war, perhaps you heard? My husband I have not seen since the war began. My son not since January."

"I'm sorry, Mrs Swanepoel....I mean.....Jacoba."

"Don't be sorry yet, they are still sending men home from the overseas camps. They may yet arrive to surprise me," I replied with a confidence I did not feel.

I sipped my tea, staring out of the window at the hotel opposite. It had been so long since I had sat in civilised surroundings and been treated with respect. I could see the table where Fanny and I last sat, discussing what to do with our money, as if that were the most important thing in the world. My reverie was interrupted by Peter.

"Now. Is this a social call or is there something I can do for you?"

"Yes. Yes, there is. I have two foster children, five and seven years old, orphans from the camp, my neighbour's sons. I am afraid for their inheritance, the Government is desperate to buy their farm to lease to British settlers. I am afraid they will be made wards of court and then it will be up to the court to decide what is in their best interests. I am sure they will sell the farm."

"It might be in their best interests, Jacoba. They are so young, would it not be better if they had a sum of money put by for when they are older?"

"We are Boers, Peter, without our land we are nothing. I must preserve it for them."

"That may not be easy. If you are not related to them you have no claim."

" I have this."

Poor Anna had written a letter, leaving her two children to me in the event her husband did not return.

"Ah. This changes things. It is fortunate that she was able to make her wishes so clear."

More fortunate that Mary was there to hold her hand and force it across the page, while she raved in her final delirium, I thought

"I will draw up the papers and you can come back next week to sign them, and at the same time I will set up a trust for the children. You will need a man to be joint trustee and I am willing to do that if it suits you?"

"Yes, of course. And there is one more thing. I have very little money. I must ask you to wait until after my next harvest to be paid."

It almost choked me to say it.

Peter's grey eyes were full of sympathy.

"I would not take your money, even if you had it. I do not intend to make a living out of the misfortunes of war," he replied.

A month later I had ten thousand morgen of land with not a living thing on it and no *plaasmense* to work it with.

My next trip was in the opposite direction, to the military remount depot next to the railway line at Orange River Station, which had been taken over by the Repatriation Board. Here we were to collect our rations. How we were to bring them home without wagons or animals to pull them was anybody's guess. The depot comprised five large sheds, each a hundred feet long, with paddocks, forage store and several *kraals*. The condition of the horses and mules was appalling. Mange was rampant, they were thin and restless, their skin bald and dry like parchment, laid about the shoulders and neck into thick folds and wrinkles. I was disgusted that anyone could allow any animal, let alone these that had endured such hardship and served so faithfully, to fall into such a state of neglect. There was a seventeen hand mule, who had seen service with the Royal Field artillery, I was told. I could not imagine who would want to buy him, he was too big for any kind of work. I stood at the *kraal* for a while, watching them rub and scratch themselves and suddenly one small pony caught my eye. It was the little Shetland, very thin now, with scabs all over his flanks, that I had ridden briefly during my time with the commando. I whistled and he turned his head and whinnied. I climbed over the fence and as I was walking towards him I saw a group of six ponies standing together. There was something familiar about them and then I saw my brand on their hairless shoulders. The

Shetland was nuzzling my hand, looking for something to eat and I gave him a pat on the neck.

"I'll be back for you in a minute," I said

One of the sheds was stacked from floor to roof with meal, meat, seed and grain and a man sat inside the doorway behind a desk, his thin pencil moustache bristling with authority. I did not recognise him, he must be one of the Englishmen with which the British were now populating our country.

"Yes?" he said, looking me up and down. Had he never seen a woman in breeches before?

"You have my horses in your *kraal*,"

"Those horses belong to the army, madam,"

"Six of them are mine, they carry my brand."

I could see he did not believe me.

"Well, you'll have to prove it. If I go giving out horses to any Tom Dick and Harry that comes along I'll be out of a job."

"You can ask anyone around here. Everyone knows my brand," I said but as soon as the words were out of my mouth I remembered that most of my neighbours were dead or imprisoned. I could see I would get no further with this man and I was tired. In those days it did not take much to knock me back and everything I did sucked the energy out of me. I put my ration card down on the desk.

"You will give me food, at least?"

He picked it up with both hands and studied it carefully, turning it over to look at the back, before handing it back to me.

"You are living on the farm Nooitgedacht?"

"Is that not what it says on the card?"

He pursed his lips. I could see he was biting back a retort but by then they had been told to be polite to us and treat us respectfully, as if that would make us forgive them for what they had done.

"I'm afraid you do not qualify for the free grant,"

"What?"

He opened a big black book and turned the pages until he arrived at a page which was headed, Nooitgedacht Farm, District Jacobsdal, Jacoba Swanepoel.

"According to my records this is one of the wealthiest farms in the district," he said, leaning back in his chair and folding his arms across his chest.

"You are surely making a joke. Have you seen the state of my farm? I might have been wealthy once but your soldiers have reduced me to nothing. I have no money, no house to live in, no stock and no crops and yet you tell me I am wealthy?"

"According to our records you own an unmortgaged farm of five thousand morgen."

"I cannot eat my farm," I replied

This was obviously something that had not occurred to him but it did not soften his attitude.

He told me that I might buy on credit, a thing I had never done, a thing my Oupa warned me against in the strongest terms. I might repay my debt after my first harvest.

"And how am I to plough and plant a crop with no mules or oxen and no seeds?"

"The Board will shortly be sending teams with seed to help you. I will put your name on the list."

As I was leaving a woman arrived driving a cart, with a treetrunk as a *disselboom* and a biscuit tin as a seat. Four planks sat on several old wheels of various types tied together with wire. I recognised her from when I had helped out at the Jacobsdal hospital at the beginning of the war and she stopped to talk.

"How are you Jacoba?"

"As you see me. Alive at least."

A shadow passed across her face.

"Yes. We can be thankful for that but not for much else."

I did not enquire about her family as we used to do. Nobody asked about family any more, we were too afraid of the answers..

"I must get back to the farm. Will you call in for coffee when you next come for rations?"

"I will."

I passed a large marquee where they were cobbling together sets of harness taken over from the army. Standing outside the door, smoking a cigarette was Nicholas Papenfus, the joiner. I felt my temper flare and I was about to walk past him when it occurred to me that he might be of use.

"Nicholas," I said, choking back my contempt, "*Hoe gaan dit met jou*? Are you working here."

"*Goed, mevrou.* Yes, I am in charge of the harnessmaking."

He was surprised I was talking to him, nobody else did. The joiners and *hensoppers* who either fought with the British or surrendered at the earliest opportunity, had had to start their own church, so high was the feeling against them for their treachery.

"Perhaps you can do me a favour, Nicholas?"

"Anything, Mrs Swanepoel, just say the word."

"I need you to go and tell that man inside that those six horses are mine. Will you do it?"

He walked with me to the *kraal,* where I pointed them out to him.

"Yes. I can see your brand. I will inform him straight away, *mevrous*. Are there any others you want? I could tell him they are yours too."

"No, but you can tell him I will take the Shetland pony and the mule as well."

"Yes, *mevrou.*"

I drove my battered little herd towards Nooitgedacht, the Shetland scampering along at the head, kicking his heels joyously. Out of these poor animals I had start rebuilding my fortune.

NOVEMBER 1902

CHAPTER FORTY FIVE

I waited almost four months before I took my rifle and rode Swart Lawaai along the boundary of my land. It took me three days.

I was one of the lucky few whose grass had not been burnt by the soldiers. It was too late to sow wheat but we had enough time to sow maize and there would be sufficient grazing for sheep if we could get some. I found the remains of a cooking fire and some discarded Mauser cartridges at the top of Bleskop. This was all that was left of our struggle. From up there there the house looked even more forlorn but there were more important things to do than rebuild a house. It was almost December and we had to plant our *mielies* or risk another year of starvation and still no sign of the *verdomde* Repatriation Board ploughing team. But I knew my land and as I looked up at the sky I was thinking we might be in for another drought.

I returned with a springbok. He was quite small but he would feed us for a few days before his meat started to go off. I gained great pleasure out of reviving all the skills I had learned as a child. Next year, when I could afford to buy pickling barrels and spices and muslin, we would put meat by, just as we had done in Zululand

I bought sheep on credit but when they arrived I soon discovered it was not only jackals we had to contend with. Packs of dogs, abandoned during the war, had gone completely wild and were attacking the flocks, made worse by the fact that, unlike the jackals, they had very little fear of people. I was forced to shoot a number of them, fine boerbuls and little terriers, which upset me greatly.

The new government said we were now only allowed to keep five families on our farms where before I had twelve. How did they expect me to manage a ten thousand morgen farm with only five families?

Bywoners came. Most of them were idle, landless families who expected me to assist them when I could barely help myself.

"*Mevrou*, everyone in the district knows you made your fortune selling diamonds with the *Joodse vrou*," one said, accusingly.

"Is that what they say? I can assure you that even if it were true, that money is long gone."

"We are only asking for a small plot of land on which to live, *mevrou*."

"And what do you intend to give me in return?"

It was clear he was shocked by my question.

I offered him work clearing the *khakibos* weeds and Scotch thistles which the British had brought here mixed in their hay bales but he turned up his nose.

"That is *kaffirs* work,"

"Perhaps. But if I can do it so can you."

"Never."

"Well then you will never live on my farm."

Nooitgedacht was next to the road to the depot and each month I joined the convoy of carts and wagons going to get their rations. At first we were so dazed by our suffering that we could do little more than load our carts and go home immediately but by the third month the women began to break their homeward journey at Nooitgedacht and we shared our coffee and sugar and talk. Some were young widows, some were old widows, some were the widows of *hensoppers* and joiners, shunned by the Church and their neighbours through no fault of their own. And some, like me, did not yet know whether or not they were widows.

At first all our talk was about the war. Twenty six thousand Boer women and children and twenty thousand of our *kaffirs* had died in the camps. Thirty thousand Boer homesteads had been burnt down, stripped of livestock and crops. Millions of cattle, horses and sheep had died. The British alone lost almost half a million horses, mules and donkeys. It had cost the British taxpayer two hundred million pounds. It had cost us an entire generation. Our bitterness was unquantifiable and our hatred of Lord Kitchener universal. Before the War, the Orange Free State had been a prosperous Republic. Now we were impoverished, second class citizens in our own country and thousands of poor Whites were flocking to the cities to try to find employment. The British had inherited a wasteland.

We disagreed on many things, we were, after all, by nature an argumentative people but on one thing we all agreed. We were never again going to be told what to do by men. We were tired of being characterised as silent martyrs. We wanted the right to vote.

When they started dismantling the blockhouses and offering them to us for five pounds apiece I bought two of them and with these and the surprising number of handpressed Kimberley bricks which had survived the fire we were able to rebuild most of the house. We had no wood for a door, nor even enough for a frame, every bit of wood for miles around had been plundered by one side or the other. To make the floor, we broke down anthills and hauled them back in the Scotch cart I had bought on credit from the depot. If we were lucky the aardvarks and pangolins had been there first and broken them up. My seventeen hand mule came into his own then. Frikkie and Mouton had named him Koos de la Rey.

But my instincts about the weather proved right. Instead of good rain at decent intervals, we had heavy downpours followed by dry weather, which continued until my crop of maize was nearly dead. And then the locusts came. I heard the whirr of millions of wings in the distance and as the sky darkened I thought it was a freak thunderstorm. We watched in horror as the hideous swarm stretching from horizon to horizon swept overhead, consuming everything in its path. They landed on the thatched roof of the house, thousands upon thousands of wriggling, ravenous, khaki coloured bodies, seeking out every living thing. For two hours we sat inside, listening to the methodical scratching and when we came out, not a blade of grass, nor a *mielie* stalk was left.

"It will never rain again. Too much blood in the land," said Nandi.

DECEMBER 1903

CHAPTER FORTY SIX

The war had been over for over eighteen months and I had accepted that Conor and Quartus would never return. I had done my grieving and written their names in my oupa's *Statenbijbel*, so it came as a great shock to me when, early one morning, I found my son standing on the *stoep*, carrying a little bundle of clothes, and for a moment my mind refused to recognise him. And then I burst into tears and my sobs brought Mary rushing out of the house.

"Your son?"

I nodded as I collapsed into her arms.

Word spread quickly and Lukas came running across the garden, Bloody Fool hard on his heels, swearing about his trampled flowerbeds. Nandi was hugging him as if he were her own child, Frikkie and Mouton just kept punching him on the arm, and everybody was talking at once. And then there was silence and into that silence Quartus dropped the words I was dreading.

"Pa is dead."

He told us that he had found his father not long after I was taken to the hospital, and spent the rest of the war blowing up trains along the line from Port Elizabeth to Bloemfontein. When news of the peace came they had said goodbye to the rest of the commando, only fifteen of them by then, and were heading home when they were surprised by a British patrol. Conor had held up his hands and told Quartus to do the same, telling him they would be alright, the war was over. But Conor was wearing a khaki shirt and an officer pulled out his revolver and shot him in the head, he had not known that Kitchener had given orders that anyone found wearing an English uniform was to be shot on sight. The officer rode away then and a soldier told Quartus to take whatever he wanted from his body, before they buried him and then they took him prisoner and sent him to Saint Helena Island.

He held out Conor's bloodstained notebook.

"It was all he had, ma. This and a pencil, which I have used up."

When, years later, I could bring myself to read it I would find all my husband's good intentions in that notebook. I would also find an account of my father's last hours and discover the place where Conor had buried him.

But Quartus was not finished yet.

"It was the same officer that burned the farm, Mama."

I am not, by nature, a vengeful person but this last piece of information awakened in me a murderous fury that made me nauseous and I had to sit down on the *stoep* while I tried to compose myself. Was it possible that a single human being could have wreaked so much destruction on my life?

The next morning I set Bloody Fool to making a coffin out of the planks remaining from the blockhouses I had bought and told Lukas to hitch Koos de la Rey to the Scotch cart.

"Mama? What are you doing?" said Quartus.

"We are going to fetch your father," I replied. "You know where he is, don't you?"

I could see by the look on his face that he thought I had gone mad.

"It is too far, mama, and he has been too long in the ground."

I turned to look at him. He was only twelve years old but the boyish look was gone from his eyes. He was a man now, a bitter man, who hated all things English. It was the only thing we would ever fully agree upon.

"I will tell you a story, Quartus, which I have not told you before. My father, your *oupa* was killed by the Zulus at Isandlwana and we had no body to bury. I do not even know how he died, because your great grandfather would not speak of it. *Nou klim in*. We are going to bring your father home."

It took us a week and it was a horrible business but we found where they had buried him and we brought what was left of him home, in Bloody Fool's coffin and buried him next to the dam where I would see him more often than I ever did when he was alive. I went in to Jacobsdal and brought the *predikant* out to hold a proper service and afterwards we held a wake because I knew that's what Conor would have wanted. I was tempted to take a drink myself but I knew that if I did I might never stop. Between them, Asjas and Bloody Fool more than made up for my abstinence.

The war had ended but it was not over. English was made the sole official language in the Free State and Transvaal. Everything, civil service, courts, schools, police, was run by Englishmen lured to

South Africa by Milner's promises of land and wealth. All the teaching in the schools was done in English. Dutch was used to teach English and English to teach everything else. I had a battle on my hands to persuade Quartus to go to school at all, he had been in the company of grown men for too long and thought himself too old for it. Frikkie and Mouton were in awe of him and it was not long before I had a full scale rebellion on my hands which was only put down when Mary and Nandi flung them bodily into the mule cart, took them into Jacobsdal and asked the schoolmaster to give them each three stripes for truancy.

Not long after Quartus returned, a wagon so familiar that I will never forget it, rumbled across the *veld* and my heart skipped a beat. It drew to a halt in front of my house and Tannie van Tonder climbed slowly down. She was older and heavier but her smile was as warm as I remembered it. She held out her arms to embrace me and I choked down my guilt and fear. Then she held me away from her, pushing a stray wisp of hair away from my face.

"Jacoba. You have grown into a fine young woman. Your mother would be proud of you if she could see you now."

No she wouldn't. Not if she knew what I did all those years ago.

She saw Quartus watching us from the verandah.

"And this is your son? He looks just like your *oupa*."

"I have a daughter, too. She is in Johannesburg with a friend," I replied, trying to keep the conversation away from Jaap, for I was sure she had found out what I had done and this was why she had come.

"Come, *tannie,* let us sit. You must be tired after your journey. How are Fanie and Tielman? Their children must be grown up by now?"

"Both killed at Spioen Kop," she replied and I could hear the heartache in her voice.

"Oh. I am so sorry *tannie*."

She shrugged.

"No doubt you have also lost someone, Jacoba. I can see it in your face."

"Yes. My husband."

We were silent then, both lost in our own thoughts, and when she spoke again my world stood still.

"I know about Jaap."

"I can explain...."

"You don't have to. I knew what he was like. There had been an incident in the Cape. That's why he never went back to school."

"Oh."

"I am old now, Jacoba, and my heart is broken. I do not want to die and leave you guiltstricken for the rest of your life. We have all endured too much suffering."

"I am so sorry for what I did, Tannie. He came to the ...."

Tannie van Tonder raised her hand and I trailed off into silence.

"Do not tell me Jacoba. He was my favourite, you know that, perhaps because he was so different to the others. I was unwilling to believe what he had done in the Cape. When I heard *Oom* Danie giving him the sjambok I walked away from the house until it was finished. Jaap was never the same after that. I should not have sent him to you. Can you forgive an old woman?"

"I am so sorry, *tannie*. In twenty three years not a day has gone past that I have not regretted what I did."

"You should not waste your life on regrets, Jacoba. I ask only one thing. That you tell me where he is buried that I may finally say goodbye to him."

I winced and turned to look away.

"He is under my Oupa,"

Tannie van Tonder smiled. A wry smile.

"I am glad to hear it. If anyone could spend eternity talking sense into him it is Gerrit Swanepoel."

"You will stay a few days, *tannie*? Before you go home?"

"One night. To rest the oxen and then I must go back to Natal. The sons that are left are not a patch on their older brothers."

We talked into the night. Of the *oudae* and the carefree days at *Nagmaal*, before the British came to Zululand and began the ruin of our lives. We remembered my mother and father and Oupa and everyone who had perished because of the British and when she left the following evening she turned to me

"One day we shall have our land back again. Perhaps not in my lifetime, but certainly in yours."

I marvelled at her optimism, but she was right. We would get our land back and we would both be alive to see it.

I watched the wagon sway across the *veld* and felt a weight lift off my shoulders. It didn't make me any less of a murderer but at least I could stop looking over my shoulder. And I had killed many more since the day I shot Jaap.

After she had gone, I sat down to draw up my claim for compensation. How should I claim for the loss of my entire life? I had receipts from both Boer and British for stock and food taken. These amounted to just over a thousand pounds. They were saying we would get two shillings in the pound. One hundred pounds? It was laughable.

MARCH 1904

CHAPTER FORTY SEVEN

I rode Swart Lawaai to the dam. I had grown fond of the old mule and I felt safe on him. My days of reckless galloping across the *veld* were over since I broke my leg. It still ached in cold weather. Asjas, who had rarely let me out of his sight since my return, scampered alongside me. His face was grey and his broken arm bothered him when it was cold and I wondered how long it would be before he died too. He still drank as much as he ever did. I did not know where he got hold of it, for I kept all my liquor securely locked away.

I had erected a fine tombstone on Conor's grave and I had just finished pulling out weeds when I saw a solitary rider making his way towards the dam and I cantered down to cut him off. Heavier than when I had last seen him, his hair starting to thin, the livid white scar on his temple, I could not fail to recognise him and the sour taste of bile filled my throat.

"What are you doing here?"

"Why, Mrs Swanepoel," he replied, removing his hat, "I am the Claims Officer for this district. I have come to assess your claim.

"Oh no. You get off my land this instant!"

"You had best mind your manners, madam, it very much depends on me as to whether your claim will be accepted."

"Do you think I will mind my manners for a hundred pounds?"

He rode past me up the hill and I turned to follow him.

"Did you not hear me? You are trespassing."

"I thought I might do a little painting while I am here. Such a splendid day don't you think?"

I saw the easel and paintbox tied to the back of his saddle.

"Don't get off your horse," I warned him.

Ahead of us Conor's tombstone was now visible in the long grass and I felt my anger ignite. Looking back, it was well for all of us that I had not brought my rifle with me because I know that I would have shot him in that moment.

The path narrowed and he rode up next to me so that our stirrups were touching and as I nudged Swart Lawaai to the side a stone flew past my head. And another one and suddenly we were under fire and Swart Lawaai started to bray. One stone hit Herbert's horse square on the side of the head and it leapt sideways, dislodging a rock at the edge of the dam, and losing its footing. I watched as its hind legs scrabbled at the crumbling rim of the dam and Herbert laid into it with his whip, trying to drive it forward. Suddenly it fell onto its belly and slid backwards, plunging into the green depths below. Herbert flung himself clear before it hit the water and I dismounted and walked forward to the edge.

"Damn this clumsy horse" he called out, "Throw down a rope, would you?"

The horse was beginning to panic, as it swam around the confined space, thrashing around in the water and knocking its head against the sheer rock walls.

"For the love of God, woman, throw me down a rope."

"Why would I do that, Colonel?"

"To save me from drowning, for God's sake!"

"And why would I want to do that?"

And then he knew and his terror was written all over his face.

"You cannot mean to let me drown?"

"I can assure you that is exactly what I mean to do."

The horse was tiring by then, sinking lower into the water and I raised my rifle to my shoulder.

"Please! Don't shoot me!"

"No fear of that," I replied as I shot the suffering horse behind the ear. "I intend to see how well you can swim."

Herbert swam well, it was more than an hour before he finally sank beneath the surface of the water. I thought I would get some pleasure out of it but I didn't. There is nothing pleasant about watching a man drown, but still I felt I owed it to Conor to see the job through to the end. If Herbert had been a mining man he would have seen the hand and footholds cut into the side of the dam and perhaps been able to save himself. As it was, he did not.

I was about to leave when I heard a noise and when I looked around Nandi was there. She sat down next to me and began to speak in Zulu.

"When I was a young girl in Zululand, I had twin sons by a white man. Twins are unlucky, you know this, *ntombazana*, because you yourself grew up not far from my own place. My mother took one twin out into the veld and I had to flee my home with the other one. When my son was eight years old he was taken to Cetshwayo's kraal to be a baggage carrier for his uncle. I followed the army to Isandlwana and when the fight was over I went onto the field to look for my son. I did not find him but there was plenty of food there, left by the soldiers, and I had nowhere else to go, the English had burned all our *kraals*, so I stayed and built myself a little *pondokkie* out of the English wagons. I was there for months and then they came to bury their dead and that man found me and tied me up and left me for the hyaenas and the jackals. They did this to me."

She held up her thumbless hand.

"Afterwards I went back to Ulundi, to see if my son was there and after the big battle where they ate us up, I saw that man take him away. I have never seen my son again."

She got up then and I watched her walk back down the hill towards the house. It would be many years before we spoke about her son again.

Asjas eventually tired of pelting me with stones and I waited for him to come down from the *koppie* where he had hidden himself. He appeared clutching an empty square face in his hand and I heaved him up onto the saddle in front of me, where he lay semiconscious and reeking of gin, all the way back to the farmhouse.

"Pa was wrong about you," I said, "You are not stupid at all. You have turned out to be a very clever baboon indeed.

In a little village in the Cape, called Matjesfontein, Amelia sat in the lounge of the Lord Milner Hotel reading a letter from Mabel's solicitor. Mabel had contracted typhoid and she was now buried in the cemetery outside the village, near General Wauchope and George Lohmann, the Yorkshire cricketer whom she had so admired. The letter begged to inform her that Mabel's entire estate had been left to her. She was, at last, free to do as she pleased. She put the letter aside and, for the one hundredth time, picked up the photograph she had taken at the camp in Bloemfontein. Half a dozen grimy children stood in a little group holding toys they had made from scraps of wire and cloth. Some distance behind them was a large marquee where a woman stood in the doorway. The image was unclear, the woman's features fuzzy, but the height was right and there was something about the way she carried herself. Surely it had to be Jacoba? There was only one way to find out. She walked down to the station and booked a seat on the next train to Kimberley.

THE END

Printed in Great Britain
by Amazon